I0632293

William Archer

William Charles Macready

William Archer

William Charles Macready

ISBN/EAN: 9783337423117

Printed in Europe, USA, Canada, Australia, Japan

Cover: Foto ©Raphael Reischuk / pixelio.de

More available books at **www.hansebooks.com**

BY

WILLIAM ARCHER

.

LONDON
KEGAN PAUL, TRENCH, TRÜBNER & CO., Lᵀᴰ.
1890

(The rights of translation and of reproduction are reserved.)

PREFACE.

THE chief authority for a Life of Macready is, of course, his *Reminiscences, Diaries, and Letters*, edited by Sir Frederick Pollock. His *Reminiscences*, unfortunately, come to an abrupt end at the close of the year 1826. Up to that point, my main task has been to check his statements (which I find surprisingly accurate, even where he had only childish memories to draw upon), and to supplement them by extracts from contemporary documents. From 1826 onwards—that is to say, during the last twenty-five years of Macready's life as an actor—the *Diary* affords only fragmentary information. It is valuable rather as an expression of character than as a record of events. In the following pages, then, the story of Macready's whole career is told for the first time, with, I hope, reasonable fulness and accuracy.

My guiding principle has been to avoid vague and second-hand statements, and, as far as possible, to give precise information founded on first-hand evidence. For instance, I have examined every London play-bill on which Macready's name appears, except those belonging to one or two seasons at the very close of his career, which are absent from the British Museum collection. His performances during these years are fully recorded in the newspapers, to which I have also referred for details as to his rare visits to suburban theatres. I have naturally given special attention to his four seasons of management. They form, as it were, the central point in the stage-history of this century; in them the traditions of the " palmy days " and the tendencies of our own time met, and clashed. Therefore I have tried to write their annals at large, in the spirit of the painstaking Genest.

In the course of my inquiries I have incurred many obligations. With a generosity not always characteristic of collectors, Mr. E. Y. Lowne, a warm admirer and personal friend of Macready, gave me free access to his vast store of Macreadiana, now in the possession of Mr. Henry Irving. Mr. Lowne's unwearying kindness at once lightened my labour and placed within my reach much interesting material not otherwise accessible. My thanks are also due to the late Mr. Robert Browning, for some very valuable notes as to his relations with Macready; to Mr. George Scharf, F.S.A., Director of the National Portrait Gallery, and Mr. Henry Howe of the Lyceum Theatre, who have favoured me with interesting personal reminiscences; to Mr. Joseph N. Ireland, the learned historian of the New York stage ; to Mr. Samuel Timmins, and the officials of the Birmingham Public Library ; to Mr. F. W. Dendy of Newcastle, and Mr. W. E. Adams, editor of the *Newcastle Weekly Chronicle ;* to

Mr. James Macready Chute, of the Prince's Theatre, Bristol ; to the editor of the *Bath Chronicle ;* to Mr. J. Evans of Manchester, and Mr. E. R. Dibdin of Liverpool, who were good enough to make some researches on my behalf into the early history of Macready's parents ; to Mr. Sketchley of the Dyce and Forster Libraries ; and last, not least, to the ever-obliging officials of the British Museum Library.

CONTENTS.

c

WILLIAM CHARLES MACREADY.

CHAPTER I.

BOYHOOD.

1793–1808.

WHEN Charles Macklin paid his last visit to Dublin, in 1785, Daly, the manager of the Smock Alley Theatre, was to have played Egerton to his Sir Pertinax McSycophant. He took offence, however, at the veteran's overbearing manner of directing the rehearsals, and recalled a young actor from Waterford to take his place. The actor's name was William Macready. He was the son of a well-to-do Dublin upholsterer, who afterwards became "Father of the Commons" (a municipal dignity, I take it), and, dying, left £20,000 to be frittered away in a Chancery suit. Before taking to the stage, young Macready is said to have served an apprenticeship to his father's craft. He now held a respectable position in the Smock Alley company, and "had figured in many first-rate parts" in the Irish provinces. In selecting him for Egerton, Daly may have had the intention of pitting Turk against Turk, for Macready's temper was of the hottest. The experiment, in any case, succeeded, for Macklin was much pleased with his Egerton. In a letter, preserved in the British Museum, he writes to Macready at Waterford (August 18, 1785)—

"Dear Sir,

"I am obliged to you for your civility, by your journey to Dublin, and your kind attention. . . . Mr. Mattocks, of the Liverpool company, desired me to learn whether there was any young man that would play Gentlemen Fops and Tragedy for his company at Liverpool and Manchester —were there such to be had, I think it might be a step towards his being introduced to Covent Garden Theatre. I play four nights at Liverpool, and such a person might travel with me thither."

The old man (he was at least eighty-six) evidently had Macready himself in his eye, desiring, perhaps, to secure an attentive travelling-companion. In this he seems to have succeeded. Macready did not appear along with him in Liverpool, where his performances took place between the 7th and the 17th of October; but in the following month we find "Mr. M'Cready" a member of the Liverpool company. In the course of the winter he played in Liverpool such parts as Trueman in *George Barnwell*, Altamont in *The Fair Penitent*, Pylades in *The Distrest Mother*, and Stephano in *The Tempest*.

In Manchester, where Mattocks also reigned, he made the acquaintance of a Miss Christina Ann Birch, who played such parts as Goneril in *Lear*, the Queen in *Hamlet*, Mrs. Dangle in *The Critic*, and Lady Medway in Mrs. Sheridan's comedy *The Discovery*, at the Theatre Royal, Spring Gardens. How this young lady became an actress we do not know. The traditions of her family went back to the Civil War, when her great-grandfather

is said to have been disinherited for espousing the
Cavalier cause. Her grandfather, Jonathan Birch, was
Vicar of Bakewell, in Derbyshire; two of her paternal
uncles were clergymen; her father was a surgeon; her
mother was a daughter of Edward Frye, Governor of
Montserrat; so that all her antecedents were at least
"genteel." Her birthplace was Repton, near Derby,
where her father died, overwhelmed by pecuniary
disaster, before she was three years old. She was now
in her twenty-first year, and an attachment soon sprang
up between her and Macready, who was ten years her
senior. We find them taking a joint benefit on April 7,
1786, Macready playing Bob Acres, and Miss Birch
Julia, in *The Rivals*. At the close of the season they
were married, the ceremony taking place at the Collegiate
Church, Manchester, on Sunday, June 18, 1786.

Macklin was as good as his word in procuring
Macready a London engagement. On September 18,
1786, just three months after his marriage, he made his
first appearance at Covent Garden, as Flutter in *The
Belle's Stratagem*. For ten consecutive seasons he
remained a useful, but not a brilliant member of Harris's
company. A list of his chief Shakespearian parts will
show the estimation in which he was held. They were
Gratiano (to Macklin's Shylock), Paris (to Holman's
Romeo), Fenton, Borachio, Malcolm, Cassio, Le Beau
(or, as it was then spelt and pronounced, "Le Beu"),
Edmund, Antonio (*Merchant of Venice*), Poins, Page,
and others of even less importance. He made no
advance in status or authority. Edmund, indeed, is a
good part; but as we find him cast for Guildenstern in
the same season, we can only conclude that he was
regarded as an actor-of-all-work. Among his non-Shakespearian parts were Young Marlow, Figaro, Fag in *The

Rivals, and Tattle in *Love for Love.*   He also tried his hand at authorship, producing, in 1792, a farce named *The Irishman in London,* and in 1795 a comedy named *The Bank-Note,*—both mere adaptations of older plays. At the close of the season 1796–97 he quarrelled with the management over a question of salary, and resigned his position.   He left behind him a reputation summed up in the following couplet :—

> " Tho' than Macready there are many better,
>   Who, pray, like him, so perfect to a letter ? "

In other words, painstaking, but mediocre.

His wife, so far as I can ascertain, did not appear on the London stage.   Three children were born to them, who died in infancy ; then a daughter who lived to reach her seventh year, and dwelt in the memory of her younger brother as an "angelic influence," intervening "between his infant will and the evil it purposed."   The child whose precocious depravity she thus restrained was WILLIAM CHARLES MACREADY, born on Sunday, March 3, 1793, in Mary Street (now part of Stanhope Street), Euston Road.   As this is Macready's own statement, apparently on the authority of an entry in his mother's Prayer-book, it may be taken as conclusive. He was baptized at St. Pancras Parish Church, January 21, 1796, the date of his birth being given in the register as 1792 ; but this he explicitly declares to be a mistake. London remained his parents' head-quarters long enough for the boy to be sent to a preparatory school in Kensington, but he cannot have been more than six when the scene of his life changed to Birmingham.

Two years before his secession from Covent Garden, the elder Macready had become a provincial manager. Here is his first manifesto—.

"Theatre Royal, Covent Garden, June 11, 1795.

"MR. M'CREADY, with profound Respect, begs Leave to acquaint the Ladies and Gentlemen of Birmingham and its Vicinage that . . . he purposes opening the spacious THEATRE erected [after an incendiary fire] in New Street, on Monday, the 22nd inst., with

A PLAY AND ENTERTAINMENTS

. . . MR. M'CREADY respectfully pledges himself to have a succession of the most capital Performers on the London Stage during the Summer;—for he will only presume to solicit encouragement from the Public so long as his Exertions shall prove that it is his greatest Ambition to merit their Favour and Protection."

The name of Mrs. M'Cready appears in a subordinate place among the company. If not a great actress, she was certainly versatile. In the course of seven seasons, besides playing pretty constantly in farce, she supported almost all the "capital Performers" whom her husband, in pursuance of his promise, brought to Birmingham. She played Charlotte in *The Gamester*, to Mrs. Siddons's Mrs. Beverley, Celia to her Rosalind, Andromache to her Hermione, Elizabeth to her Mary Queen of Scots. She played Blanche to Elliston's Sir Edward Mortimer, and Countess Wintersen to Kemble's Stranger. Among her other parts were the Queen in *Hamlet*, the Countess Almaviva, Evelina (the Spectre) in *The Castle Spectre*, Betty in *The Clandestine Marriage*, and Lucy in *The Rivals*. She never, even for her benefit, attempted a leading part, and whenever the company included another actress who was competent to undertake "seconds," the manager's wife at once resigned in her favour. From this, and from the absolute silence of all records as to the merit of her performances, I conclude that she was a "utility" actress in the strict sense of the word. Her son does not mention that she was on the stage at all.

The Birmingham season lasted from June to September. In the winter of 1797, after his quarrel with the Covent Garden management, Macready made an attempt to run the Royalty Theatre, in Well Street, Wellclose Square, Whitechapel, as a sort of music-hall. Failing in this, he shook the mud of London off his feet, and devoted himself to his Midland circuit, which he extended, in the winter months, so as to include Sheffield and other northern towns.   In all probability, then, it was early in 1798 that William Charles was taken from his Kensington school and handed over to an irascible pedagogue named Edgell, in St. Paul's Square, Birmingham.   Here he distinguished himself chiefly in recitation, learning by heart long extracts from Shakespeare, Milton, Pope, and Young, "which," he says, "have been of some service to me in accustoming my ear to the enjoyment of the melody of rhythm."   His mother had great difficulty in teaching him to use, without abusing, the letter *h*. "The line, ''Appy, 'appy, 'appy pair !' was for some time an insuperable obstacle to progress."   In the holidays he hung about his father's theatre, observing and remembering much.   He was awed by Mrs. Siddons, who visited Birmingham almost every year; he saw King, the original Sir Peter Teazle and Lord Ogleby, dressed for the latter part; and Gentleman Lewis, the great Mercutio, left his face engraven on the boy's memory.   He remembered, too, the appearance, in 1802, of the beautiful Mrs. Billington.   The same season left another vision still more deeply impressed on his mind. During the Peace of Amiens, the Hero of the Nile made a triumphal tour of the provinces.   On August 30, 1802, he reached Birmingham, and went to the theatre in the evening, where one Blisset, an actor of provincial fame, was playing Falstaff in *The Merry Wives*.   The per-

formance must have pleased him, for the next day's play-
bill announced, "By desire of the Right Honourable
Lord Nelson, *King Henry IV. ; or, The Humours of Sir
John Falstaff.*" The theatre was crowded with hero-
worshippers, and Macready records their frantic enthusiasm. An improvised act of homage to the popular
idol included the singing of a song with this refrain—

"We'll shake hands and be friends ; if they won't, why,
    what then ?
We'll send our brave Nelson to thrash 'em again ! "

which Lady Hamilton applauded with uplifted hands,
kicking with her heels against the foot-board of her seat.
It is wholesome to be reminded that the heroes of the
glorious past did not escape, and perhaps did not
altogether disdain, the homage of the music-hall lyrist.

Under the heading of " Midsummer, 1803," the register
of new pupils at Rugby School contains the following
entry :—

"Macready, William Charles, son of Mr. W. Macready,
Master of the Birmingham, Leicester, and Stafford Theatres,
&c., aged 10. March 3."

He boarded with his mother's cousin, William Birch,
one of the masters of the school, who treated him with
great kindness, and did much to alleviate the trials which,
at a public school of that period, must have beset a boy
of his temperament. Oddly enough, his schoolfellows
do not seem to have bantered him about his father's
calling. Had they done so, Macready would have taken
care to record the fact. On the contrary, as his school
career advanced, he acquired popularity by reason of his
father's readiness to lend dresses and properties for the
boys' theatricals. His own abilities as an actor and
reciter procured him some consideration. He began by

playing small female characters, but rose eventually to
such parts as Zanga in *The Revenge*.   A programme of
the Rugby speech-day of 1808 has been preserved, with
comments on each recitation by one of the audience.
His remarks run the whole gamut of blame and praise,
from "Horrible," up to "Surprisingly well indeed"—the
last being reserved for the so-called "Closet-Scene" from
Hamlet, with Skeeles as the Queen, and Macready major
as the Prince of Denmark.   (His younger brother, Edward, had joined him at Rugby in the previous year.)
The Latin prize poem on this occasion was *Shakspearus*,
by Robinson major (afterwards Master of the Temple),
who was Macready's only rival in recitation.   It is clear
that there was a marked theatrical bias in the Rugby
mind.   Macready, indeed, declared to Dr. Inglis that he
"very much disliked the thought" of the stage, and
approved of his father's design of sending him to the
bar.   But when, speaking of his last recitation at Rugby,
he notes what "inward elation he felt in marking, as he
rose slowly up, the deep and instant hush that went
through the whole assembly," we cannot but recognize
the young war-horse scenting the battle afar off.

His first home-coming from Rugby was a sad one.
He arrived in Sheffield to find that his mother, whom he
deeply loved, had died the day before.   Her health had
been failing for some years.   In the season of 1802 she
does not seem to have acted at all, though a benefit was
given her, at which she spoke an address.   During the
following season Mrs. Macready's name is again absent
from the bills, and on December 12, 1803, *Aris's Birmingham Gazette* contains the following announcement
in its list of deaths :—

"Saturday se'nnight [Dec. 3], at Sheffield, aged 38, Mrs.
M'Cready, wife of the worthy manager of our theatre, after

a severe and lingering illness, which she bore with the most Christian fortitude and resignation, leaving a disconsolate husband and four young children, as well as all who knew her and her exemplary character, to bewail the loss of so amiable and so good a woman."

She seems, from the little we know of her, to have been not only an amiable, but a brave and wise woman, and the loss of her counsel probably paved the way for her husband's subsequent misfortunes. Her memory was an abiding influence for good in the life of her son.

The elder Macready's day of disaster was distant as yet. The next season, indeed, witnessed his chief managerial triumph, which was thus heralded—

" The Ladies and Gentlemen of Birmingham and its Vicinity are respectfully informed that the celebrated

YOUNG ROSCIUS,

Who has performed with such astonishing Excellence, Attraction, and Applause, at the Theatre Royal, Dublin, Cork, Belfast, Edinburgh, Glasgow, &c., &c., is engaged here for EIGHT NIGHTS, the first of which will be

This present MONDAY, *August the* 13th, 1804."

This was Master Betty's first appearance in England, and the Birmingham people greatly appreciated their manager's enterprise in securing for them so marvellous a novelty. He was two years older than young Macready, who, however, found him, at the height of his renown, a congenial and very boyish playfellow. A return visit of the phenomenon in 1805 was again brilliantly successful, and there is no evidence that the seasons of 1806 and 1807 were other than prosperous. Macready had certainly saved some money when, in 1806, the lesseeship of the new Theatre Royal, Manchester, was put up for competition. In an evil hour, Macready outbade his rivals, offering the extravagant rental of £1600 a year. In order to complete the decorations of the house and make a start, he took into partnership a certain Galindo, a Dublin fencing-master, whose wife afterwards made herself notorious by publishing a defamatory pamphlet concerning Mrs. Siddons. Galindo was to have invested £3500 in the enterprise, £1000 of which he borrowed from Mrs. Siddons; but the conditions of the partnership were of the quaintest. The theatre, a large and very handsome one, was opened on June 29, 1807. Things went badly from the very first. The company was voted unworthy of Manchester, and though some attractive stars appeared—Mrs. Siddons, Munden, the Young Roscius (then in his decline), and Elliston—nothing availed to turn the tide of ill luck. Macready's own performances were but little relished. One critic denounces him as a "delirious Daggerwood" (Sylvester Daggerwood was the Crummles of the period), foisting himself on the public in the whole round of the drama, and playing his own panegyrist in the newspapers. Even his brogue—unkindest cut of all!—was declared to be bad. When it became evident that the undertaking could not prosper, Galindo not only refused to pay the last instalments of his £3500, but claimed prompt repayment of the sum actually advanced. The claim, it appears, was justified by the terms of this odd partnership, and Macready found ruin staring him in the face. Having given up his Birmingham theatre at the close of the 1807 season, he struggled on gallantly in Manchester; but his exchequer was so low that he could not pay his sons' school-bills for the second half-year of 1808.

The sons, as yet, knew nothing of their father's difficulties. Passing through Birmingham on his way from Rugby to Manchester for the Christmas holidays of 1808, William Charles found a box-ticket for the theatre awaiting him—an act of courtesy on the part of his father's successor, Watson of Cheltenham. The bill of the evening (December 16) consisted of *The Busy-Body*, and "Dibdin's much-admired ballet d'action, *The Bridal Spectre; or, Alonzo and Imogine.*" The Baron St. Clare was played by the star of the evening, "Richer, the funambulist;" the Fair Imogine found an obese representative in the manager's wife; and "a little mean-looking man in a shabby green satin dress appeared as the hero, Alonzo the Brave," Knight of Calatrava. Six years later, this mean-looking little man leaped into renown, and the name of Edmund Kean became a synonym for "Génie et Désordre." Had Macready been in Birmingham four days earlier, he might have seen the little man play Joseph Surface and Alonzo the Brave on the same evening.

Arrived at Manchester, he was soon made aware of his father's distresses. The pride, which was his blessing and his bane, at once asserted itself. He formally renounced all thought of the bar, and stated his intention of seeking his career on the stage. His father made some show of resistance, but was in reality only too glad to find a burden thus transformed into a prop.

Behold him, then, at the age of sixteen less two months, embarked as his father's lieutenant in the multifarious and adventurous enterprises of provincial management. He left Rugby with a fair smattering of the classics. Latin he seems to have read fluently, and he knew enough Greek to astonish a dinner-party with a quotation from Homer; but the tragic poets are notably absent from his lists of reading. He never suffered his classics to rust, but was always rubbing them up; mainly, no doubt, from a genuine love of literature, but partly, we may suspect, because a little learning is a gentleman-like thing, and served to mark him off from the common herd of actors.   It was his habit to note "business" on his parts in Latin, so that his comrades might not understand it.   His public school training was in a sense his chief misfortune, for to it we may surely trace the morbid sensitiveness on the subject of his social status that tortured him in after-years.   "My father," he says pathetically, in speaking of this first turning-point in his life, "was impressive in his convictions that the stage was a gentlemanly profession.   My experience has taught me that . . . in other callings the profession confers dignity on the initiated; on the stage the player must contribute respect to the exercise of his art."   He found, in other words, that a clergyman or a soldier was rated a gentleman because of his profession, an actor in spite of it; and this caused him "many moments of depression, many angry swellings of the heart."   In the mean time, however, he was insensible to the mighty difference between the prefix "Mr." and the affix "Esq."   He faced his new career, if not with enthusiasm, at least with resolute composure.

CHAPTER II.

1809–1816.

IT was not till a year and a half after he thus cast in his lot with his father that Macready actually "commenced actor." He was too old for a Young Roscius, too young for a mature tragedian; and he had no idea of serving an apprenticeship in minor parts. After a miserable six months in Manchester, helping his father to dodge the sheriff's officers, he undertook the supervision of the Newcastle Theatre for a short summer season, and "fell desperately in love with one of the actresses." In the autumn he went to London to learn fencing under Angelo, and study the leading actors of the day. His father forbade him to see John Philip Kemble, lest he should imitate his style; but the prohibition was needless, as the O. P. riots, which broke out on September 18, the evening before Macready's arrival in town, banished that noble Roman from the boards during his whole stay. On nights when the O. P. party did not begin their orgy until half-price time, he saw G. F. Cooke, Young, Charles Kemble, Munden, Fawcett, Emery, and Liston; at the Lyceum he saw the burnt-out Drury Lane company; and at the Surrey he saw Elliston in the "Grand Ballet of Music and Action founded on *Macbeth*," with which he opened his first transpontine management.   Returning to Manchester, he was present, and " burst into tears," when his father surrendered himself to a sheriff's officer to be lodged in Lancaster Castle.   Next day he assumed the management of his father's company at Chester, and found himself for the first time battling single-handed with the serious troubles of life.

His lines had not fallen in pleasant places.   The lot of a strolling manager in difficulties was laborious and anxious, shifty . and sordid.   He lived from hand to mouth, watching with eager eyes the rise and fall of the shallow stream that flowed through his treasury, and knowing that some caprice of the crowd might at any moment cause it to run dry.   He had to be obsequious to the County, submissive to the Garrison, conciliatory to the Civic powers.   His company was inadequate and often turbulent, the inevitable jealousies and discontents being embittered and emboldened when pay-day became a movable feast.   Macready, it is true, had but a short experience of the pinch of managerial poverty.   He escaped absolute bankruptcy at Chester, and got himself and company transported to Newcastle in time to open the theatre on Boxing Day, 1809 ; though to do so he left his own watch in pawn in Chester, and the watches of three of his company at a posting-house on the road. The Newcastle season was fairly successful, the gigantic Conway, beloved of Mrs. Piozzi, proving a great attraction.   Before it closed, the elder Macready was out of durance, and once more at the helm.   But even these few months of strain and stress must have been a hard trial for a boy not yet seventeen, inclined by disposition and training to regard the *Roman Comique* from its tragic rather than its comic side.

As a manager, the elder Macready was popular with his audiences, but not with his actors. He had catered liberally for the Birmingham public, and had earned their esteem. Local critics were apt to make merry now and then over the flowery style of the manager's advertisements. When *Pizarro* was about to be produced as the latest London novelty, he heralded it with a glowing description of "the pervading effects of its resistless power." "The sense," he wrote, "aches with pleasure, while at the same time the heart melts with sympathy, and the mind is entranced with a something bordering upon vision supernatural." Such literary foibles, however, were easily pardoned, and we have ample evidence of the respect in which he was held, even by his creditors. With his actors the case was different. He was obstinate, violent, overbearing, and anything but open-handed. Already in 1796 a libellous pamphlet entitled, *The Dissection of a Bir—g—m Manager* was hurled at his head. In the spring of 1807 he got into a miserable pamphlet war with an ex-officer calling himself John Prosser Edwin, whom he had dismissed from his Newcastle company. Edwin's two pamphlets rank with Cape Everard's *Memoirs of an Unfortunate Son of Thespis* in the deplorable records of itinerancy. The first, *An Appeal to the Public relative to the Conduct of William M'Cready, Esq.*, was answered by the manager in a manifesto entitled, *Fact versus Fallacy;* to which Edwin rejoined with *Candour versus Calumny; being an Ample Refutation of the Malignant Falsehoods and Despicable Misrepresentations lately published by the* MAN-*ager, William M'Cready*. The whole affair is simply squalid. Beside it the Crummles episode in *Nicholas Nickleby* seems dignified and almost idyllic. There are two gleams of humour in the story of debt, drunkenness, and unseemly wrangling. The first is Mr. Edwin's preliminary note : "To avert the imputation of egotism, I shall narrate in the third person ; " the second is his complaint that the manager would not suffer him to correct the grammar of that distinguished playwright Mr. Cherry, but insisted on a singular subject being followed by a predicate in the plural, if it stood so in the prompt-book.

This species of obstinacy is exemplified on a larger scale in one of the anecdotes related by his son. At Berwick, in 1814, on the summer evening appointed for an illumination to celebrate the fall of Napoleon, Macready senior determined to open the theatre, though warned on all hands that it would be empty. He announced Reynolds's comedy *Laugh When You Can*, with himself as Gossamer. The players dressed, the musicians assembled, and seven o'clock struck. "Shall I ring in the music, sir?" inquired the prompter; "there is no one in the house." "Certainly, sir; ring in the music," replied the manager. When the curtain rose there were two boys in the gallery, one man in the pit, and William Charles Macready in the centre box, watching his father "very gravely, and indeed sternly, begin the part of the laughter-loving Gossamer." Even filial piety could endure but little of this entertainment, so the young man went out for a walk, and returned about nine, to find the play just over. The man in the pit disappeared, but the two boys remained in the gallery until the musicians began the overture to the afterpiece. Then one of them leaned over the balustrade, made a violent gesture with his arm, and called out, "Oh, dang it I give over!" whereupon they both walked out, leaving the theatre empty. A manager subject to such aberrations was not likely to be popular with his subordinates. At a later period, in Bristol, he dismissed a too-convivial scene-painter, saying to him, " I was told you were a blackguard, Mr. Atkins, and I was not deceived ; " on which the artist retorted, " I was told *you* were a gentleman, and I *was* deceived. That's all the difference, Mr. Macready." Anecdotes and allusions of a like nature abound in the theatrical gossip of the period, showing that, in the lower ranks of the profession, the manager was but little beloved. In short, his reputation with the public of his district was such as to enable the elder Macready to give his son an excellent start ; but his domineering temper rendered it highly improbable that the two should long continue to work together in harmony.

The summer of 1810 found the elder Macready once more manager in Birmingham, which was naturally selected as the scene of his son's first attempt. It was thus announced—

" On Thursday Evening, June 7, will be presented the
Tragedy of

ROMEO AND JULIET

(Written by Shakespear).

The Part of Romeo by a YOUNG GENTLEMAN, being his
first appearance on any Stage ;
Friar Lawrence, Mr. Harley ; and Juliet by Mrs. Young.

In Act I. *A GRAND MASQUERADE.*

In Act V. THE SOLEMN DIRGE.

To which will be added (for the first Time this Season)
the Farce of

THE IRISHMAN IN LONDON;
or, THE HAPPY AFRICAN
(Written by Mr. M'Cready).

Murtoch Delany, MR. M'CREADY ; Edward, MR. MANSEL ;
and Louisa, MRS. CLIFFORD."

C

A rare portrait by De Wilde, taken two months later, shows us the young Romeo as he appeared in the Balcony-Scene—a chubby-faced boy in a close-fitting white satin tunic and knee-breeches, slashed with purple on the breast and thighs. He wore a broad flowered sash almost under his armpits ; an upstanding ruff close to the neck ; white kid gloves, white silk stockings and buff-leather dancing-pumps ; and he carried in his hand a large black hat with a forest of white plumes.

He had rehearsed very diligently and " had got by rote, as it were, every particular of place, gesture, feeling, and intonation." His opening speeches he went through mechanically, " like an automaton moving in certain defined limits." The first burst of applause scattered the mist which clouded his faculties ; he gained his self-possession, entered into the spirit of the character, and " felt the passion he was to represent." Every round of applause heightened his inward elation, and the curtain fell upon a complete success. " Well, sir, how do you feel now ? " said one of the company, who crowded around him with their congratulations. " I feel," he replied, " as if I should like to act it all over again."

Here is the first printed criticism that greeted the young actor—the harbinger of a mighty host. It appeared in *Aris's Birmingham Gazette* for Monday, June 11, 1810—

" THEATRE ROYAL.—The Tragedy of *Romeo and Juliet* was brought forward at our Theatre on Thursday last, for the purpose of introducing (a young candidate not eighteen years of age) MR. WILLIAM M'CREADY to the stage, from whose performance we have no hesitation at predicting his future fame and prosperity ; indeed, we never witnessed a better first appearance. He looked the character admirably ; the elegance of his figure, the expression of his countenance, and the very great ease of his deportment, united in forming a perfect representation of what Romeo should exactly appear. He received the most encouraging and flattering applause through the four first acts, and at his dying scene there were *several distinct peals*, testifying surprise and the highest admiration of talents which have been seldom equalled, if ever surpassed."

On June 11 the "young gentleman" made his second appearance as Romeo, and on June 13 his third appearance, as Lothair in "Monk" Lewis's *Adelgitha*, to the Robert Guiscard of Conway. Three days later the same play was repeated, the name of "Mr. William M'Cready" this time figuring in the bill. He next appeared as Young Norval and as Zanga (in which, according to *Aris's Gazette*, he "evinced a mind far beyond his years") and played Romeo a third time. The play-bill of Friday, July 27, bears the following announcement:—

"Mr. William M'Cready, with Gratitude to a liberal Public for the fostering encouragement and cheering Applause bestowed on his *first Dramatic Efforts*, laments that his other engagements will not admit of his appearing here THIS SEASON after Monday next, July 30th, on which Evening will be presented the historical Play of

GEORGE BARNWELL;
Or, THE LONDON MERCHANT."

His performance of Lillo's homicidal hero was, by his own account, the best of these early attempts.

Had it been Macready's habit to look at the bright side of things, he must have recognized, in later life, that his upward path was from the first made singularly smooth for him. He did not, like Garrick, awake one morning to find himself monarch of the theatrical globe; but except Garrick, whose genius made him a perpetual exception to all rules, few actors have been more uniformly fate-befriended. When we compare Macready's apprenticeship with that of Kemble or Mrs. Siddons, Edmund Kean or Mr. Irving, we see how little cause he had to chide with Fortune. He stepped at once into "the lead." For four years he held the chief place in his father's companies, working hard, indeed, and playing at least seventy-four parts, but always the best parts in the repertory of the day. Then he passed two seasons at Bath, still successful and applauded ; and from Bath to London was but a single step. No fitter method could well have been devised for the complete and rapid development of his powers. He was spared the soulless drudgery in which so many actors have wasted their best years. It was not his fate to eat his heart out while awaiting tardy opportunity. The career was open to his talents from the first. To some natures the very facility of the course would have been ruinous ; but Macready was a born worker ; sloth had no charms for him. His hunger for self-improvement was commensurate with his means of satisfying it. Had he been capable of happiness, he might have been the happiest of men.

The sympathies of Macready senior were all with the older generation. Macklin and Henderson were his idols, and his soul delighted in the pompous iambics of eighteenth-century tragedy. His son, accordingly, went through a very "legitimate" course of training, escaping, in a great measure, the influence of German romantic drama and its home-made imitations, which were then at the height of their popularity. Yet his second series of performances, at Newcastle, added Rolla in *Pizarro* and Earl Osmond in *The Castle Spectre* to his repertory —Teutonisms both. During a return visit to Birmingham, at the close of 1810, his most important character was Luke in Sir James Bland Burgess's alteration of Massinger's *City Madam*, entitled *Riches*. This was a problem indeed for a lad of seventeen to attempt. Early in the following year, at Newcastle, he made his second Shakespearian essay, in Hamlet—a performance which led him to the often-quoted reflection that "a total failure in Hamlet is of rare occurrence." The Duke Aranza in Tobin's *Honeymoon* (his first comedy part), Posthumus in *Cymbeline*, and Orestes in *The Distrest Mother*, made him "the established favourite of the Newcastle audience." It was during the Newcastle season of 1811–12 that he encountered two members of the Clan Kemble—first, Mrs. Whitlock, a caricature of her elder sister, Mrs. Siddons, with something more than her bulk and infinitely less than her genius; and then the imperial Siddons herself. He played Beverley in *The Gamester* (a new part) to her Mrs. Beverley, and Young Norval to her Lady Randolph. In his first scene with her his awe overcame him, and he broke down for a moment in his part. She kindly whispered the word to him, and he gradually regained confidence, playing so well in the last scene that, as she stood at the wing awaiting her cue, she called out, "Bravo, sir! bravo!" and loudly applauded him in sight of part of the audience. After the performance of *Douglas* she summoned him to her room, and gave him some parting words of advice. "You are in the right way," she said; "but remember what I say: study, study, study, and do not marry till you are thirty!" The admonition was not thrown away. Macready study-study-studied, and married at thirty-one. "Her acting," he says, "was a revelation to me, which ever afterwards had its influence on me in the study of my art."

With the awe of Melpomene fresh upon him, Macready passed under the charm of Thalia. After an uneventful summer at Birmingham, he spent the autumn of 1812 at

Leicester, where, on the opening night of the season, he played Don Felix in *The Wonder* to the Violante of Mrs. Jordan. " Oh, the words laughed on her lips ! " he cries. " With a spirit of fun that would have out-laughed Puck himself," she combined a discrimination of character and a careful elaboration of effect which impressed the young man scarcely less than the majesty and passion of Mrs. Siddons. " Her common speech had more sweetness in it than any other woman's singing," says Robson, the " Old Playgoer ; " and Macready almost echoes his enthusiasm, adding that she could vary her common speech by certain bass tones " that would have disturbed the gravity of a hermit."

The winter season (1812–13) at Newcastle was marked by the addition of three Shakespearian parts to his repertory—Richard II., Richard III., and Cleopatra's Antony. Macready was under the impression that *Richard II.* had not been acted since Shakespeare's time, but that was a mistake. It was revived at Covent Garden in 1738, and garbled versions of it had been produced at earlier dates. Oddly enough, it was the success of the season ; whereas it was barely accepted in London three years later, when Kean played Richard II., and Elliston Bolingbroke. Macready's Richard III. was received with approbation, but he felt no satisfaction in playing it, because " a hump-backed tall man is not in nature." Yet this was the part which afterwards confirmed his leading position on the London stage. Antony he played for his benefit (April 9, 1813) " with little effect." On the morning before the performance an anonymous paper was affixed to the box-office door, accusing him of having " shamefully misused and even kicked " the young lady who was to act Cleopatra. The house was nevertheless crowded, for " Mr. William " was very popular. At the first entrance of Antony and Cleopatra, he led the lady down to the foot-lights, and asked, "Have I ever been guilty of any injustice of any kind to you since you have been in the theatre ?" "No, sir," she replied. "Have I ever behaved to you in an ungentlemanlike manner ?" "No, sir." "Have I ever kicked you ?" "Oh no, sir !" This little dialogue was received by the audience with laughter and loud applause, and the play proceeded. The idea of Antony calling Cleopatra to witness that he had never kicked her is sufficiently quaint, but provincial audiences of that date were accustomed to such episodes.

The summer and autumn of 1813 were passed in Glasgow, whither the elder Macready had now extended his operations. Here William Charles added to his list of parts Captain Plume, Doricourt, Puff, Young Marlow, and Mark Antony in *Julius Cæsar*. W. H. Betty, no longer the Young Roscius, had now emerged from his period of seclusion at Cambridge. The two young men appeared together in Glasgow, as Charles II. and William Wyndham in *The Royal Oak*, and as Warwick and Edward IV. in *The Earl of Warwick*, the combination proving very attractive. Macready speaks in high terms of Betty's talent. He especially praises his Osman (Orosmane) in Aaron Hill's translation of *Zaïre*, and his Sir Edward Mortimer in *The Iron Chest*. Had he studied and persevered, according to Macready, he might have taken a permanent and honourable place on the stage; but he "deteriorated by becoming used up in the frequent repetition of the same parts." During a visit to Dumfries, in the autumn of 1813, Macready played one part at least which he has forgotten to put on record—Count Rostopschin in the "celebrated new drama" *The Burning of Moscow*.

The first serious quarrel between father and son took place at the close of the Glasgow season. Each possessed a temper which rendered him (as Carlyle's mother said of her son) "gey an' ill to live wi'." In his heart the elder Macready was very proud of his son's talent. Before the boy's first appearance, his father saw him, one day, instructing a stage Indian how to make a tiger-spring upon his enemy, and then suddenly fall back in astonishment on seeing his own figure reflected in his adversary's shield. "If you can do anything like that on the stage," cried the manager, taken by surprise, "there will be few come near you." . In later days, when William Charles was rising into metropolitan fame, Macready senior, it is said, overheard an actor of his company comparing him unfavourably with Kean and Young, and dismissed the impertinent critic on the spot. To his face, however, he was systematically cold and discouraging, and this ill-advised surliness tended to place the pair on a false footing. Moreover, the elder man was apt to resent correction, remonstrance, or even the slightest difference of opinion, and in moments of passion "there was no curb to the violence of his language." "God's blood!" an oath more ancient than elegant, was his favourite expletive, and he allowed himself an unbridled licence of insult and innuendo. "You fool, William!" was one of his formulas of address. It was not in human nature, least of all in the nature of William Charles Macready, to refrain from kicking against such pricks.

Soon after the first quarrel Macready returned to Newcastle for the season of 1813–14. He went into lodgings of his own, and was placed on a salary of £3 a week. His chief individual effort was a careful revival of *King John*, in which he played Faulconbridge. The grown-up Roscius paid a short visit to Newcastle in January, 1814, when the Glasgow experiment of a "combined attraction" was repeated with success. After the departure of his younger brother to join the army in the Netherlands, Macready returned to the paternal roof, but his father soon withdrew to Carlisle, leaving "Mr. William" to carry on the prosperous season at Newcastle. For his own benefit he acted Benedick and Marmion in an adaptation by himself of Scott's poem. For his father's benefit he adapted *Rokeby*, in which he played Bertram of Risingham. The summer and autumn were passed at Berwick, Dumfries, Leicester, and Carlisle. The Newcastle Theatre was temporarily reopened during the race-week in June, and the assize-week in August. Mr. and Mrs. Charles Kemble were the attraction of the race-week, Macready playing Pierre to Kemble's Jaffier, Colonel Briton to Kemble's Don Felix and his wife's Violante in *The Wonder*, and (strange to relate) Captain Absolute to their Faulkland and Julia in *The Rivals*. These parts, which modern actors can scarcely be bribed to undertake, were then the star-parts of the comedy! It is in speaking of this engagement that Macready sums up Charles Kemble's merits in the phrase, "He was a first-rate actor in second-rate parts." During the assize-week Charles Young and Emery were engaged, Macready playing Alonzo to Young's Zanga in *The Revenge*, and Wilford to Young's Sir Edward Mortimer and Emery's Orson in *The Iron Chest*. Young took occasion to warn him against over-acting—a hint for which he was afterwards grateful, though he regarded it at the time as an attempt on Young's part to impose on others his own cold and declamatory manner.

The beginning of the winter season of 1814–15 brought Macready once more to Newcastle. A new disagree-

ment with his father soon followed, and, remembering
that Dimond of Bath had offered him an engagement
for the previous season, Macready now wrote to inquire
whether his services were still in demand. The manager
answered in the affirmative, and it was arranged that the
young tragedian should appear in Bath shortly after
Christmas. Before he left Newcastle he played a part
in a singular real-life melodrama. On December 16,
1814, a fearful hurricane swept over Newcastle. The
two Macreadys were sitting over their wine after dinner
in their lodging in Pilgrim Street, when a sudden crash
shook the house to its foundations, and the room was
filled with dust and smoke. A chimney had fallen in,
and, breaking through the roof, had wrecked one of the
upper bedrooms in which the landlady's two children
were playing. The distracted mother was already be-
moaning their fate, when Macready junior rushed up
to the room, and found them safely ensconced under a
large mahogany table, which had protected them from the
avalanche of bricks and mortar. The myth of the child
rescued from a burning cottage, which, as we shall see,
haunted Macready all his life through, probably arose
from some perverted rumour of this incident.

During a week of farewell performances in Newcastle
he added the Stranger and Othello to his list of characters.
He played Beverley and Benedick on December 20 and
21, and eight days later we find him on his new scene
of action.

Bath, if not quite in its glory, was not yet obviously
in its decline. Forty years had passed since Sir Anthony
Absolute and Sir Lucius O'Trigger were to be met on
the North Parade, and the memorable sojourn of Mr.
Pickwick and Sam Weller was not to be until twenty
years later. It was the Bath of Miss Austen—the Bath

of *Northanger Abbey*. Catherine Morland, an assiduous theatre-goer, must certainly have seen Macready. If he was playing on the evening of her tiff with the Tilneys, he probably found her a sadly preoccupied spectator. His first appearance took place on December 29, 1814, when he played Romeo. " The manager paid him the compliment," says Genest, who was no doubt present, "of new-casting *Romeo and Juliet* to the best advantage, and ensured him a good house by bringing out *Aladdin* on the same night." There is, perhaps, a touch of malice in Genest's curt comment, "*Aladdin* was very success-ful ; " for the clerical critic thought little of Macready. His Romeo, however, was applauded by the public and praised by the press. The Earl of Essex was his next character, and he subsequently appeared as Hamlet, Orestes, Hotspur, Richard II., Beverley, Luke in *Riches*, and other characters. Genest preferred Macready's arrangement of *Richard II.* to Wroughton's adaptation, in which Kean appeared at Drury Lane some six weeks later ; but he notes that it was acted only twice, to bad houses. Macready's engagement came to an end on February 18, 1815, but Dimond retained him for the following season, at an increased salary.

The news of his success soon reached London, and led to a correspondence with Harris of Covent Garden, which would probably have ended in a three-years' engagement, but for a blundering interference on the part of the elder Macready. During a short visit to town on business connected with this negotiation, Macready saw Kean for the first time since his rise to eminence, and was much impressed by his Richard III. He also met him at supper, and records " his unassum-ing manner . . . partaking in some degree of shyness," the "touching grace" of his singing, and the extraordinary humour of his mimicry.   He saw Miss O'Neill, too, in Juliet, and wrote of her in after-years, when he had himself been her Romeo, "Through my whole experience hers was the only representation of Juliet I have seen. . . . 'She is alone the Arabian bird.'" Some time afterwards, a negotiation with the Drury Lane committee likewise fell through, on the question of terms.   The Rev. J. Noel, a relation of Lady Byron's, had been commissioned by Macready's Rugby friends to plead his cause with Lord Byron, then the leading spirit of the Drury Lane management.   After descanting for some time on the young actor's merits, his clerical advocate wound up, with ingenious infelicity, "And besides all this, Mr. Macready is a very moral man." "Ha! then," replied Byron, "I suppose he asks five pounds a week more for his morality!"

In the early spring of 1815 he played a short engagement in Glasgow, rendered memorable to him by his first meeting with his wife, then "a pretty little girl, about nine years of age."   She played one of Rosalvi's children to his Felix in *The Hunter of the Alps*, and he scolded her for being imperfect in her part.   In April he made his first appearance in Dublin, being engaged, on the strength of his Bath reputation, at the large salary of £50 a week.   Then came a round of short engagements in England and Scotland, in the course of which (at Newcastle) he added Henry V. to his list of parts, with no great success.   The winter season found him once more at Bath.   Genest notes his reappearance as follows : "Dec. 9. *Much Ado.* Benedick = W. Macready—very bad."   His Benedick, however, gained him the friendship of the Twiss family (Mrs. Twiss was a younger sister of Mrs. Siddons), through whom he obtained an introduction to the best circles in Bath.   It was his first experience of " society," in the narrower sense of the word. He seems to have entered into it with zest, and with less false sensitiveness than he sometimes displayed in later life. Among many local notabilities, he encountered one lady of a wider fame—that "lively little lioness," as he calls her, Mrs. Piozzi, her hair still black, and her cheek still (artificially) red, at the age of seventy-five.

His principal new parts during this season were Mentevole in Jephson's *Italian Lover* (which added greatly to his reputation), and Kitely in *Every Man in his Humour*. For his benefit he played Leontes in *The Winter's Tale*, and then, towards the end of February, 1816, set forth to fulfil a thirteen-weeks' engagement in Dublin. For so long a visit he could not expect the high salary of the previous year, but contented himself with £20 a week. The only part of any importance which he added to his repertory was Lord Townly in *The Provoked Husband.* He found the Dublin audience apt to be unruly, but keenly sensitive and warmly sympathetic when once their attention was seized. He played Pierre on one occasion, to the Jaffier of a portly and drawling local actor, who dragged out his dying speech unconscionably. At last, unable to endure it any longer, one of the gods called out loudly, "Ah, now! die at once!" to which another immediately replied, "Be quiet, ye blackguard!" then, turning to the lingering Jaffier, added encouragingly, "Take your time!"

Meanwhile negotiations had been renewed with Harris of Covent Garden, Macready's friend Fawcett, the stage manager, acting as intermediary. . A five-years' engagement was the result, at a salary of £16 a week for the first two seasons, £17 for the second two, and £18 for the last season of the term. Macready's demand for a veto on characters he considered " derogatory " was fortunately not conceded—fortunately, because, if he had had the power, he would certainly have declined several parts which helped to establish his reputation. Starring engagements at Wexford and Galway, and an unprofessional tour in Wales, occupied the time between the close of his Dublin engagement and his first appearance in London, which was fixed for September 16, 1816.

MACREADY'S CHARACTERS BEFORE HIS APPEARANCE IN LONDON.

1810–1816.

[Here, as in subsequent lists, parts which Macready " created " are marked with an asterisk.]

Romeo ; Lothair (*Adelgitha*) ; Young Norval ; Zanga ; George Barnwell ; Achmet (*Barbarossa*) ; Osmond (*Castle Spectre*) ; Rolla ; Alwin (*Countess of Salisbury*) ; Luke (*City Madam*) ; Hardyknute (*Wood Demon*) ; Earl of Essex ; Roderick Dhu ; John of Lorne (*Family Legend*) ; Julian (*Peasant Boy*) ; Hamlet ; Duke Aranza ; Posthumus ; Orestes ; Frederick (*Natural Son*) ; Phocyas (*Siege of Damascus*) ; Charles II. (*Royal Oak*) ; Percy (in Hannah More's tragedy) ; Daran (*Exile*) ; Chamont ; Edward the Black Prince ; Alexander the Great ; Fitzharding (*Curfew*) ; Rover ; Beverley ; Rolla (*Virgin of the Sun*) ; Hastings ; Zaphna (*Mahomet*) ; Don Felix ; Richard II. ; Dorax (*Don Sebastian*) ; Oroonoko ; Richard III ; Antony (*Antony and Cleopatra*) ; Captain Plume ; Tangent (*Way to get Married*) ; Lovemore (*Way to Keep Him*) ; Doricourt ; Puff ; Young Marlow ; Antony (*Julius Cæsar*) ; Count Villars (*Education*) ; Magician (*Aladdin*) ; Frederic (*Lovers' Vows*) ; Rostopschin (*Burning of Moscow*) ; William Wyndham (*Royal Oak*) ; Edward IV. (*Earl of Warwick*) ; Faulconbridge ; Nourjahad (*Illusion*) ; Aladdin ; Benedick ; *Marmion ; Gingham (*The Rage*) ; Lackland (*Fontainebleau*) ; Beverley (*All in the Wrong*) ; Belcour ; *Bertram (*Rokeby*) ;

Pierre; Colonel Briton; Captain Absolute; Wilford (*Iron Chest*); Alonzo (*Revenge*); Vincent (*Education*); Stranger; Othello; Hotspur; Gustavus (*Hero of the North*); Cheveril (*Deserted Daughter*); Henry V.; Leon (*Rule a Wife*); Mentevole (*Julia*); Kitely; Leontes; Lord Townly; *Edward Gregory (*Changes and Chances*); Octavian (*Mountaineers*); Bertram: eighty-two characters.

POSTSCRIPT.—Parts played in Newcastle in 1813, not mentioned in *Reminiscences:* Charles I. (*Royal Martyr*); *Oswald, the Noble Foundling (Dr. Trotter's tragedy, *The Noble Foundling; or, The Hermit of the Tweed*); Doricourt (*Belle's Stratagem*); Frederick (*School of Reform*).

CHAPTER III.

FORGING AHEAD.

1816–1823.

THOUGH Macready did not at first (or perhaps at last) recognize the fact, his arrival in London was certainly well-timed. The poetic drama, it is true, was entering upon a period of disruption and decline. Throughout his career, the state of the theatre was a perpetual source of torture to his artistic susceptibilities; but for his personal fame and fortune the conditions were, on the whole, as favourable as could be desired. In 1816 the stage was rapidly clearing, as though in preparation for a new actor of the first magnitude. Mrs. Siddons had formally retired four years earlier; John Philip Kemble was entering upon his farewell season; Miss O'Neill's short and brilliant career had only three more years to run. It was now nearly three years since Edmund Kean had taken London by storm, and he was still at the height of his reputation. His talent and his fame alike may fairly be said to have culminated in his terrible performance of Sir Giles Overreach, which took place in January, 1816. He was only six years older than Macready, and was in every way a rival to be feared. But the brandy-bottle was already doing its work, and

though Kean's great name was a power in the land even
to the day of his death, seventeen years later, his genius
was a mere wreck before Macready's had reached
maturity. Charles Young, cold, stately, estimable, and
Charles Kemble, the first-rate actor of second-rate parts,
had neither the talent nor the force of character to prove
serious obstacles in Macready's path. The unpre-
possessing youth of three and twenty could scarcely
hope to conquer London at one blow, as Kean and
Garrick before him had done. His gifts, as he very
well knew, were not of this overwhelming order. But he
had not unreasonably long to wait for a fair share of
popularity, which gradually increased until he stood without a rival at the head of his profession.

In what play was the new actor to make his first
venture? Kean's parts were barred, the semi-mythical
"Wolves" being leagued, it was thought, to fall upon
and rend any pretender to their hero's laurels. This
put the leading Shakespearian characters out of the
question, as well as Massinger's Luke, whom Macready
would himself have chosen. A timid policy finally prevailed, and Orestes in *The Distrest Mother* was fixed
upon. The play was a translation of Racine's *An-
dromaque*, by Ambrose Philips—the poet whose name,
satirically corrupted, has given us the term "namby-
pamby." It had not been revived for several years, so
that Macready, who had acted Orestes with applause
in the country, would not have to contend against
the vivid recollection of any great predecessor. Charles
Kemble would make an admirable Pyrrhus, but the
importance of the female parts was a great drawback.
Miss O'Neill had not yet returned to town; Miss
Foote and Miss "Sally" Booth were not to be thought
of in such heavy characters. There remained Mrs.

Egerton, an excellent Meg Merrilies, who was cast for the haughty Hermione; while Mrs. Glover, one of the first comic actresses of her time, was specially engaged to appear as the tearful Andromache.   Abbott, a heavy walking-gentleman, played Pylades.

The opening of *The Distrest Mother* is excessively trying for a nervous aspirant.   Orestes has to dash upon the stage in high elation the moment the curtain rises, crying—

> "O Pylades ! what's life without a friend ?
> At sight of thee my gloomy soul cheers up ! "

Macready clasped Abbott's hand convulsively, as, with hyacinthine curls flowing over his shoulders, an ample and most unclassical chlamys streaming behind him, and legs bare to three or four inches above the knee, he hurried to meet his fate,   He had not a single personal friend among the audience, and the mere play-bill announcement of "Mr. Macready, from the Theatre Royal, Dublin," can have aroused no special predisposition in his favour.   He was cordially received, however, and proceeded nervously with the scene.   His first eighty lines or so were heard in silence.   It is even stated that a dangerous tittering commenced on the first bench of the pit, which might have been fatal had it extended a little further.   But at last the phrase—

> "O, ye gods !
> Give me Hermione, or let me die ! "

was greeted with "loud and long plaudits ; " and this applause, by restoring his self-possession, assured his success.   The mad-scene at the close—considerably amplified in the English version—brought down the house, though the critic of the *News* thought it " one continued, bustling, incoherent rave."   It was not yet the custom (at Covent Garden, at any rate) to call players before the curtain; but the announcement that the play would be repeated on the following Friday and Monday was received with cheers. Edmund Kean, who was "conspicuous in a private box," applauded loudly; and Harris delighted his new recruit by saying, "Well, my boy, you have done capitally; and if you could carry a play along with such a cast, I don't know what you cannot do."

The critics were unanimous in condemning the selection of the play, praising the new actor's power and passion, and declaring his face his misfortune. Hazlitt (in the *Examiner*) moralized in the strain of the Great Marquis—

> " He either fears his fate too much
>   Or his desert is small
> That dares not put it to the touch
>   To gain or lose it all."

Orestes he described as "an ambiguous character," in which, if great success was impossible, total failure was unlikely. At the same time, he " had not the slightest hesitation in saying that Mr. Macready was by far the best tragic actor that had come out in his remembrance, with the exception of Mr. Kean." He praised the power, harmony, and modulation of his voice, approved of his declamation, defended him against the accusation of excessive violence and deficient pathos, but had nothing to say for his face. The *Times* held that he would scarcely supersede Young, and that Charles Kemble, even in tragedy, had little to fear from him; but allowed him "a large quantity of vocal and brachial force," and admitted that, at the right moments, he knew how to produce his effects with "a speaking eye or a deep and broken murmur." The critic of the *News*

had seen Macready " so often and in so many characters
in every exhibition of paintings at Somerset House,"
that he was inclined to class him with the incompetents
who "wriggle themselves" forward by means of puffing.
The performance of Orestes dissipated this prejudice.
" Mr. Macready," the critic proceeded, " is one of the
plainest and most awkwardly made men that ever trod
the stage. His voice is even coarser than his person.
And yet . . . he is undoubtedly an actor, . . . and an
actor in many points superior to Mr. Kean." The *Globe*
discerned in him " a man of mind," praised his voice,
and remarked that his eyes were so " full of fire " as to
divert attention, at critical moments, " from the flatness
of the features they irradiate." The *European Magazine*,
on the other hand, admitted the gracefulness of his
action and the excellence of his voice, but added that, in
spite of the fire in his eye, " the vacuity of his countenance lessened the illusion."

"I'm told he's a capital actor, but a devilish ugly
fellow," said a playgoer one evening, little dreaming that
Macready was sitting at his elbow; " they say he's an
ugly likeness of Liston." John Kemble, when his
brother Charles prophesied great things of the new
actor, took a pinch of snuff, and rejoined with a signifi-
cant smile, " Oh Charles ! *con quel viso !* " These
testimonies to Macready's lack of personal beauty are
borne out by the portraits of the period, which show a
small but rather scowling mouth, an irregular nose, and
a chubbiness of contour which was doubtless apt to seem
coarse. His face seems to have been one that improved
in aging. The furrows of time and the lines of thought
strengthened and ennobled it until, in old age, it
became venerable and most impressive.

Orestes was repeated twice, and then, on September

30, Jephson's *Julia ; or, The Italian Lover*, was revived, with Macready as Mentevole. This tragedy was produced in 1787, with John Kemble and Mrs. Siddons in the principal parts. It is well-knit and powerfully written, but intolerably sombre, Mentevole being a lurid and volcanic personage, who sticks at no crime in the pursuit of his desires. The performance increased the new actor's reputation. "It was impossible," the *News* declares, " to look the dark burning slave of passion better than Mr. Macready. . . . Passion quivers at his finger-ends." "Subtlety, terror, rage, despair, and triumph," says the *Times*, " were successively displayed by him with truth and energy." Hazlitt praised him highly, but thought that his behaviour, when accused of the murder of Claudio, was too obviously that of conscious guilt. The play-bill announced that his Mentevole was "greeted with shouts of rapturous applause ;" but the tragedy was repeated only once. In a sense, it did Macready a disservice, for his personal success in so villainous a part probably helped to procure him that reputation for consummate (theatrical) villainy under which he writhed for so long.

A sterner trial was at hand. Weary of exhibiting his recruit in plays that would not draw, Harris announced him to appear alternately with Young in the parts of Othello and Iago. Othello was, of all his Shakespearian parts, the one with which he was least familiar, and Iago he had never played at all. Nevertheless, he had to make the plunge, playing the Moor on the 10th, and his Ancient on the 15th of October. His Othello was surprisingly successful, and his Iago was not disastrous. The *Times* was enthusiastic over Othello, especially praising "his practice of employing all his force in passages of noiseless but intense feeling." Several critics

(Hazlitt among them) found him effeminate, and, in the pathetic passages, inclined to be "whimpering and lachrymose." His address to the Senate, according to the *News*, was "stilted and studiously eloquent;" and in repeating Desdemona's words of commiseration, he mimicked her. On the whole, however, his Othello produced a favourable impression. He was certainly not outshone by Young, whose Iago was "jocular and sarcastic—nothing more." When the parts were reversed, Hazlitt compared Young's Othello to a great humming-top, and Macready to a mischievous boy whipping it. The *News* complained that he "resolved Iago's character into one of simple, unmixed impulses;" and the *Times*, admitting that he had some "great and superlative" moments, found him in the main faulty and unimpressive. The simple truth was that he had had no time to master the character. Othello he repeated once, Iago not at all.

In the mean time Miss O'Neill had returned to her duties, and John Philip Kemble's farewell round of performances was announced. It began with Cato on October 25, and closed with Coriolanus on June 23, 1817. There was no room for Macready in any of the legitimate plays acted by Kemble and Miss O'Neill, Young and Charles Kemble being in possession of all the secondary parts. On two occasions, indeed, Macready acted Beverley in *The Gamester* to the Mrs. Beverley of Miss O'Neill, but the part reverted to Young. Another circumstance which tended to keep him in the background was the appearance (February 12, 1817) of Junius Brutus Booth, "of the Brighton and Worthing Theatres." His marked physical resemblance to Edmund Kean—a similarity of temperament as well as of appearance—led the Covent Garden managers to hope that

they might find in him an effective counter-attraction to
the Drury Lane tragedian. Booth's Richard III. was
enthusiastically received; but a quarrel as to salary
enabled Kean, with apparent generosity and real astute-
ness, to lure his simple-minded rival to Drury Lane, in
the hope of quietly shelving him. Booth soon awoke to
Kean's design, alleged illness as an excuse for not
appearing a second time at Drury Lane, and returned to
Covent Garden. Here his reappearance led to a riot,
his vacillating behaviour having displeased "the town."
Several nights passed before he was listened to with
patience, and then, the excitement having subsided, he
sank into comparative obscurity. The management,
nevertheless, did their best to force him upon the public;
and it filled Macready's soul with bitterness to find himself elbowed to the wall, not only by the established
favourites, but by a raw and inexperienced youth. This
fact explains his undue contempt for Booth's talents.
There can be no doubt that in later years he was a great
actor, and the man who, at twenty-one, could in the eyes
of Hazlitt hold his own for a single night against Kean
in the splendour of his genius, cannot have been a mere
charlatan.

But if Macready's loftier aspirations were held in
check, he soon fell in with a stirring part in the lower
walk of the drama. This was Gambia, the African
Bayard, in Morton's musical drama of *The Slave*, produced on November 12, 1816. Its success was not
exactly a personal triumph for Macready. Liston and
Emery played the comic parts of Fogrum and Sam
Sharpset, while Miss "Kitty" Stephens, as the quadroon
heroine Zelinda, lent the aid of her lovely voice and
great personal charm. Yet Gambia, in which, according
to the *Times*, he found ample room for "the broad and

boisterous ostentation of tempestuous passion," was the
first part which made Macready really popular.   It is
tragi-comic to think of him with "black body, legs, and
arms, short white cotton trunks, and coloured beads
round arms, neck, and ankles," uttering such sentiments
as this : "There is a state worse than slavery !—liberty
engendered by treachery, nursed by rapine, and in-
vigorated by cruelty."   The chief situation of the piece
is thrilling in the extreme.   Clifton and Zelinda (whom
Gambia hopelessly adores) are fleeing from Somerdyke
and his myrmidons.   They cross a stream by a rope-
bridge, and the pursuers are about to follow when Gambia
scrambles up the tree from which the bridge is sus-
pended, and cuts the rope.   "We are safe, my husband !"
cries Zelinda; but alas ! at the sound of her voice her
child, who has been concealed hard by, runs out from its
hiding-place, on the wrong side of the river.

Child. It was my mother's voice !   Mother ! mother !
Zelinda. Alas ! my child !
Somerdyke. Her child !   Then we triumph—seize him !   (*A
slave seizes the child, and, running up a point of rock, hands
it to Somerdyke, who continues.*) Move one step further, and .
you will see him buried in the waters.   Submit, or this instant is his last.   (*Holding him up in the act of precipitating
him.*)
Zelinda. I do submit.
Gambia. Never !   (*Gambia, who has concealed himself in
the branches, snatches the child up into the tree.*)   Father,
receive your child !   (*Throws the child across the stream.*)
They have him !   He is safe !   Ha ! ha ! ha !   [*Curtain.*

On January 18, 1817, he played Demetrius in a poor
adaptation of *The Humorous Lieutenant.*   The play was
a failure, but the actor was praised.   For the sake of its
one effective scene, he volunteered to play Robert in
Tobin's *Curfew* to the Fitzharding of Booth.   Again he

succeeded. On April 15 a romantic play by Dimond, named *The Conquest of Taranto ; or, St. Clara's Eve*, was produced for the first time, Young playing a Moorish Admiral, Booth the heroic Rinaldo, and Macready the traitor Valentio. It was sorely against his will that he undertook this odious character, but in the fine situation of the last act (the one good point in the play) he entirely outshone Booth, and scored a personal success. " His by-play," says the *European Magazine*, " was excellent. If his features could but display the agony of his heart, it would be perfect." The piece was a failure ; but a more successful venture of the same order soon followed it. Richard Lalor Sheil, afterwards the Right Honourable, and the most luxuriantly eloquent champion of Irish Nationalism, was at this time a briefless barrister of twenty-six. He had found a friend in his countrywoman, Miss O'Neill, who had secured the production of his first play, *Adelaide*, in the previous spring ; but it was acted only once. On May 3, 1817, his second effort, *The Apostate*, was produced, Charles Kemble playing the feeble and vacillating Hemeya, Young the strong and telling part of Malec, Miss O'Neill the fair Florinda (whose impassioned outburst, " This is too much for any mortal creature !" excited a good deal of ridicule), and Macready the cruel and sinister Pescara, Governor of Granada. This character, too, he vehemently rebelled against ; yet it earned him a distinct access of reputation. Ludwig Tieck, who saw little merit in Kemble and none in Kean, declared that Macready's Pescara •took him back to "the best days of German acting," and prophesied that the young actor had a career before him. Miss O'Neill's acting being pronounced "shockingly good," and " terrifically horrible " (she enraptured Tieck), the play attained a fair success. The author, on

the first night, was a prey to painful nervousness.   After
sitting out the first two acts, he could endure no more,
but betook himself to the green-room, which he found
deserted.   An attendant, entering shortly afterwards,
found him pacing the narrow platform in front of the
divan which ran round the room, absorbed in thought.
At last he became alive to the fact that he was not alone,
and, turning sharply, said in a tone of earnest anxiety,
"Can you tell me, sir, about what time they generally
begin to hiss tragedies at this house?"   That fatal hour
fortunately passed without a murmur, and *The Apostate*
was played twelve times during the last weeks of the
season.

Before leaving town for the recess, Macready was
present at a dinner given by the English actors to Talma,
who had come to London to assist at John Kemble's
leave-taking.   On this occasion Kemble paid Macready the honour of a special invitation to drink wine
with him—a distinction of which the young actor was
vastly proud.   He had left London for a professional
tour round his father's northern circuit, before the date
(June 27) fixed for the farewell banquet to "the noblest
Roman of them all."

His first appearance for the season of 1817–18 took
place on October 15 in the part of Gambia.   The
Covent Garden company was practically unaltered,
except that Booth appeared only once ; and Macready's
position, in respect to the line of parts assigned him,
was in no way improved.   He was forced to play in
wretched melodramatic after-pieces, in which his con-
scientiousness earned the esteem of the public and the
amused wonder of his comrades.   The season, however,
was by no means barren of advantage to him.   An illness
of Charles Kemble's gave him an opportunity of playing

Romeo to Miss O'Neill's Juliet (Monday, December 15, 1817) with great distinction.* "In the very opposite feelings of tenderness and energy," said the *Theatrical Inquisitor*, "the powers of this gentleman are perhaps unrivalled, and his Romeo exhibited that superiority in a gorgeous and conclusive manner." He had no part in Milman's *Fazio*, produced on February 5, 1818; but on March 12 he created the part of Rob Roy in Pocock's adaptation of Scott's novel, which had been published on the last day of 1817. Liston played Bailie Nicol Jarvie; Mrs. Egerton, Helen Macgregor; and Miss Stephens, Diana Vernon. "It seems odd to me," Scott wrote to Daniel Terry, on April 30, "that *Rob Roy* should have made good fortune." Perhaps he thought the theme too Scotch to please a London audience; but Liston's Bailie, though excessively humorous, did not reproduce the dialect of the Sautmarket with such fidelity as not to be understanded of the people. Rob Roy remained for many years one of Macready's most popular parts. He studied it, he tells us, from the original, so that he was not only Pocock's Rob Roy, but Scott's. A writer in the *Examiner* (whom I suspect to have been Leigh Hunt) found him "improved since *The Slave*—less loud and declamatory;" and Barry Corn- wall addressed to him a sonnet, praising "the buoyant air, the passionate tone, that breathed about him." Another poetical tribute came from Charles Lloyd, the friend of Lamb, who, after having been afflicted for four years with "a torpor of feeling," found the springs

---

* Macready represents that, but for an illness of his own, he would have repeated Romeo on the following Monday; but his memory seems to have been at fault. The play-bill of Thursday, the 18th announced, "On Monday the Tragedy of *Venice Preserved*," and Macready was playing on Friday, the 19th; so that Monday's bill was fixed before his illness declared itself.

of emotion suddenly touched by Macready's Rob Roy, and wept healthful and refreshing tears. The improvement continued for several years, but at last the cloud of melancholia descended immovably upon his mind. Macready's remaining creations of this season were villains of the deepest dye—Chosroo in John Dillon's feeble tragedy of *Retribution*, and Amurath or Sinano in Sheil's *Bellamira; or, The Fall of Tunis*, which was fairly successful. The *Examiner* praised Macready above all his comrades (Young, Charles Kemble, Terry, and Miss O'Neill), alleging that " he gave the malignant villainy of Amurath its best because most quiet effect." " He performed one scene," said the *European Magazine*, "in a style which would have added honour to the greatest master of the art." At one of the rehearsals of *Bellamira*, Young inquired of the author what he was to do at the line, " My scimitar, my scimitar ! my child ! " seeing he had given up his scimitar in the previous scene. Thus appealed to, Sheil explained the situation : " Now observe : here's Mr. Young ; here's Mr. Kemble. Well, the guard comes on ; Mr. Young draws his sword, and finds that he hasn't got it ! "

Though Macready found himself, at the end of the season, greatly advanced in reputation, its petty annoyances had been a sore trial to him. At one time he thought seriously of taking Ben Jonson's advice, and leaving " the loathèd stage," to enter what would doubtless have been in some respects a more congenial calling —the Church. But just as he was debating this question in his mind, a sum of money was suddenly required for the military advancement of his brother, to whom he was romantically attached. This put an end to his hesitation. A friend had offered to lend him a certain sum to support him at Oxford while studying for orders. This

sum he now borrowed to supply his brother's need, and
in order to repay it he was forced to stick to his profession. Such a trait of true generosity goes far to
explain the affection with which his friends regarded
him, all faults of temper notwithstanding.

Friends were by this time beginning to gather round
him. Among the earliest was William Wallace, barrister
and journalist, who, until his death in 1839, may be said
to have acted as Macready's literary adviser. At Wallace's
rooms, shortly before the production of *The Apostate*, he
met Lalor Sheil, who remained for over thirty years one of
his firmest friends. The "unaccustomed gush" of tears
over Rob Roy led to a friendship with Charles Lloyd ;
and Lloyd introduced him to that greater Charles, who
was not yet known as Elia. "I have been indulged with
a classical conference with Macready," says Lamb, in
Barbara S——, enumerating the actors he has known.
On June 27, 1820, Crabb Robinson writes, "Went to
Lamb's, found the Wordsworths there, and, having walked
with them to Westminster Bridge, returned to Lamb's,
and sat an hour with Macready, a very pleasing man,
gentlemanly in his manners, and sensible and well-
informed." It was Lloyd, too, who made him acquainted
with Talfourd, one of the most prominent members of his
circle in later years. About the same time we find him
on friendly terms with Procter, Alaric Watts, Jerdan, and
other literary men of the younger generation. Dickens
and Forster, the intimates of his later life, were not yet
in their teens.

During the summer of 1818 Macready received £100
for a week's engagement with Elliston at Birmingham,
and gave a gratuitous series of performances at his
father's theatre, in conjunction with Miss O'Neill. Returning to London for the season 1818-19, he reappeared

on September 11, in the character of Rob Roy. On the previous evening William Farren, "from Dublin," had made his first appearance in London as Sir Peter Teazle, with instant and unmistakable success. Farren's well-known vaunt that he could always command his own price, as he was "the only cock-salmon in the market," suggested to the much-tried manager a nickname for Macready. "If Farren is the cock-salmon," Harris used to say, "Macready is the cock-grumbler." The preponderance of villainy in the business assigned to him was an unceasing ground of complaint. Michael Ducas in Monk Lewis's *Adelgitha* seemed a particularly bitter pill to swallow. His old friend Fawcett replied to his remonstrances, "Why, William, you grumble at every part that is given you, and you succeed in them all! Set to work at this, and, though it is rather an odious gentleman, you may make something of him by hard study." Fawcett's encouragement was more than justified by the result. "For myself," says Macready, "the part was a great step in public opinion. . . . Indeed, from this performance I date an elevation of style and a sensible improvement in my acting." Miss Somerville, otherwise Mrs. Bunn, whom Kean had driven from Drury Lane because she overtowered him in stature, was the Adelgitha of this revival; and she subsequently played Alicia to Miss O'Neill's Jane Shore, Macready winning fresh laurels in the part of Dumont. Forty-four years later, Macready's friend George Wightwick thus recorded his impressions of that performance—

"In the second scene Belmour and Dumont entered. There was some applause, as the greeting of a favourite, but I should not have known to which it applied if the actor of Dumont had not slightly bowed. . . . His tone of voice, enunciation, and action . . . struck me at once, and 'nipp'd me into listening.' Here was the homage of admiration without any prompting of antecedent expectancy. I felt that an actor, great, or destined to become so, was before me. . . . But when, on his over-pressed familiarity with Jane Shore, the advances of Hastings are prevented by Dumont, and the seeming servant of 'venerable aspect' disarms the proud and irate nobleman, down came such plaudits as had not been heard before. . . . I had no play-bill. I had but come to see Miss O'Neill, and no play-bill was necessary for that. 'Who *is* this actor?' said I to my neighbour. It was a Mr. Macready!"

A comedy by Kenney, entitled, *A Word for the Ladies*, was unsuccessful, though Macready, Charles Kemble, Young, Liston, and Farren all appeared in it. On February 10, 1819, however, Sheil's *Evadne; or, The Statue*, was produced with complete success. According to the play-bill, it was "universally admired for the classic beauty of its poetry;" but we may suspect that it was rather the strong situation of the last act which carried it through thirty performances. The idea and several of the scenes were suggested by Shirley's tragedy of *The Traitor*. The terrible conclusion of the older play, where the profligate duke, rushing to an unholy tryst with Amidea, finds her corpse awaiting him, is altogether suppressed. The earlier passage, in which Amidea defends her chastity at the dagger's point, is replaced by a much finer scene, founded on the idea which Victor Hugo utilized, ten years later, in the portrait-scene in *Hernani*. Sheil's play is much better knit than Shirley's, though its style is conventional and flaccid. Miss O'Neill found in the heroine a character after her own heart, and Macready gained much credit as the traitor, Ludovico, the counterpart of Shirley's Lorenzo de' Medici, afterwards so marvellously embodied by Alfred de Musset in his *Lorenzaccio*. A villain of yet deeper

dye fell to Macready's lot in Maturin's *Fredolfo*, a
piece of romanticism run mad, which did not survive
its first performance. In the last act Charles Kemble,
as Adelmar, yielded up his sword to Macready, as
Wallenberg, who immediately plunged it into the bosom
of his defenceless foe. "A yell of indignation," says
Macready, "greeted this atrocity, such as, I fancy, was
never before heard in a theatre. Not another syllable
was audible." George Robertson in *The Heart of
Midlothian* (to Miss Stephens's Effie Deans and Liston's
Dumbiedikes) was Macready's only remaining creation
during this season. When Young played Brutus for his
benefit, Macready supported him as Cassius. For many
years he and Young were in the habit of exchanging
these services of courtesy. "Our rivalry," says Macready,
"was always maintained on the most gentlemanly
footing."

Two great actresses made their last appearances on
the stage at the close of this season—Mrs. Siddons at
the age of sixty-four, Miss O'Neill at the age of twenty-
eight. Mrs. Siddons appeared, on June 9, as Lady
Randolph, for the benefit of Mr. and Mrs. Charles
Kemble. Macready, who played Glenalvon, may be
said to have received the last expiring flicker of her
genius, at the lines—

> "Thou look'st at me as if thou fain would'st pry
> Into my heart. 'Tis open as my speech!"

In this one phrase, he says, she was once more at her
greatest; having delivered it, she sank into apathy. A
month later (July 13), Miss O'Neill acted Mrs. Haller,
the play-bill announcing that this would be her last performance before Christmas. It proved to be her last
appearance in London. On December 18 she married

Mr. (afterwards Sir) William Wrixon Becher, and retired from the stage. She died on October 29, 1872, just six months before Macready.

During the summer recess Macready visited Scotland, appearing for the first time in Edinburgh, where, says Mr. Dibdin, in his "Annals" of the local stage, he "was not cordially received." The Edinburgh public, indeed, never took very kindly to him. He made a three-weeks' walking-tour in the Highlands, visiting Rob Roy's country with special interest, and then took his way southward to play an engagement with his father on the western circuit. From Easter, 1819, until his death in 1829, the elder Macready was prosperously established in Bristol, where his descendants (by his second marriage) are still connected with theatrical affairs.

The season of 1819–20 opened disastrously for Covent Garden. Young had left the company, Miss O'Neill and Miss Stephens were absent (the former, as we have seen, never to return), and illness disabled Liston for more than six weeks. At Drury Lane, on the other hand, Kean, Munden, Dowton, Harley, Miss Kelly, and Mrs. Glover were assembled under the command of Elliston, who opened his management with characteristic energy. The first night at Covent Garden (September 6) was inauspicious, Charles Kemble's Macbeth being received with open disfavour. Two nights later Macready appeared as Joseph Surface, and, though this was afterwards one of his popular parts, it seems at this time to have made little impression. The critic of the *News* hoped never to see him again in this character, adding that "his looks certainly would not have been dangerous to Sir Peter's peace." Mordent in *The Steward*, an alteration by S. Beazley of Holcroft's *Deserted Daughter*, was his first original part, in one scene of which he was

E

likened by the *Times* to Kean in Sir Giles Overreach.
The first six weeks of the season dragged slowly along,
Macready playing Othello, Henry V., Hotspur, and other
parts to miserable houses, salaries falling into arrear, and
Harris (as he afterwards declared) not knowing in the
morning whether he should not shoot himself before
night.   At last he determined upon a less desperate
course.   He had in Macready an actor of undoubted
ability : why not give him a chance to establish himself
in popular favour as a tragedian of the first rank ?
Accordingly, Macready was announced to appear on
October 25 as Richard III.   He approached the adven-
ture with many misgivings.   His figure was unsuited to
the character, and he feared to affront comparison not
only with Kean, but with the still vivid memory of Cooke.
There was no help for it, however ; he braced himself
to the effort, studying the text of Cibber, but trying to
inform it with the spirit of Shakespeare.   The event was
a complete success.   The house was crowded, and the
applause was loud.   Twice the pit literally " rose at "
the new Richard, shouting, cheering, and waving handkerchiefs.   They would not hear the subordinate whose
duty it was to announce the repetition of the play, but
insisted on Macready himself appearing before the
curtain.   This " raising of the dead," as conservative
playgoers called it, was an innovation at Covent Garden,
though it had occurred more than once at Drury Lane.
The critics were no whit behind the public in their
enthusiasm.   With scarcely a single reservation, they
accepted Macready's Richard as a worthy counterpart to
Kean's.   It was " perfectly original," wrote James Haines,
in the *Morning Chronicle ;* " yet there was no apparent
struggle after originality, no laborious effort to mark a
difference in passages of small importance."   " We did

not perceive one servile imitation of Kean," said the
News; "all Kean's defects were studiously avoided, and
even his beauties given in a different form." Leigh
Hunt, in the *Examiner*, remarked that Macready presented "the livelier and more animal part" of Richard,
Kean, "the more sombre and perhaps deeper part." He
blamed in Macready a tendency to whining in the scenes
of remorse, but declared that he "never saw the gayer
part of Richard to such advantage." All the other
papers followed suit, and Macready found himself, by
general admission, the leading actor of the theatre, and
the peer of Kean. One studious and evidently impartial critic published a forty-page pamphlet, entitled,
*A Critical Examination of the respective Performances
of Mr. Kean and Mr. Macready in . . . Richard the
Third*, summing up, on the whole, in Macready's favour.
Their rivalry, though not friendly (for they knew little of
each other personally), was generous and as yet unem-
bittered. A newspaper paragraph of the period represents Kean saying, with reference to Macready's Richard,
"Such a man could do nothing short of excellence," and
Macready owning, in return, that he could not appear
as Othello without "blushing through his black" at his
inferiority to Kean.

The success of *Richard III.* saved the theatre, proving
that Harris's company was still able to hold its own against
Elliston's; and the return of Liston and Miss Stephens
completely re-established the balance of power. On
November 29 Macready appeared as Coriolanus, con-
firming, but scarcely increasing, the reputation gained
by his Richard. It was easier to compete with Kean
in the flesh than with the memory of Kemble. "Mr.
Macready," says the *News*, "aware, no doubt, that his
figure, face, and manner combined would not inspire

awe in vulgar souls, or strike a plebeian dumb by a single
motion, gave excessive bitterness to his words and violence
to his actions." Other critics were more favourable, but
Coriolanus was acted only thrice, whereas *Richard III.*
furnished nine performances.

In March, 1820, Macready "groaned and snarled"
through the part of Front de Bœuf in a drama founded
on the latest of the Waverley Novels, Charles Kemble
playing Ivanhoe; Miss Stephens, Rowena; Miss Foote,
Rebecca; Liston, Wamba; and Farren, Isaac of York.
The death of poor old George III. having removed
the long embargo upon *King Lear*, the play, was announced for revival at Drury Lane, with Kean in
the title part. Harris determined to take the wind out
of his rival's sails, after the ungenerous fashion of the
times, and asked Macready to prepare himself in Lear
with all possible speed. Respect for Shakespeare and
for his own reputation led him to decline the task, but
he offered to take any other part in the revival that
might be assigned him. Booth was accordingly engaged for Lear, and Macready cast for Edmund.
The revival took place, unsuccessfully, on April 13;
and Kean's performance, eleven days later, was scarcely
more fortunate. Henri Quatre, in a musical romance
of that title by Morton, provided Macready with a
pleasant and effective character, "in which," says the
News, "he relaxed in a great degree his usual stern-
ness." It remained for several seasons among his
most popular parts. But a more noteworthy triumph
was at hand—the "crowning mercy" of this eventful
season.

Early in 1820 a Glasgow acquaintance of Macready's
begged him to read a tragedy named *Virginius*, which
had been acted with success at the local theatre. The

author was an Irish schoolmaster, known to his pupils as Paddy Knowles. He had been a strolling player in his time, and had acted with Edmund Kean at the Waterford Theatre. It was Kean who suggested the theme of *Virginius*, which Knowles scribbled in fragments upon a schoolboy's slate, in his rare moments of relaxation ; for his teaching occupied thirteen hours out of the twenty-four. In earlier years, in London, he had known Lamb, Hazlitt, and others of the literary set, but Macready had not even heard his name. He read the tragedy, was delighted with it, and secured its acceptance by Harris, who entrusted to him the entire care of the mounting. Charles Kemble was cast for Icilius, Terry for Dentatus, Abbott for Appius Claudius ; and Virginia was assigned to "the elegant, the swanlike, the fascinating Maria Foote."

On May 17 (after the Lord Chamberlain, at the express command of George IV., had cut out some lines on tyranny) the production took place. It was a complete success, both for the author and for the actors When we compare *Virginius* with other tragedies of the time—the works of Maturin and Sheil, for example, not to mention obscurer names—we can understand the enthusiasm awakened by the frank humanity of its subject and the rhetorical vigour of its style. To sophisticated ears, its pseudo-Shakespearian phraseology, its "broad and boisterous ostentation of passion," seem perilously like mere fustian. We are apt to laugh when we hear Virginius, at the height of his agony, describe his baby-daughter lying

> " At the generous
> And sympathetic fount, that, at her cry,
> Sent forth a stream of liquid living pearl
> To cherish her enamell'd veins."

Genest remarks, very aptly, that this description of the simple operation of suckling a child "would have done vastly well in a burlesque tragedy," and compares with it the exquisite simplicity of Lady Macbeth's—

> " I have given suck, and know
> How tender 'tis to love the babe that milks me."

But merit is, after all, comparative, and *Virginius* was far more truly alive than any play of its kind that had appeared for years. · John Hamilton Reynolds, the poet whom Leigh Hunt introduced to the world in company with Keats and Shelley, provided a prologue; Barry Cornwall wrote the epilogue ; and Lamb, in a poetical address, exclaimed—

> " With wonder I
> Hear my old friend (turn'd Shakespeare) read a scene
> Only to *his* inferior in the clean
> Passes of pathos : with such fence-like art—
> Ere we can see the steel, 'tis in our heart."

When so fine a critic further compliments the poet on attaining his effects almost without the aid of "that huffing medium, *words*," we, who know very certainly that Knowles was not a word-sparing dramatist, cannot help transferring to the actor a large share in the eulogy.

He met with praise on all hands. "Austere, tender, familiar, elevated," said the *Morning Herald*, "mingling at once terror and pathos, he ran over the scale of dramatic expression with the highest degree of power." "Faults hitherto attributed to his style," the *News* declared, "were studiously avoided ; his love of sudden transition was controlled within the bounds of propriety, and his rich manly voice, which has too frequently tempted him to rant, was subdued and mellowed down to a tone of exquisite touchingness." Virginius estab-

lished him firmly in the distinguished position he owed
to his Richard III., and remained one of his favourite
characters to the end of his career. For his benefit
(June 9) he appeared for the first time in Macbeth,
and was greeted with enthusiasm. It was on this
occasion that he rebelled against the long-established
custom which permitted an actor, on his benefit day, to
accept gifts of money from distinguished " patrons."

In the course of his provincial tour this summer (1820)
he visited Aberdeen, Montrose, Dundee, and Perth,
with a company under the management of Ryder, playing
Macbeth, Coriolanus, Romeo, Virginius, and other parts.
His Virginia was Miss Catherine Frances or " Kitty"
Atkins, the girl whom he had scolded in Glasgow, five
years before, for being imperfect in a child's part. She
was now not quite fifteen, but the local critics already
discovered in her a " correctness of taste and accuracy of
judgment" which encouraged them to hope that she was
" destined to a high degree of eminence." Macready was
brought into frequent contact with this young lady, and,
as he quaintly puts it, " grew less and less desirous of
avoiding her." He found her graceful, amiable, intelligent, and docile—and to a man of his character, docility
was a crowning charm in womanhood. He procured her
a situation, a few months later, in his father's company
at Bristol, and from this time onwards he never lost sight
of her.

The season of 1820–21, though remunerative to the
management, was comparatively unexciting. Macready
created three new characters, which failed to take a
permanent place in his repertory. The first was Wallace
in a turgid and feeble tragedy of that name by a young
man named C. E. Walker, which met with a success
far beyond its deserts. The second was the Duke in

Barry Cornwall's *Mirandola,* in the construction of which Macready may be said to have collaborated. Its style is lighter and more graceful than that of most contemporary plays, but the conduct of the story is unskilful—a female Iago, with a clerical familiar, playing an equivocal and ineffective part in the action. The third original character was Damon in Banim and Sheil's tragedy, or rather romantic play, *Damon and Pythias.* This is a really strong and stirring drama, and the fact that it was less successful than the puling *Wallace* can only be attributed to some unaccountable caprice of public taste. Macready also added four Shakespearian parts to his list. His Iachimo was described by the *News* critic as "the worst he had ever seen," and Macready himself admits that it was ineffective. Prospero, in a further maltreatment by Reynolds of Dryden and Davenant's perversion of *The Tempest,* was a performance of small account; but Hamlet, which he acted for his benefit, was received with enthusiasm. Finally, on June 25, 1821, he made a remarkable success as the King in the second part of *Henry IV.,* revived for the sake of introducing a Coronation Spectacle, which was so attractive as to lead to a prolongation of the season. Charles Kemble was the Prince of Wales; Fawcett, Falstaff; Farren and Emery, Shallow and Silence ; and Mrs. Davenport, Mrs. Quickly — an excellent cast. Earlier in the season, at Macready's instance, an attempt had been made, with small success, to revive the original text of Shakespeare's *Richard III.*

"Of the Tragedy hitherto acted under the title of *King Richard the Third,*" said the play-bill, "more than half is the exclusive composition of Cibber. The present is an attempt to restore (in place of his ingenious alteration) the *original character and language of Shakespeare;* in which no more extraneous matter is retained than the trifling passages necessary to connect those scenes between which omissions have necessarily been made for the purposes of representation."

In spite of these protestations, several of Cibber's most famous claptraps were retained; but they were not sufficient to reconcile the general public to the new face of their old friend.

Macready's original five-years' engagement had now expired, and he re-engaged with Harris for a similar period, on terms to be stated presently. Young's return to Covent Garden combined with several other circumstances to render the season 1821–22 an idle and inglorious one for Macready. He appeared only three times before the New Year—twice as Virginius and once as Gambia; and during the remainder of the season he created no new character, and appeared only some forty-five times in all, as against a hundred and twenty appearances in 1819–20, and a hundred and thirty in 1820–21. The public taste, whetted by the pomp and circumstance of the previous summer, was insatiate in its demand for spectacle. Reynolds's "melodramatic opera" *The Exile* revived for the sake of the " grand public entry of the Empress Elizabeth ;" *The Two Gentlemen of Verona*, treated as a spectacular opera ; and Pocock's *Montrose ; or, The Children of the Mist*, with Liston as Dugald Dalgetty, were all extremely popular ; so that, for Macready, the season was practically barren. The only noteworthy event was a successful revival of *Julius Cæsar*, with Young as Brutus, Charles Kemble as Antony, and Macready as Cassius. To this character he now devoted renewed study, and made it, he says, " one of his most real personations."

In the spring of 1822 Charles Kemble, who was now

(by his brother John's gift) a co-proprietor in the theatre, obtained a preponderating share in its management. It soon became evident that he and Macready could by no means pull in the same boat. They had at one time been on good terms, and in after-years, when the causes of friction no longer existed, they professed much mutual esteem; but the relation of actor-manager and actor led to perpetual misunderstandings. There were, no doubt, faults on both sides; but it is clear that Macready worked himself into a state of unreasonable irritation which often warped his saner judgment. Open warfare broke out soon after the change of management, which took effect on March 11, 1822. On May 1 Macready writes to "— Forbes and Willett, Esqrs.," Charles Kemble's co-managers, a long and angry letter of complaint. "My fortunes," he says, "are surrendered to the single sway of an actor whose aspirations to supremacy in his profession must render my reputation but of secondary moment to him, while he who has the. motive is also armed with the power to molest and distress me." His specific complaint is that, Kean having promised to play for his benefit, Charles Kemble has maliciously revived an obsolete rule, forbidding the enlistment on such occasions of performers from the other theatre. The rule, if it ever existed, has been set at nought, Macready declares, by Farren and Miss Stephens: why, he asks, should it be enforced in his case alone? "If Mr. C. Kemble," he proceeds, "be permitted to exercise his influence without control over the course of a contemporary actor, the Committee must expect to see him the single supporter of the Covent Garden stage, as no gentleman of talent or feeling can brook so irrational and so partial an autocracy." The remonstrance was without avail. Macready had to content himself with Young's support on his benefit night, when they played Othello and Iago to a large house.

Towards the end of June, 1822, Macready set forth on a tour to Italy. He passed through Paris, Geneva, Lausanne (where he called on John Kemble, but did not see him); up the Rhone valley, over the Simplon to Domo d'Ossola, Lago Maggiore, and Milan; thence to Verona and Venice, Bologna and Florence; from Florence to Naples without pause; back to Rome, which he "did" with laudable diligence; then by way of Bologna to Parma and Milan; thence to Turin, and over the Mont Cenis to Geneva and Paris. He had a letter of introduction to Byron, but some difficulty as to his route compelled him to leave Pisa unvisited. He does not seem to have heard while in Italy of the death of Shelley, which occurred just a week before he crossed the Alps. In Paris he saw Mdlle. Mars on his outward, and Talma on his homeward, journey. Of both he speaks with enthusiasm.

An Englishman whom he met in Paris assured him that he had recently seen Young play Hamlet at Drury Lane. Macready politely but confidently insisted that he must be mistaken, for Young was engaged at Covent Garden, and, even if any disagreement had taken place, he could not yet have appeared at Drury Lane, as there was a convention between the theatres that no performer leaving the one should be engaged at the other until a year had elapsed. His informant, as it turned out, was in the right. The unwise economy of the Covent Garden management, and the no less unwise extravagance of Elliston at Drury Lane, had led to a revolution in the theatrical world. Young, Liston, and Miss Stephens demanded that their salaries at Covent Garden should be raised from £20 to £25 a week. The management

demurred, and Elliston, regardless of the unwritten
compact, seized the opportunity to offer the seceding
artists, not £25 a week, but £20 a night, for at least
three nights a week.   This trebled their Covent Garden
salary, and they naturally accepted without hesitation.
The result was a complete overthrow of the balance of
power.   Kean, Young, and Elliston, Munden, Liston, and
Dowton, Miss Stephens, Madame Vestris, Mrs. Glover,
and Mrs. W. West—a company of unusual strength—
were opposed to Macready, Charles Kemble, Farren, and
Fawcett—a company of unexampled feebleness.   Drury
Lane was crowded, Covent Garden deserted ; but the precedent of enormous salaries, thus established by Elliston,
was ultimately ruinous to both houses.

The Covent Garden season was naturally dull.   Sheil,
who was anxious to secure an actress for the leading part
in his *Huguenot*, thought he had discovered a new O'Neill
in a Miss F. H. Kelly from Dublin, who was, at his
request, tutored by Macready, and brought forward in
Juliet.   This part she performed about a dozen times,
with some success, but her subsequent efforts fell far short
of her promise.   *The Huguenot* was duly produced on
December 11, 1822, and was duly massacred.   Abbott,
at rehearsal, declared that the name, which he pronounced " You-go-not," was one of ill omen, and secured
the fulfilment of his prophecy by refraining from learning
his part.   The play was altogether miscast, and though
Macready thought it the best of Sheil's works, and
devoted much study to his own part of Polignac, it was
acted only three times.   Miss Mitford's *Julian*, produced
March 15, 1823, met with somewhat better fortune.
Poor Miss Mitford had an evil time of it for many months
between the contending Kemble and Macready factions,
but at last cast in her lot with Macready, for whom she

had at that time the warmest admiration. One of his letters was "the prettiest letter I ever read in my life, . . . quite the letter of a scholar and a gentleman, not the least like that of an actor. . . . He is just such another soul of fire as Haydon—highly educated, and a man of great literary acquirements — consorting entirely with poets and young men of talent." Her tragedy was well written and not uninteresting, but there was a womanishness in the character of Julian that sapped its otherwise undeniable merit. It evidently led to some friction between the poetess and the actor, for she writes on May 13, "That Macready likes me I know; but I have, perhaps, suffered even more from his injustice and prejudice and jealousy than from the angry attacks of the Kembles." Their relations, in after-years, were far from amicable.

The new Shakespearian parts which Macready this season essayed were Cardinal Wolsey and King John, both undertaken, it would appear, with reluctance, yet both reckoned afterwards among his best performances. Macbeth, too, which he had not acted since the spring of 1820, was now revived; and for his benefit he played Shylock for the first time, along with Delaval in Kenney's comedietta of *Matrimony.* It was his general custom, on his benefit night, to choose some afterpiece affording him a light-comedy part—Almaviva, Sir Charles Racket in *Three Weeks after Marriage*, or Delaval.

In the mean time Macready's hatred for Charles Kemble was growing more and more bitter. It blinded him even to his merits as an actor, which he afterwards freely acknowledged. Kemble was to have played at a benefit on behalf of the Philanthropic Society, when the news of his brother John Philip's death forced him to withdraw his name. In this difficulty a deputation was sent to Macready. As soon as their spokesman broached the business to him, he interrupted him, saying, "So, sir, because the CORPORAL refuses to do his duty, you apply to the COMMANDER-IN-CHIEF!" This extravagant piece of arrogance is vouched for by an ear-witness; and certain it is that Macready's tone led the Philanthropic Committee, perhaps with a spice of malice, to advertise that he had "condescended" to play Hamlet for their benefit—a phrase which, being attributed to Macready himself, gave him much annoyance. About the same time he wrote to an aspiring dramatist that "he wished to avoid anything that would bring him into collision with a person for whose talents and judgment he had such a contempt as he bore for those of Mr. C. Kemble." With the other managers his relations were scarcely happier. In an undated note dashed off at the Box Office (probably on February 15, 1823)—

"Mr. Macready informs the Committee of Management . . . that he CANNOT undertake the character of King John for Monday se'nnight. If it should be his ill fortune to have any concern with them so long as the following Monday, he will endeavour to be ready in the part; but neither his spirits nor his powers of mind are, under their conduct, what they have been. . . . Mr. Macready desires to know of the Committee why his name, whilst he has the misery of belonging to their theatre, is omitted on the Play-Bills for Cardinal Wolsey, and why they will suffer their agents to disgrace them by breaking a promise, given at least ten times, of the performance of Macbeth as a recompense for undertaking Wolsey."

The Committee could scarcely be eager to retain the services of a performer who favoured them with such missives as this, and the breach which soon followed was clearly inevitable. Macready's written agreement with Harris for a second term of five years placed his salary at £20 a week, but was supplemented by a verbal promise that he should have the highest salary in the theatre—in other words, if any regular performer received more than £20, his salary should at once be raised to the same amount. This stipulation, a common one at the time, was made in the presence of a witness, and in handing over the management to Forbes, Willett, and Kemble, Harris explicitly informed them of its terms. During the season 1822–23, however, Macready found them attempting to shuffle out of it. Correspondence and interviews led to no settlement. The question was to be referred to arbitration, but the Committee delayed and delayed until Macready at last gave them notice that, as they declined to ratify his engagement, he held it void. This was, perhaps, the very thing the Committee desired. Macready issued a pamphlet, dated June 16, 1823, in which he set forth his wrongs. Among other things, he accused Charles Kemble of having offered Miss Stephens £25 a week, on condition that she should keep the fact secret, and so defraud him (Macready) of the additional £5 a week to which, by his agreement, he would have been entitled. This may or may not have been true ; but it is evident, from the correspondence Macready prints, that the Committee shuffled and paltered most unjustifiably. Elliston offered him the same terms he had given to the other refugees from Covent Garden, and Macready engaged with him for the ensuing season at £20 a night.

MACREADY'S CHARACTERS.

1816–1823.
(With the number of performances.)

COVENT GARDEN : 1816-17 : *Gambia (*Slave*), 33 ; *Pescara (*Apostate*), 12 ; *Valentio (*Conquest of Taranto*),

6 ; Demetrius (*Humorous Lieutenant*), 5 ; Orestes (*Distrest Mother*), 3 ; Othello, Mentevole (*Italian Lover*), Beverley (*Gamester*), 2 ; Iago, Robert (*Curfew*), 1.

1817-18: *Rob Roy, 34 ; *Amurat (*Bellamira*), 13 ; *Dumont (*Father and Children*), *Berndorff (*Illustrious Traveller*), 9 ; *Salviati (*Castle of Paluzzi*), 8 ; *Chosroo (*Retribution*), 7 ; Pescara, 6 ; Gambia, 4 ; Romeo, Glenalvon (*Douglas*), Pizarro, Hotspur (second act of *Henry IV. Part I.*), Posthumus, 1

1818-19 : *Ludovico (*Evadne*), 30 ; *George Robertson (*Heart of Midlothian*), 16 ; Rob Roy, Dumont (*Jane Shore*), 15 ; *Romani (*Proof Presumptive*), Ducas (*Adelgitha*), *Winterland (*Word for Ladies*), 3 ; Cassius, 2 ; Pescara, Earl of Warwick (Francklin's play), Hotspur, Pierre, *Wallenberg (*Fredolfo*), Glenalvon, Gambia, 1.

1819-20 : *Henri Quatre, 28 ; *Front de Bœuf, *Virginius, 14 ; *Mordent (*The Steward*), 13 ; Rob Roy, 11 ; Richard III., 9 ; Joseph Surface, Coriolanus, Jaques, Edmund, Macbeth, 3 ; Rolla, Biron (*Isabella*), *Leicester (translation of Schiller's *Maria Stuart*), *Montoni (*Montoni; or, The Phantom*), Gambia, 2 ; Othello, Henry V., Hotspur, Clytus (*Alexander*), Bajazet (*Tamerlane*), Peregrine (*John Bull*), 1.

1820-21 : Henry IV., 21 ; *Wallace, 17 ; *Mirandola, 15 ; Rob Roy, 14 ; Virginius, Henri Quatre, 11 ; Prospero, 10 ; Gambia, 9 ; *Damon, 7 ; Pierre, Joseph Surface, 4 ; Iachimo, Richard III., 2 ; Zanga, Jaques, Hamlet, Sir C. Racket (*Three Weeks after Marriage*), and Captain Irwin (*Every One has his Fault*), 1.

1821-22 : Rob Roy, 9 ; Cassius, 8 ; Gambia, 4 ; Virginius, Daran, Henri Quatre, 3 ; Romeo, Othello, 2 ; Joseph Surface, Prospero, Wallace, Henry IV., Hubert, Almaviva, Antonio, Posthumus, 1.

1822-23 : *Julian, 8 ; Rob Roy, 7 ; Wolsey, King John, Macbeth, Jaques, 5 ; Joseph Surface, 4 ; *Polignac (*Huguenot*), Pierre, Virginius, 3 ; Henri Quatre, Wallace, Daran Gambia, 2 ; Othello, Earl of Essex, Hamlet, Shylock, Delaval, Duke Aranza, 1.

CHAPTER IV.

1823–1837

THE DOLDRUMS.

WE come now to what may be called the doldrums of Macready's career—"a region of calms, squalls, and light baffling winds." Hitherto he had gone steadily ahead; for the next thirteen years, during which he made Drury Lane his head-quarters, his progress, though real, was slow and intermittent, while annoyances in the shape of hostile criticism and personal enmity beset him on every hand. These thirteen years brought him no great and inspiriting triumphs like Rob Roy, Richard III., and Virginius. They added only two really enduring creations to his record—William Tell and Werner—and they were fruitful in semi-successes, disappointments, and humiliations. It is true that, if he made enemies during this period, he also made staunch and devoted friends—the "clique" who were so often accused of ministering unduly to his self-esteem. But if he had died or retired from the stage in the winter of 1835–36, it might have been said with apparent truth that he had for some time been losing ground, and had not fulfilled the promise of his early years. Oddly enough, it was his bitterly-rued assault upon the Poet

F

Bunn that seemed somehow to dissipate the spell. His migration to Covent Garden after the outbreak gave a fresh impetus to his career, and marks in every sense a new departure.

On Monday, October 13, 1823, Macready made his first appearance at Drury Lane, as Virginius, Wallack playing Icilius; Mrs. W. West, Virginia; and Mrs. Glover, Servia. The aforesaid annoyances commenced at once. In the *John Bull* of October 19 the following paragraphs appeared :—

"At Drury Lane, Mr. Macready opened his career in *Virginius*, one of those melodramatic tragedies which peculiarly suit the ventriloquism of what are called *natural* actors, and his reception was very flattering.

"Mr. Macready is a clever performer, and moreover a clever man—he is a scholar, and, as we are told, a person of refined manners, gentlemanly habits, and classical pursuits— it must therefore be extremely painful to him to witness the ill-judged *puffery* with which he is bedaubed in all the morning papers. We do not allude to his gallant preservation of a fellow-creature, or his own modest concealment of the fact— *there* he cannot be too much lauded."

The writer then goes on to quote an apparently extravagant, because ill-written, eulogy from the *Courier* (edited by Macready's friend Mudford), and to remark that if Mr. Macready were not known to be "above such conduct," it would seem as though the "empty praises" were founded on solid pudding.

Here I must digress to explain "the gallant preservation of a fellow-creature." In May, 1821, appeared the first number of an obscure theatrical paper, containing what purported to be a biography of Macready. It related how, during an engagement at Birmingham, he had heroically rescued a child from a burning house. There was not an atom of foundation for the story,

which may, however, have been a distorted version of
the quite unheroic incident during the storm at Newcastle
in 1814. Macready at once contradicted the legend, but
in vain. In August, 1823, it cropped up in a Southampton
newspaper. Mudford copied it into the *Courier*, from
which it was disseminated through half the papers in the
kingdom. I have not been able to procure the original
magazine, but it was in the following form that the story
went the round of the press :—

" . . . He had left the house after the tragedy of *Hamlet*,
in which he had delineated, with his accustomed ability, the
romantic and philosophic Prince, and was proceeding on foot
to his lodgings in the suburbs, when he approached a small
cottage in flames, surrounded by a concourse of people. The
flames were bursting out of the front door, and a cry of
distress was heard from within ; he instantly threw off his
coat, waistcoat, and hat, and, with the agility of a harlequin,
sprang into the parlour window, from whence he soon issued
with an infant in his grasp. The flames had caught his
'clothes, which, however, were soon extinguished, and the
infant was received by the speechless mother in an agony no
words can describe. The hat, coat, and waistcoat of the
adventurous hero were gone, and he darted through the
crowd as he was, to his lodgings."

The myth then relates how his identity was discovered.
" A fellow " was caught next day selling " a handsome
coat " with Macready's name marked in the sleeve, and
the modest hero was forced to confess that this was
the coat he had thrown off in order to facilitate his
harlequin leap through the window. A £10 note, sent
him anonymously on his benefit night, " as a tribute
to his humanity and courage," he at once handed to the
parents of the rescued child, " promising to assist the
infant as it advanced in years." In vain Macready tried
to strangle this terrible infant, which came trailing clouds

of most unwelcome glory. It continued to haunt him at intervals, on both sides of the Atlantic, until the very end of his career.

This was the "gallant preservation of a fellow creature," which the *John Bull* admitted to be above praise. Macready's explanations led to the following paragraph in the next issue : " Our observations upon the fulsome praises of Mr. Macready . . . have drawn from that gentleman a letter which he wishes us *not* to publish. . . . Mr. Macready seems equally with ourselves to feel the injurious effect of such overstrained praise; and requests us to contradict the statement of his having saved a child from a burning house . . . and informs us that he himself contradicted the story some months ago." The writer then goes on to protest that the paragraphs " were directed, not against his acting, but against a system likely, as he says himself, to do him incalculable mischief." Macready believed that Theodore Hook, then editor of the *John Bull*, deliberately misrepresented his letter in order to involve him in difficulties with the friendly portion of the press. It is certain that he would be the last man to despise or reject favourable criticism, even if a little overstrained. Yet it seems probable that Hook carelessly misunderstood some expression in his letter, and wrote without malice. A week or two later the *John Bull* makes a similar attack on the extravagant panegyrists of Mrs. Bunn, whom, nevertheless, it praises warmly, and to all appearance sincerely. I find no sign in the *John Bull* of any animus against Macready at this period, except such as might arise from his habitually appearing in the " democratic, ranting, trashy plays" of Knowles. In May of the following year the *John Bull* eulogizes Macready's Richard III. at the expense of Kean's, declaring Macready to be the greater attraction of the two. It seems, therefore, that he was wrong in supposing himself the victim of deliberate malice on the part of Theodore Hook. None the less was the paragraph calculated to injure him with the press in general. It cost him years of effort, he says (perhaps with some exaggeration), to "live down" the hostility it excited.

His second part at Drury Lane was Rolla, his third Hamlet, his fourth Macbeth, with Wallack as Macduff, and Mrs. Bunn as Lady Macbeth. Then came a tolerably successful revival of *The Winter's Tale*, in which he appeared, for the first time in London, as Leontes. Mrs. Bunn made a stately Hermione ; Wallack played Florizel ; Mrs. W. West, Perdita ; Mrs. Glover, Paulina ; Munden, Autolycus ; and Harley, the Clown. A fortnight later (November 18), "in consequence of the Sanction of the Licenser having been at length obtained," Knowles's *'Caius Gracchus* was performed for the first time. The interest of this play is entirely political, Cornelia and Licinia serving merely as a plaintive chorus. Moreover, its whole action turns upon the fickleness of the tedious pseudo-Shakespearian mob, who keep on veering about through the whole five acts with imbecile unanimity. Caius Gracchus himself is represented as a singularly feeble politician, loquacious, yet unpersuasive, devoid alike of foresight and of temper. The cast, too, was anything but strong, so that failure was inevitable. Macready represents that Bunn, who was Elliston's stage-manager, brought the run to an untimely end because his wife was unsuccessful as the Mother of the Gracchi. But it was not in the nature of things that such a play should become really popular.

On December 8 Kean appeared and Macready disappeared. Elliston had intended to make their joint performances the great attraction of his season, but Kean flatly declined to be seen on the same stage with Macready. He " did not mind Young," whose method served as a foil to his own, but shrank from facing a fierier rival. Elliston was consequently forced to restrict Macready's engagement to the stated minimum of forty nights. He reappeared after Easter (1824) to finish his tale of performances ; but the remainder of the season was uneventful, save for Munden's retirement from the stage on the last day of May. The only part added to Macready's repertory was that of the Duke in *Measure for Measure.*

His last appearance for the season took place on June 23, and on the following morning he was married at St. Pancras Church to his Virginia of four years ago, Miss Catherine Frances Atkins. Miss Atkins had held the " juvenile lead " in his father's Bristol company from January, 1821, to June, 1822. Here she had played Lady Anne to Macready's Richard III., Virginia to his Virginius, Isidora to his Mirandola. Among her other parts were Ophelia, Celia, Dorinda in Dryden and Davenant's *Tempest*, Calanthe in *Damon and Pythias*, and Zelinda in *The Slave.* The "lead" was held at this time by a Miss Desmond, who, towards the close of 1821, became the wife of the elder Macready. On leaving Bristol, Miss Atkins and her father and mother migrated to Dublin ; and on March 26, 1823, her father was drowned, with seventy other passengers, in the wreck of the Liverpool packet *Alert* off the Welsh coast. Up to this time the relation between Macready and Miss 'Atkins had been that of guardian and ward, or preceptor and pupil. Her father's death brought matters to a point. They became formally betrothed, and in the autumn of 1823 Miss Atkins came to England to make the acquaintance of

Macready's sister Letitia, who had for some time resided with him. This lady seems to have possessed a full share of the family temper, and Macready gives a tragi-comic account of her more than ungracious reception of her sister-in-law to be. In time, however, this difficulty was got over, and the two became friends. Miss Atkins spent the winter studying assiduously to fit herself for the high estate and dignity of Macready's spouse. He him-self was in his element in the part of guide, philosopher, and friend to his "lovely and docile Griselda." Accord-ing to the newspaper gossip of the time, he might, had he so pleased, have married "the daughter of a noble Earl"—what noble Earl I do not know. He preferred the obscure country actress to the high-born dame (if she ever existed), and was rewarded by conjugal happiness as perfect as his nature would allow, throughout the twenty-eight years of their married life.

His second season at Drury Lane (1824–25) opened on November 15 with Macbeth. *Der Freischütz* had been produced five days earlier—the fifth adaptation of Weber's opera performed in London within the space of four months. It was the rage of the season, and was played seventy-two times. Macready performed Leontes, with Harley as Autolycus; Jaques to the Rosalind of Mrs. Yates, the Orlando of Wallack, and the Touchstone of Harley; and King John to Wallack's Faulconbridge and Mrs. Bunn's Constance. On January 5, 1825, Massinger's *Fatal Dowry*, expurgated and adapted by Sheil, was produced with great success, Macready playing Romont; Wallack, Charalois; Terry, Rochfort; and Mrs. W. West, Beaumelle. It was repeated on January 7, and bade fair to prove a great attraction, when a serious illness which befell Macready interrupted its career. He suffered from inflammation of the diaphragm, was for some time in imminent danger, and, on rising from his sick-bed (as he himself tells us), left the vivacity of youth behind him.   An anecdote, recorded by his enemy Bunn, but doubtless founded on fact, relates to this illness.   Elliston, on calling one day to inquire for him, "was admitted into the chamber of the sick tragedian, who faintly implied a belief in his approaching dissolution."   The manager, deeply impressed, spoke some words of encouragement, and glided on tiptoe from the room.   He had not reached the bottom of the staircase when some one, in a whisper, called him back.   He approached the sufferer's bedside, "in the conviction that some posthumous attention was about to be required of him ;" when, to his astonishment, the dying man feebly but eagerly whispered, "Elliston, do you think that *Rob Roy*, reduced to two acts, would be a good afterpiece for my benefit?"   Elliston, no doubt, left the house reassured as to Macready's chances of life.

It was more than three months before Macready was able to resume duty, and in the mean time many things had happened.   The notorious case of Cox *v.* Kean had been tried while his illness was at its height ; Kean's ill-advised attempts to outface British pharisaism had occupied the public mind; and yet another theatrical scandal, the case of Miss Foote *v.* Hayne, had intervened to divert attention from the drama proper. Reappearing as Romont on April 11, Macready found that the success of three months before had been forgotten, and the piece was soon withdrawn.   On the other hand, Knowles's *William Tell*, produced on May 11, survived the insufficient rehearsal of the first performance, and proved a lasting success.   Though turgid and long-winded even beyond the playwright's wont, it contains some effectively overwrought scenes which suited Macready's style. Mrs. Bunn played Tell's wife, and the infant prodigy, Clara Fisher, created the important part of the boy Albert. For his benefit (June 2) Macready acted Henry V. and Rob Roy (the play-goers of those days liked to have their money's worth), and for Harley's benefit he resumed his old part of Gambia, for the last time in London.

The remainder of the year 1825 and the first three months of 1826 were devoted partly to provincial engagements, partly to rest in a country retreat near Denbigh. An article in *Blackwood's Magazine* for June, 1825, embittered the commencement of this partial holiday, causing Macready at least as much annoyance as his dispute with the *John Bull*. It was entitled, *A Letter to Charles Kemble, Esq., and R. W. Elliston, Esq., on the Present State of the Stage*, the signature of " Philo-Dramaticus " being assumed by the Rev. W. Harness. Inquiring into the depressed state of the national drama, the author laid the fault at the door of "your GREAT ACTORS—I mean your *soi-disant* GREAT ACTORS—Messrs. Kean, Young, and Macready." Their refusal to attach themselves permanently to a stock company, their demand for short engagements at high salaries, and their self-seeking tyranny over dramatic authors, constitute the head and front of their offending.

"They must have tragedies written to suit their personal tricks—I beg pardon, their peculiarities. . . . The history of the lately rejected tragedy of *Rienzi* [by Harness's intimate friend, Miss Mitford] is strikingly illustrative of the evils that attend the operation of the present system. . . . The play was completed and shown to Mr. Macready. He was delighted with the production. The chief part was very effective both in language and situation, and only required a very *few* and slight alterations to render it worthy the abilities of any of the *great* actors. He wished an entirely new first act; this was indispensable that Rienzi might be introduced striking to the earth an injurious Patrician, . . . because this circumstance had peculiarly pleased Mr. Macready's fancy when a boy at school. To make room for the introduction of this new incident, the second and third acts . . . were to be compressed into one. The fifth act, was to be rewritten, that the character of Rienzi might, to the very dropping of the curtain, hold its paramount station on the stage. All these alterations were to be made *in a fortnight;* the authoress was then to . .¯. superintend in person the rehearsals and *getting up* of the piece. . . . In a fortnight she called on Mr. Macready with the manuscript. To her utter astonishment he received her with the greatest coolness : 'There was no hurry for her play. The managers had another piece at the theatre which must at all events be produced first ; and it was very improbable her play could be acted at all.' This other piece was *The Fatal Dowry* of Massinger. . . .

"Persons of. distinguished ·talent . will cease, as they have ceased, to write for the stage. . . . Who are your successful authors ? Planché and Arnold, Poole and Kenney ; names so ignoble in the world of literature that they have no circulation beyond the green-room. . . . It is no longer, the play, but the actors, that the public are called to see. . . . I have seen Mrs. Siddons go through the part of Constance, of Isabella, of Belvidera, of Mrs. Beverley, almost without a single burst of applause ; there have been nothing but tears and sobs to interrupt the silence. . . . But this style of simple and natural acting has passed away. The actor of forty pounds a night comes forth to astonish. He is a sort of rhetorical Merry Andrew ; and all his excellence consists in the exhibition of a certain round of tricks. . . . Every start, every rant, every whisper, is followed by rounds of applause, and by these [the audience] estimate his merits. The mob are collected to see an enormously paid actor, who acts only for twelve nights, and their expectations must not be disappointed. If they returned home without having been wonderfully astonished, without having something extra-ordinary and monstrous to relate, they would begin to suspect that the performer did not deserve his wages. The consequence is that Messrs. Young, Kean, and Macready—Mr. Young in a degree less than the other two—have introduced a manner of acting more forced, heavy, exaggerated, and unnatural than perhaps ever disgraced the stage since England had a regular theatre to boast of."

I have quoted this long passage because, in spite of obvious exaggerations, it contains a certain leaven of truth, and at least represents the views then held with regard to the stage by a large number of educated men. Macready declares the account of his dealings with Miss Mitford to be "false and libellous;" but it was certainly not quite unfounded. What the writer failed to see was that the weakness of the authors, rather than the egoism of the actors, lay at the root of the evil. No playwright of really commanding talent was ever tyrannized over by his actors, though the greatest playwrights, from Shakespeare downwards, have not disdained to fit particular actors with parts "cut to their measure."

In the spring -of 1826 Macready played a short engagement (April 10 to May 19) at Drury Lane, now nominally under the management of William Gore Elliston, a son of the Great Lessee. He attempted no new character. He was the Hotspur in *Henry IV. Part I.* when Elliston made the attempt to play Falstaff, which brought his career at Drury Lane to an inglorious close. At rehearsal Macready thought Elliston the best Falstaff he had ever seen, but on the night of performance (May 11) he was feeble and ineffective. When the play was repeated, four nights later, he struggled on until, in the last act, he reeled and fell upon the stage. The disaster was generally attributed to drink, but Macready avers that it was really due to physical weakness combined with an overdose of ether.

After fulfilling some provincial engagements, Macready,

with his wife and sister, sailed from Liverpool for New York on September 2, 1826, arriving on the 27th of the same month. As to the details of this tour I have not been able to learn much, but there is no doubt that it was thoroughly successful. His impresario was Stephen Price, one of the first of a long line of American speculative showmen, who was lessee of Drury Lane Theatre during this very winter. Macready made his first appearance at the Park Theatre, New York, on October 2, in the character of Virginius, and was warmly received both by the public and the press. He may not have been much gratified on finding himself described in one of the leading papers as " second only to Mr. Cooper ; " * but there must have been solace in the fact that another critic credited him, not only with genius, but with great personal beauty. It seems to have been recognized, on the whole, that of all the tragedians who had appeared on the American stage, only Cooke and Kean were to be regarded as his peers. Though it was five years since Junius Brutus Booth had crossed the Atlantic, he had not yet attained the height of his fame ; Forrest, the first native-born tragedian, was but a youth of twenty, though already rising into note ; and such actors as Holman and Conway were evidently on a lower plane of talent. Kean's second American tour, ill-advised and humiliating, had taken place during the previous winter, and it is possible that the unpopularity of his predecessor may have reacted to the advantage of Macready, whose conduct, both in private life and towards his audiences, was so different. At Boston, where the most serious anti-Kean riots had occurred, Macready was received

* Thomas Abthorpe Cooper, the pupil of William Godwin. He was an actor of fine endowment, marred by carelessness and defective training.

with enthusiasm, both on his first visit in November,
1826, and during a return engagement in the following
March. He also appeared at Baltimore, Philadelphia,
and Albany, and seems to have visited Niagara. In New
York he played no fewer than five short engagements
—in October and December, 1826, and in February,
April, and May, 1827. In the third series of performances Conway appeared with him, playing Jaffier to
his Pierre, Charalois to his Romont, Faulconbridge to
his John, the Prince of Wales to his Henry IV., and
Brutus to his Cassius. He took his farewell benefit in
New York on June 4, playing Macbeth and Delaval, and
seems to have returned to England shortly afterwards.

During the season 1827–28 Drury Lane was still
under the management of Stephen Price. On the opening night Charles Kean made his first appearance on
any stage in the part of Young Norval, and continued
to perform at intervals throughout the season, while
Liston, Wallack, Ellen Tree, and Miss Foote also belonged to the company. Macready appeared on November 12 as Macbeth, to the Lady Macbeth of Mrs. W.
West. It was at this time that the German traveller,
Prince Pückler-Muskau, saw him in Macbeth, and recorded * his striking excellence in the murder-scene, the
banquet-scene, and the last act. He praises the stage
management, but ridicules the fashionable flowered-
chintz dressing-gown which Macready threw over his
armour in obedience to Lady Macbeth's advice that he
should get his nightgown on.

Early in 1828 Macready played Ribemont, Marshal
of France, in an historical play by Reynolds, "founded on
Shirley and Beaumont and Fletcher," entitled, *Edward
the Black Prince.* A gentleman informed Genest that

* "Briefe eines Verstorbenen," iv. 255.

the plays of Fletcher from which Reynolds borrowed
were *Philaster, Bonduca,* and *The Two Noble Kinsmen.*
" He could not pretend to describe *how* Reynolds had
contrived to jumble his materials together—he only
knew that the thing was *done,* and that he witnessed
the damnation of the piece." No better fate awaited
Lord Porchester's tragedy of *Don Pedro,* in which (March
10) Macready played Henry of Trastamar. There were
one or two strong situations in the piece, but it was on
the whole tedious and ineffective. Macready played
Posthumus for his benefit (May 23), to Miss Foote's
Imogen and Cooper's Iachimo. Bunn states that Price,
finding him unattractive, sacrificed sixteen nights of his
engagement, though he had nevertheless to pay the
stipulated £20 for each night. As Macready played
only twenty-four times (not counting his benefit), Bunn
is no doubt right. There was certainly no love lost
between actor and manager. Macready one evening
suggested to Price that, as the bill was unusually long,
he might cut out the music in *Macbeth.* " I can't very
well do that," replied the manager; "but I'll cut out the
part of Macbeth, if you like."

During this season (1827–28) a company of English
actors, under the management of Abbott, gave a series
of performances in Paris, which has left its mark upon
the history both of the French drama and of French
music. Their first play was *The Rivals* (Odéon, September 6, 1827), in which Liston played Acres; Chippen-
dale, Sir Anthony; and Miss Smithson, Lydia Languish.
Two days later Liston appeared as Tony Lumpkin; and
on September 11 Charles Kemble played Hamlet to the
Ophelia of Miss Smithson. This was the fateful evening
which revealed to Alexandre Dumas the full possibilities
of the romantic drama, and inspired Hector Berlioz with

the great passion of his life. Harriet Smithson (the
French called her Henriette) was regarded in London
as a third-rate performer with an Irish brogue; in Paris
she found herself a great actress, a second O'Neill.
"The success of Shakespeare," wrote Berlioz, "heightened by the enthusiastic efforts of all the new literary
school, whose leaders were Victor Hugo, Alexandre
Dumas, and Alfred de Vigny, was surpassed by the
success of Miss Smithson;" and, though Berlioz is
scarcely an impartial historian, contemporary documents
fully bear out this statement. Yet the success of Shakespeare was undoubtedly great. He came in the nick
of time. The romantic revolution had set in (Victor
Hugo's *Cromwell* was the literary event of this very
winter), and its ringleaders were prepared in advance to
accept the name of Shakespeare as a watchword. "It
was the first time," wrote Dumas, "that the stage had
shown me real passions animating men and women of
flesh and blood."

Miss Smithson played Juliet and Desdemona, to Charles
Kemble's Romeo and Othello. Then Miss Foote appeared as Lætitia Hardy, Lady Teazle, and Violante,
and was pronounced (to her no small disgust, we may
believe) an imitator of "la belle Smidson." On October
4 the company removed to the Théâtre Italien (Salle
Favart), but afterwards returned once or twice to the
Odéon. Miss Smithson made her chief success in Jane
Shore, about the middle of October, and afterwards
played Belvidera, Portia, and Cordelia. On April 7,
1828, Macready made his first appearance, as Macbeth.
The house was crowded, the places of honour being
occupied by "S.A.R. Mgr. le duc d'Orléans et toute
sa famille, et S.A.R. Madame, duchesse de Berry."
The majority of the French public was not yet reconciled

to the "strange inequalities which disfigure the master-
pieces of Shakespeare." They rebelled against the
Witches in *Macbeth*, and the handkerchief in *Othello*.
But Macready's personal success was great. The *Journal
des Débats*, noticing his first appearance, spoke of him
as a fine actor, full of skill, energy, fire, and intelligence.
His play of expression, said the critic, redeemed the
irregularity of his features, while his voice, in its lower
register, possessed tones which penetrated to the very
soul. He did not fulfil the writer's ideal of Macbeth,
perhaps because that gentleman credited himself with
a singularly profound insight into Shakespeare's inten-
tions. "Abbott," he continued, "dans le rôle de Mac-
dulph, est pur, correct, et élégant;" but Miss Smithson's
Lady Macbeth he admitted to be feeble. Between the
7th and the 25th of April Macready played Macbeth
thrice, and Virginius four times. After Virginius, says
Jules Janin, "on trouva, pendant vingt-quatre heures,
que Macready était l'égal de Talma." "Who would
believe," cried the critic of *La Réunion*, on paradox
intent, "that this man, to whom Nature has refused
everything — voice, carriage, and, physiognomy — could
rival our Talma, for whom she had left nothing undone?
This prodigy, which is related of Lekain, was yesterday
realized by Macready." The general complaint was that
the performance was too harrowing. Towards the end
of April Macready returned to London, and Kean took
his place, being received with comparative coolness.
After the close of his Drury Lane engagement, Macready
paid a second visit to Paris, appearing eight times between
June 23 and July 21. His parts were Virginius, William
Tell, Hamlet, and Othello, in all of which his success
was great. "At his entrance as William Tell," says the
Débats, "and more than thirty times during the perform-

ance, salvos of applause proved to him that a French
pit has ears for the language of truth in whatever idiom
it may be couched. Protracted acclamations pursued
him even after the fall of the curtain." At the close of
his last performance as Othello, a police ordinance forbidding actors to appear before the curtain was evaded
by a number of enthusiastic young men, who haled him,
still in costume, from his dressing-room into the orchestra,
and thence lifted him over the footlights. Well might he
write to his wife, " I am considerably fatigued, as I play
in earnest here, and feel it for some days afterwards; but
I am more than repaid in the sort of transport that seems
excited among the literary and fashionable."

During the seasons of 1828–29 and 1829–30 Macready
did not appear in London, but devoted himself, with
intervals of rest, to starring engagements in the provinces.
On April 11, 1829, his father died at Bristol, aged seventy-
four, and Macready seems to have afforded a good deal
of aid to his widow, who retained the management of the
theatre. It is reported that in January, 1830, he one night
played Macbeth in Portsmouth to ten persons in the boxes
and a proportionately scanty audience in the pit; and a few
weeks later we find him selling an Irish engagement to
Alfred Bunn for £600, and then remitting £100 of the
price, " in consequence of the ill-success of the engagement." Yet, on the whole, his provincial rounds must have
been fairly remunerative. His total income amounted, in
1828, to £2361, and in 1829 to £2265; so that even if
we suppose his investments to have brought him in £500
a year, his professional receipts would still come to the
respectable sum of over £1750. As his first child,
Christina Letitia, was not born until December 26, 1830,
he was spared, at this period, the morbid anxiety to secure
a provision for his family which tortured him in after-years.

G

On October 18, 1830, he made his "first appearance these two 'years" at Drury Lane, now under the management of Captain Polhill, a wealthy amateur, and Alexander Lee, a musician. Virginius was his opening part, to the Icilius of Wallack, and the Virginia of Miss Phillips. For fourteen successive weeks he played Joseph Surface every Tuesday to Farren's Sir Peter, Dowton's Sir Oliver, Wallack's Charles and Miss Chester's Lady Teazle. Among other legitimate parts he acted Pierre, King John, and Hastings, to the Belvidera, Constance, and Jane Shore of a new actress, Miss Huddart, who was afterwards, under the name of Mrs. Warner, closely associated with his career. Wallack's performance in *The Brigand* was the great popular attraction of the autumn ; but on December 15 Macready added to his repertory a part which was destined to rank among his great achievements—the gloomy and conscience-stricken Werner. The fact that he was able to breathe life into Byron's dull, diffuse, and ill-written play appears to me, I confess, one of the most convincing proofs that he was really a great actor. Two other "creations" belong to this season—Don Leo in *The Pledge; or, Castilian Honour* (April 8, 1831), and Alfred the Great in Knowles's play of that name (April 28). *The Pledge* was a bald version, by James Kenney, of Victor Hugo's *Hernani*, produced in Paris more than a year before amid the tumultuous scenes so vividly described by Théophile Gautier. In London it was well received, the *Times* according it the then unusual honour of a whole column of criticism. The mounting, however, was miserable, and the managers seem to have been anxious to shelve the piece. Macready's part was Don Leo (Ruy Gomez) ; Wallack played Hernani ; Cooper, Charles V. ; and Miss Phillips, Donna Zanthe (Doña Sol). Knowles's *Alfred* was played ten times running, and fifteen times in all, the numerous allusions to the "patriot king" being applied to William IV., and much applauded ; but the part was not strong enough to hold its place in Macready's repertory. This season, however, witnessed his first appearance as Mr. Oakly in *The Jealous Wife,* afterwards the most popular of his few comedy parts. He acted it with "careless nonchalance," said the *Times,* up to the last scene, "which cannot be too highly praised." For his benefit (May 27) he played Coriolanus, to the Volumnia of Miss Huddart, and Puff in *The Critic.*

During the following season (1831–32) Drury Lane was under the management of Captain Polhill. The attraction of the winter was the "Grand Oriental Spectacle" of *Hyder Ali ; or, The Lions of Mysore,* in which a whole menagerie of animals, including boa-constrictors and an elephant, figured on the scene. In the spring of 1832 a version of *Robert le Diable,* entitled, *The Dæmon ; or, The Mystic Branch,* was very popular. Against such competitors "the legitimate" stood a bad chance, and Macready acted only fifty-two times in all, as against ninety-nine times in the previous season. Werner (October 4) was his opening part, and was followed by a round of stock characters. On December 5 he appeared as Richard III., "first time these eight years," said the play-bill ; but, as a matter of fact, he had not played the part in London since the spring of 1821. His only new part was Scroope in *The Merchant of London,* a poor play by T. J. Serle, actor, stage-manager, and author. It was well received on the first night, but had no real vitality. For his benefit (May 14) Macready acted Leontes and Petruchio ; and on May 30, when Charles Young bade farewell to the stage at Covent Garden, Macready played the Ghost to his retiring rival's Hamlet.

The season of 1832–33 was more eventful. Macready's opening part was Rolla (September 28), and on October 1 he appeared as Colberg in Serle's tragedy, *The House of Colberg.* Though the play was feeble as a whole, the last two acts offered fine opportunities for the morose vehemence in which Macready excelled. The death of Sir Walter Scott having occurred, in September, *Rob Roy* was revived on October 13, and was followed by a grand Waverley Pageant, which curiously illustrates the taste of the times :—

" Scene I.—View of Abbotsford (the residence of the lately deceased Poet), painted expressly by Mr. Stanfield ; to which celebrated place will be introduced, in commemoration of Scotland's Immortal Bard, a Pilgrimage of the Principal Dramatic Characters his genius has created, in imitation of the honours paid to Shakespeare in the celebrated Jubilee.

" Scene II.—The Poet's Study at Abbotsford, Exhibiting an arrangement of the Characters round his Bust and Vacant Chair, concluding with a Grand Scenic Apotheosis of the Minstrel of the North, the Coronach from *The Lady of the Lake,* to be sung by Mr. Braham and full chorus.

" ORDER OF THE PAGEANT : The Bard (from *The Lay of the Last Minstrel*), *Waverley, The Fortunes of Nigel, Guy Mannering, The Bride of Lammermoor, Rob Roy, Ivanhoe, The Antiquary, The Heart of Midlothian, Peveril of the Peak, The Lady of the Lake, The Legend of Montrose, Kenilworth.*"

Macready not only acted in the drama (or opera, as it was then called), but figured as the central personage of the *Rob Roy* group in the Pageant. On November 10 he played Kitely in a careful revival of *Every Man in his Humour,* with Power as Bobadil, Farren as Brainworm, Dowton as Justice Clement, Harley as Master Stephen, and Mrs. Nisbett as Dame Kitely. Notwithstanding this strong cast, the play was repeated only once. Kean, whose race was now almost run, appeared early in November, and on the 26th he and Macready acted together for the first time, as Othello and Iago. Greatly to Macready's disgust, Kean resorted to the old trick of always standing a pace or two further up the stage than his interlocutor, who was thus forced to appear in profile to the audience. At the close of the performance, says Bunn, who was Polhill's stage-manager, Macready "bounced into my room," and vowed that he would play no more with so unfair an actor. "He finally wound up by saying, 'And pray what is the—next p—lay you ex—pect me to appear in—with that low—man?' I replied that I would send him word. I went up into Kean's dressing-room, where I found him scraping the colour off his face, and sustaining the operation by copious draughts of cold brandy and water. On my asking him what play he would next appear in with Macready, he ejaculated, 'How the blank should I know what the blank plays in?'" They appeared, as a matter of fact, in no other play; they did not even alternate the leading parts in *Othello*. Macready played Iago ten times to Kean's Othello, and once to Cooper's, Kean being too ill to act. The last joint performance took place on February 8, 1833, and on May 25 Macready was one of the pall-bearers at Kean's funeral. A new part of a ridiculous order which he performed during this season was that of Lord Bellenden in *Men of Pleasure*, by Don Telesforo de Trueba, a Spaniard who wrote in English. A German opera company, with Schröder-Devrient as its star, was one of the attractions of the season, in the course of which, too, the "matchless" and ill-fated Malibran made her first appearance on the English stage. Both these great artists sang, and Taglioni danced, on Macready's benefit-night (June 10), when he played Joseph Surface. He at one time intended to play Charles Surface, but wisely changed his mind. Perhaps he remembered the story of John Philip Kemble and " Charles's Martyrdom."

At Swansea, during the recess of 1833, Macready played King Lear for the first time. " How?" he writes in his diary. " Certainly not well, not so well as I rehearsed it; crude fictitious voice, no point—in short, a failure !" It afterwards became one of his best Shakespearian performances.

Towards the end of May, 1833, the public and the players alike were astonished to learn that the

" . . . houses twain
Of Covent Garden and of Drury Lane "

had passed into the hands of one man, and that man Alfred Bunn. As a journalist, a speculative country impresario, an experienced stage-manager, and the husband of Mrs. Bunn, this gentleman was tolerably well known in the theatrical world. He had little education, no literary culture, a shady private character, plenty of fluency and effrontery, a fine stock of ingenuous snobbishness, and withal a sort of rough good-nature, not wholly unsympathetic. We may pretty safely conjecture that Thackeray had him in his eye when he drew Mr. Dolphin, " the great manager from London," who lured the Fotheringay away from her Chatteris admirers. " He was a tall, portly gentleman, with a hooked nose, and a profusion of curling brown hair and whiskers; his coat was covered with the richest frogs-braiding and velvet. He had under-waistcoats, many splendid rings, jewelled pins, and neck-chains." I have before me a portrait of Alfred Bunn, to which this description (all but the single word " tall ") applies exactly. As a manager he was sanguine, improvident, happy-go-lucky, and (like his master, Elliston) devoted to the catchpenny methods of the showman. His character and habits, in short, were altogether antipathetic to Macready, who regarded with justified forebodings the freak of fortune which made "Bunny," as his friends loved to call him, the autocrat of the legitimate drama.

His first measure was to strike a blow at the large salaries which he considered the ruin of the stage, and to re-establish the "maximum" of Sheridan and Harris (£20 a week). This step, which naturally enraged "the profession," was a futile attempt to stem the oncoming tide of free-trade, and revert to a bygone order of things. I have not been able to ascertain whether Macready, in engaging with Bunn for the season 1833–34, consented to this self-denying ordinance. Certain it is that he joined the Drury Lane company, and appeared on the opening night of the season as Prospero in Dryden and Davenant's version of *The Tempest*, to which, "by way of being extra legitimate," Bunn added *Comus* as an afterpiece. The new manager was determined not to let his principal tragedian rust in idleness. Between the 5th and the 30th of October Macready appeared fifteen times, playing Prospero, Macbeth, Mr. Oakly, Pierre, Biron (in *Isabella*), Posthumus, the Stranger, Wolsey, Hotspur, Werner, and Leontes. As the season went on his appearances were less frequent. On November 21, struggling against illness, insufficient rehearsal, and deplorable mounting, he played Antony to the Cleopatra of Miss Phillips, but made of it only "a hasty, unprepared, unfinished performance." A few days later he offered Bunn a premium to release him from his engagement, which Bunn, in a conciliatory letter, declined to do. The horsemanship of Ducrow attracted crowds to the pantomime of *St. George and the Dragon,* and in the early spring Bunn produced a successful adaptation of Scribe's *Bertrand et Raton,* under the title of *The Minister and .the Mercer.* Thus Macready was not greatly in request until after Easter, when a grand spectacular production of Byron's *Sardanapalus* was announced. The part of Myrrha was assigned to Ellen Tree; but just as the rehearsals were drawing to a close, Bunn received a letter from Paris which altered his plans. It was an offer from Mrs. Mardyn, the actress whose name had been associated with Byron's in the scandalous chronicle of 1815, to play the part of Myrrha, which, she declared, had been written for her. "My late regretted friend," the writer stated, "ever paid me the flattering compliment that in his portraiture of the 'Ionian Myrrha,' I had been associated by his muse in every image of her trance, and that if ever the poem strayed into publicity, beyond the closet, it was his wish that the Greek girl's sandals should be worn by *me*." Bunn promptly came to terms with "Madame la Baronne de St. Dizier," as Mrs. Mardyn now called herself, and announced the postponement of the production in order that the design of the "Noble Author" might be fulfilled. But alas! one illness after another prevented Madame la Baronne from leaving Paris, and Bunn finally concluded (on insufficient evidence, I think) that the whole correspondence was a hoax, in which the real Mrs. Mardyn had no hand. The part was restored to Ellen Tree, and the play produced on April 10, with some success. According to Macready, Cooper, the stage-manager (who played Salemenes), was "as capable of directing the *mise en scène* of a play as a man devoid of information, industry, genius, or talent may be supposed to be." It was of him that Malibran said, "C'est un hôtel garni, dont l'appartement le plus élevé est ordinairement le plus mal meublé." The mounting, though far inferior to that of Charles Kean's revival of the same play at the Princess's, passed muster with the public of that day, and *Sardanapalus* had a considerable run. A revival of *Henry IV. Part II.*, with the Coronation Spectacle, was also fairly attractive, Macready resuming his old part of the King. For his benefit (May 23) he played King Lear for the first time in London, purging the text of Tate's absurdities, but not yet venturing to restore the Fool. He was "as nervous as on the first night he acted in London," and did himself no justice in the first two acts. In the third act, however, he improved, and the performance was, on the whole, a success. Before the season closed he gave three performances at Covent Garden, repeating Lear twice, and playing Hamlet once.

On Monday, July 28, Sheridan Knowles took a farewell benefit at the Victoria Theatre before starting for America. There had been some estrangement between him and Macready, who, by way of heaping coals of fire on his old friend's head, for what he called his "bad and base conduct," offered to play Icilius to Knowles's Virginius on the night of his benefit. Knowles, however, would not hear of this self-abasement, and elected to play Siccius Dentatus to Macready's Virginius, *William Tell* being performed as an afterpiece, with the author in the title-part. Macready also played Virginius for Abbott's benefit, at the Opera House, on August 18.

The winter season of 1834–35 Macready spent entirely in the country. On October 27, 1834, he wrote from Dublin to his friend Thomas Gaspey, editor of the *Sunday Times*—

"I suppose you know that *I am not engaged in London.* Mr. Bunn will not have me. I do not know the quality of

his new performer [Denvil, who made something of a success
in Manfred, but failed lamentably in Othello], but presume
he is satisfied that I may be dispensed with.   This is rather
hard, that so grievous a monopoly is to exclude an artist
from the practice of his art, where his station gives him
some right to appear.   But cheapness is the order of the
day."

During this engagement in Dublin, *The Bridal*, adapted
by Macready from Beaumont and Fletcher's *Maid's
Tragedy*, was produced for the first time, with Macready
as Melantius.   Sheridan Knowles had contributed three
scenes to the adaptation, and some misunderstanding as
to their respective shares in the work seems to have
caused the coolness between them to which I have just
alluded.

At the end of December, 1834, Macready embarked
on a managerial speculation at Bath and Bristol, in
partnership with a Mr. Woulds.   The heading of the
play-bills (written by Macready) announced a " COMBI-
NATION OF TALENT *without precedent in this or any theatre
out of the Metropolis, and at present defying competition on
the part of the London theatres.*"   Macready and Mrs.
Lovell were the tragic stars ; Dowton represented comedy ;
and Mr. and Mrs. Wood (Miss Paton), popular vocalists
of the period, strengthened the combination.   Macready
played all his popular parts, even Gambia, and at Bath,
on February 24, he added a new part to his list—that of
Ford in *The Merry Wives of Windsor ;* Dowton playing
Falstaff; and Mr. and Mrs. Wood, Fenton and Mrs.
Ford.   The " combination of talent," though Farren
joined it in the course of the spring, was not, on the
whole, successful.   Macready writes to Gaspey from
Bristol, on March 5, 1835—

"I have made up my mind not to play at the winter

theatres this season under any circumstances ; *the thing is too low down.* We are playing here to SPLENDID HOUSES —*again.* Last week the Woods, Dowton, and self played on Monday in *The Slave* to £50 (!!!) at *Bath;* on Tuesday, *Merry Wives of Windsor*—£58 (!!!). There's taste and patronage! Thursday, *Hamlet*—upwards of £100. Saturday, *Rob Roy*—turned £100 again. HERE we have played the same pieces to considerably above £100 each night, and the *boxes greatly taken* for the remaining nights. . . . Dowton's engagement has been a total failure. Bath is incapable of supporting its Theatre."

The parsimony of Bath more than counterbalanced the liberality of Bristol, and it was currently reported at the time that Macready lost £1000 by the speculation ; but this was probably an overestimate.

Captain Polhill, having lost (as he told Planché) £50,000 in four seasons, withdrew his financial support from Bunn's enterprise in December, 1834. The union of the two houses was dissolved at the end of the season, and Bunn's genius was forced to confine itself to the restricted empire of Drury Lane. With many misgivings, Macready agreed to join the Drury Lane company for the season 1835–36. His salary of £30 a week was to extend over thirty weeks and a half ; he was to act (if called upon) four nights a week ; to be subject to no forfeit or fine ; and to possess a veto on any part which he might deem melodramatic. From the first the engagement was unfortunate. On the opening night (October 1) Macready, by his own confession, played Macbeth very badly, and " felt almost desperate." His form improved as time went on, and before the 28th of the month he had played Jaques, Hamlet, Hotspur, Leontes, Lord Townly, and Othello—sixteen performances in all. But now came the great success of Balfe's *Siege of Rochelle,* followed by the still greater success of

Planché's three-act drama, *The Jewess*, founded upon *La Juive* of Scribe, "and got up with nearly as much splendour as the original." Macready's Shakespearian performances, even aided by the abnormal receipt due to a royal "command," had produced an average of less than £220 a night, and Bunn could not afford to interrupt, for Macready's sake, the run of entertainments which, combined in one bill, brought in an average receipt of £330. Macready had declined the part of Eleazar in *The Jewess*, played by Vandenhoff, and the result was that he found himself entirely shelved from October 28 until February 3. .His salary, of course, was duly paid him, though even that Bunn had proposed to reduce ; but this enforced idleness suited neither his pride nor his interest. That one of the two homes of the legitimate drama should be given up week after week to the unbroken run of an opera and a melodramatic spectacle, was undoubtedly an innovation, and in Macready's eyes a degrading one. Moreover, Bunn had broken his contract to produce *The Bridal* "immediately after Christmas," thus depriving Macready of a considerable addition to his income, on which he had calculated. Hence the relations between actor and manager became more and more strained as the season advanced. On February 3 Macready reappeared as Othello, and a week later he created the part of Bertulphe in *The Provost of Bruges*, to the Constance of Ellen Tree. This tragedy was the work of G. W. Lovell, secretary of the Phœnix Life Assurance Company, and husband of the actress to whom the English stage owes *Ingomar and Parthenia*. It was a vigorous work of the school of Knowles, and Macready, no doubt, entered heart and soul into the agonies of the merchant prince who falls from his high estate by reason of the discovery that he was

born a serf. His performance was much praised, but
the tragedy failed, being played eight nights at an
average loss of £90 a night. Meanwhile *The Jewess* was
still holding the bills, backed by Auber's *Bronze Horse*,
and a "grand chivalric entertainment," entitled, *Chevy
Chase*. Macready's appearances were consequently rare
—they numbered twenty-one in all between February 3
and April 29—and the average receipt produced by his
Shakespearian performances barely rose above £150.
It now occurred to Bunn, in an unlucky moment, that he
might combine tragedy with opera and spectacle. He
accordingly announced *The Corsair* (*Zampa*) for April
16, with Macready in *William Tell* as an afterpiece.
This was a sore indignity, but Macready submitted under
protest. Emboldened by this partial victory, Bunn next
announced for April 29 a "combined attraction," con-
sisting of the first three acts of *Richard III.*, *The Jewess*,
and the first act of *Chevy Chase*. A truncated tragedy
was almost, if not quite, as degrading as an afterpiece,
and Macready worked himself into a state of frenzy over
the matter. He thought of throwing up his engagement,
but his solicitude for his children's future forbade him
to sacrifice £250. Once more he determined to submit ;
but on April 28, the eve of the "day of wrath," he
wound up the entry in his diary with the words, "God
knows I have very few friends here. I am very unhappy."

Unhappy he was, but rather in the multitude than the
paucity of his friends. Their "obstinate condolements"
over Bunn's "scandalous and insulting proceeding"
exasperated his exasperation. Even his old antagonist,
Charles Kemble, commiserated him. He went to the
theatre on the evening of Friday, April 29, "tetchy and
unhappy ;" but "pushed through the part in a sort of

desperate way as well as he could." He left the stage a few minutes before nine o'clock to return to his dressing-room. His way lay past the door of Bunn's office, and the chance proximity to the author of all his wrongs suddenly overcame his self-control. He threw open the door—there sat the manager at his writing-table, over which a shaded lamp cast a glow of light. " I could not contain myself," he writes. " I exclaimed, ' You damned scoundrel! how dare you use me in this manner?' And going up to him as he sat on the other side of the table, I struck him, as he rose, a back-handed slap across the face." At this point we may let Bunn take up the tale—

"After an ejaculation of ' There, you villain, take that—and that!' I was knocked down, one of my eyes completely closed, the ankle of my left leg, which I am in the habit of passing round the leg of the chair when writing, violently sprained, my person plentifully soiled with blood, lamp-oil, and ink, the table upset, and *Richard the Third* holding me down. On my naturally inquiring if he meant to murder me, and on his replying in the affirmative, I made a struggle for it, threw him off, and . . . finally succeeded in getting him down on the sofa, where, mutilated as I was, I would have made him ' remember ME,' but for the interposition of the people who had soon filled the room."

It is evident from all accounts that, considering his bulk, and the fact of his being taken unawares, Bunn made a surprisingly good fight for it. He did his antagonist no great damage, beyond biting the little finger of his left hand ; but when the combatants were separated, the manager was clearly uppermost. Willmott the prompter, the call-boy, and others quickly came to the rescue. Macready retreated to his dressing-room, where his friends, Wallace, Forster, and Dow, soon arrived to hold a council of war. Bunn, on the other hand, was conveyed to bed. He did not leave the house for three weeks, and then hobbled to the theatre on crutches, to superintend Malibran's last rehearsals in *The Maid of Artois*.

Macready's part in the affair was certainly not dignified. If there had been any premeditation about it, the assault would even have been cowardly. But he more than expiated the offence in the anguish of spirit it caused him. It was a notorious victory of that worser part in his nature against which he was for ever struggling. He happened to take up Johnson's "Life of Savage" on the following day, when "the idea of murder presented itself so painfully and strongly to his mind, that he turned directly for relief to another subject." Moreover, the newspaper placards, "*Great Fight. B—nn and M——y,*" the paragraphs, the caricatures, the gossip and comment on the affair, were torture to his soul. "It makes me sick to think of it," he wrote. Yet in this respect he escaped more easily than might have been expected. Bunn was no favourite with the general public, whose verdict, on the whole, seems to have been, "Serve him right!" Osbaldiston, who was running Covent Garden Theatre at reduced prices, at once offered Macready an engagement, and on May 11, twelve days after the assault, he appeared as Macbeth. "The pit—indeed, the house," he says, "rose and waved hats and handkerchiefs, cheering in the most fervent and enthusiastic manner." He made a short speech at the end of the tragedy, alluding to the "annoying and mortifying provocations" to which he had been subjected "in cold blood," but at the same time expressed his regret for "an intemperate and imprudent act, for which he felt, and should never cease to feel, the deepest and most poignant self-reproach." It is evident that, in the end, the event brought him an access of popularity. Weighing one thing with another, the public did not actively condemn his conduct, and the whole affair was a brilliant advertisement.

At Covent Garden, Virginius followed Macbeth, and on May 18 the bill announced that " Miss Helen Faucit will act for the first time with Mr. Macready," her part being Mrs. Haller in *The Stranger.* For Macready's benefit, on May 26, Talfourd's *Ion* was performed for the first time with complete success, Miss Ellen Tree playing Clemanthe. It was suggested that Talfourd should go on the stage in response to the applause of the audience ; but to such an unprecedented proposal Macready said, "On no account in the world." As it happened to be the author's birthday, the event was celebrated by a supper at his house. "I was happily placed," writes Macready, "between Wordsworth and Landor, with Browning opposite." Happily placed, indeed ! Forster, Stanfield, and Ellen Tree were also present, along with —guests less congenial to Macready—Miss Mitford and the Rev. W. Harness. As the assault upon Bunn was not yet an "old, unhappy, far-off thing, or battle long ago," Wordsworth perhaps showed less tact than might have been desired in quoting the lines from his own *Borderers*—

> "Action is transitory—a step, a blow,
> The motion of a muscle—this way or that—
> 'Tis done ; and in the after vacancy
> We wonder at ourselves like men betrayed."

Macready, however, does not seem to have noticed the allusion. "I felt tranquilly happy," he writes.

For Osbaldiston's benefit, on May 30, *Julius Cæsar*

was revived, with Sheridan Knowles as Brutus, Macready as Cassius, and Charles Kemble in his great character of Mark Antony. The Bunn affair had led to a formal reconciliation between Kemble and Macready, who, however, writes of this performance, "I do not think my reception was quite so long as Kemble's, or I did not use sufficient generalship with it." The eighth representation of *Ion* brought the season to a close on June 11. From the second night onwards Miss Faucit had replaced Ellen Tree as Clemanthe.

It had been supposed at first that Bunn would challenge Macready, who was ready to go out if called upon. The wily manager, however, took refuge in the plea that his adversary's conduct had deprived him of all right to be treated as a gentleman. He chose the more pacific course of suing him for assault, and as Macready allowed judgment to go by default, the issue was reduced to an assessment of damages. Thesiger, afterwards Lord Chelmsford, was Bunn's counsel, while Talfourd appeared for Macready. It cannot be said that Talfourd's advocacy did much for Macready's case. His address to the jury, full of cajolery and empty rhetoric, is a fine example of the Buzfuz style.

" Shakespeare ! " cried the learned Serjeant—" the mighty magic of the name is enough—Shakespeare, in whose mighty name the British drama originated, and still has its being—Shakespeare, and Shakespeare's representative, Mr. Macready, were to be shelved, that the words of the songs of *The Maid of Artois* should be given to the public. How polite, how modest, is Mr. Bunn ! Mr. Bunn's poetry against Shakespeare's *Richard III.!* . . . Mr. Macready felt injured and insulted ; he struck Mr. Bunn ; a scuffle ensued ; genius, and right, and strength triumphed—Mr. Bunn was the sufferer !"

The attempt to represent Macready as a victim to

H

Bunn's literary vanity was too flagrant a piece of special pleading even for a British jury. The truth, though it was not Talfourd's cue to admit it, was that "Shakespeare and Shakespeare's representative" did not draw, whereas opera and spectacle did. The fortunes of the season (unforeseen, of course, at its outset) had made Macready a white elephant on the manager's hands, and he treated the haughty and supersensitive tragedian with little consideration and less tact. Macready accused him of attempting, by dint of deliberate and studied humiliations, to force him to throw up his engagement; but I find no evidence of any such far-reaching plan on Bunn's part. The player's professional position and dignity were nothing to the manager. He regarded actors as his natural enemies : they got all they could out of him ; he would get all he could out of them. We can scarcely believe that it would have done Macready's position any grievous harm had he yielded with a good grace to the requirements of a manager who, after all, had paid him a large sum and received very little in return. In any case, even if he was right to be "jealous in honour," he was obviously wrong in being so "sudden and quick in quarrel." The jury, despite Talfourd's blandishments, awarded Bunn damages to the amount of £150.

After some unimportant provincial engagements, Macready returned to Covent Garden, where he had agreed with Osbaldiston for twenty-two weeks at £40 a week. His opening part was the favourite Macbeth (October 3), with Pritchard as Macduff, and Mrs. W. West as Lady Macbeth.

Charles Kemble's farewell performances drew crowded houses during the last three months of 1836. He played his great parts of Faulconbridge, Cassio, and Antony, to Macready's King John, Othello, and Brutus, and also acted Hamlet, Macbeth, Mercutio, Shylock, and Petruchio, his last part being Benedick, to Miss Faucit's Beatrice, on December 23. Osbaldiston was running the theatre at reduced prices (boxes, 4*s.*; pit, 2*s.*; lower gallery, 1*s.*; upper gallery, 6*d.*); but the rush to see the last of Kemble induced him to announce on the play-bill of Monday, November 21 (*Julius Cæsar*), that "Stalls had been fitted up in the Orchestra," admission 7*s.*; and this arrangement was adhered to throughout the season.

On the fourth day of the new year (1837) a new dramatist made his first essay. *The Duchess de la Vallière*, "by E. L. Bulwer, Esq., M.P.," had been offered to Bunn in the spring of 1836; but the author making it a condition that the play should be accepted unread, Bunn very naturally declined to buy a pig in a poke. At Covent Garden, Vandenhoff made a most unkingly Louis XIV.; Farren was ludicrously out of place as Lauzun; Miss Faucit acted La Vallière; and Macready, Bragelone. The play met with a mixed reception, and held the bill for eight nights only. That Macready should ever have accepted the part of Brage-lone is a strong proof of his friendship for Bulwer; for the scenes between Louis, La Vallière, and Madame de Montespan in the third act are the only really effective passages in the rambling, turgid, and unhealthy play. Another new dramatist was soon to have his turn. We have seen that at the *Ion* supper Macready sat opposite to Robert Browning. "On descending the staircase," writes Mr. Browning, "he said, with an affectionate gesture, 'Will you not write me a tragedy, and save me from going to America?'" Mr. Browning responded in a letter which Macready accepted as one of the highest honours that had ever been paid him; but other occupations prevented the poet from immediately fixing on a subject.   At last he selected the story of Thomas Wentworth, and on the evening of Macready's benefit (May 1) *Strafford* was produced for the first time. While the play was in rehearsal Macready had grave doubts as to its reception, which the event did not justify.   He anticipated "considerable opposition;" but though the minor parts were badly filled, the play met with unmixed applause.   "Macready acted very finely," Mr. Browning notes, "as did Miss Faucit.   Pym received tolerable treatment.   The rest—for the sake of whose incompetence the play had to be reduced by at least one-third of its dialogue—*non ragioniam di lor!*"   Most of the critics complained of the obscurity of the action. "Events are implied, not stated," said the *John Bull;* "thoughts inferred, not uttered."   Even the more than friendly *Examiner* could not predict permanent success for the tragedy.

"It should be stated, however," the critic wrote, "that it was most infamously got up; that even Mr. Macready himself was not near so fine as he is wont to be ; and that for the rest of the performers, with the exception of Miss Faucit, they were a barn wonder to look at !   Mr. Vanden-hoff was positively nauseous, with his whining, drawling, and slouching in Pym ; and Mr. [J.] Webster whimpered in somewhat too juvenile a fashion through young Vane. Some one should have stepped out of the pit and thrust Mr. Dale [Charles I.] from the stage. . . . The most striking thing of the evening was Mr. Macready's first entrance upon the stage.   It was the portrait of the great and ill-fated Earl stepping from the living canvas of Vandyke."

The play-bill of May 3 (Osbaldiston was great in play-bills) announced that "The new Historical Tragedy of STRAFFORD, having been indeed most eminently successful and greeted with the most enthusiastic fervour by a house densely crowded in every part, will be repeated This Evening, on Friday and Tuesday next." After the fourth performance (May 9) a series of benefits intervened, and the fifth and last did not take place until May 30, when the tragedy was for the first time announced as "by — Browning, Esq."

Macready's chief parts during the spring were King John to the Faulconbridge of Vandenhoff and the Constance of Miss Faucit; Brutus to Vandenhoff's Cassius and Sheridan Knowles's Antony; Posthumus to Elton's Iachimo, Farren's Cloten, and Miss Faucit's Imogen; and Leontes to Miss Faucit's Hermione, Mrs. Glover's Paulina, and Farren's Autolycus. His last appearance took place on June 3, when he played Othello to Elton's Iago and Miss Faucit's Desdemona.

The doldrums were now fairly past, and during the remaining fourteen years of his career Macready ran before the trade-winds of success. His financial fortunes varied, but his reputation, his position, was securely established. He was "a personage," the recognized leader of his profession. He had lived down the adverse influences which beset his middle course. Though heartily hated in many quarters, he was respected in all. His unpopularity both with the press and among his fellow-actors had decidedly declined, and, on the other hand, his enthusiastic supporters were more numerous and influential than ever before. The faithful Talfourd was always at his side. He had made the acquaintance of John Forster at Kean's funeral, in 1833. Bulwer he met in Dublin in the following year, and their friendship was now confirmed. In 1835, at the house of W. J. Fox, he met "Mr. Robert Browning, the author of *Paracelsus.*" In his dressing-room at the Haymarket, in June, 1837, Forster introduced him to "Dickens, *alias* Boz," his friend till death parted them. Thus the chief members of his much-talked-of "clique" were already around him at the period we have now reached. The establishment of the Garrick Club, in 1832, somewhat extended his social relations, but its atmosphere was never very congenial to him, and he retired from it at the close of 1838. During and after his period of management he entered largely into social life, and his dinner-parties were famous in their way. "I only intend in future," writes Abraham Hayward, in 1838, "to go to dinner where I am sure of meeting people worth meeting. . . . At Macready's, for example, there was no rank, but there was hardly a person in the room but was worth knowing for something."

I am inclined to believe that his liberation from his thraldom to the bungling managers of Drury Lane led to a substantial improvement in his art. In the newspaper criticisms between 1825 and 1835 the adjectives "cold," "tame," and "measured" recur with surprising frequency. Now, if we can be sure of anything with regard to a player of the past, it is that Macready was not naturally "cold" or "tame." His temper, however, reacted strongly upon his performances, and the chronic dissatisfaction and despondency under which he laboured through so many seasons may well have begotten a slackness and apathy in his average efforts. Under these circumstances, too, he would naturally yield to his mannerisms without a struggle. He notes that on December 7, 1836, Mrs. Glover remarked to him that "she had never seen such an improvement in any person as in himself lately;" and Mrs. Glover spoke with the authority of commanding talent, and an experience which reached back to the best days of the Kemble dynasty.

No doubt his somewhat exaggerated sense of having endangered his position by his assault on Bunn served as a spur to his flagging genius; and he was soon to have the nobler incentive of acting amid worthy surroundings on behalf of an enterprise in which his own fortunes were identified with what he conceived to be the best interests of the British drama.

MACREADY'S CHARACTERS.

1823–1837.

DRURY LANE: 1823–24: Leontes, 12; *Caius Gracchus, Rob Roy, 7; Virginius, 4; Macbeth, Rolla, 3; Hamlet, Duke (*Measure for Measure*), Wolsey, Coriolanus, 2; Prospero, Almaviva, Delaval (*Matrimony*), 1.

1824–25: *William Tell, 11; Romont (*Fatal Dowry*), 7; Macbeth, Jaques, 4; Leontes, 3; King John, Virginius, 2; Wolsey, Henry V., Rob Roy, Gambia, 1.

1826: Tell, 6; Virginius, 4; Macbeth, Othello, Hotspur, 2; Leontes, Posthumus, Delaval, 1.

1827–28: Virginius, 8; Tell, 6; Macbeth, 3; *Ribemont (*Edward the Black Prince*), *Henry of Trastamar (*Don Pedro*), 2; Hamlet, Biron (*Isabella*), Jaques, Posthumus, 1.

1830–31: *Werner, 17; Joseph Surface, 16; *Alfred the Great, 15; Tell, 11; *Don Leo (*The Pledge*), 8; Rob Roy, 5; Virginius, 4; Hastings, Henri Quatre, Macbeth, 3; Henry V., Pierre, Stranger, Mr. Oakly, Coriolanus, 2; Hamlet, Hotspur, King John, Daran (*The Exile*), Puff, 1.

1831–32: *Scroope (*Merchant of London*), 9; Daran, 7; Macbeth, 6; Richard III., Rob Roy, 5; Tell, 4; Werner, Virginius, Joseph Surface, 3; Alfred the Great, 2; Hastings, Stranger, King John, Hamlet, Leontes, Petruchio, 1. At COVENT GARDEN: Ghost (*Hamlet*), 1.

1832–33: Iago, 11; Joseph Surface, 8; Rob Roy, Macbeth, 6; Rolla, *Colberg (*House of Colberg*), Tell, Mr. Oakly, *Lord Bellenden (*Men of Pleasure*), 4; Kitely, Virginius, 2; Hotspur, Hastings, Daran, Wolsey, 1.

1833–34 : *Sardanapalus, 23 ; Henry IV., 12 ; Macbeth, Werner, 7 ; Prospero, Hotspur, Virginius, 4 ; Tell, Antony (*Antony and Cleopatra*), 3 ; Hastings, Hamlet, Coriolanus, 2 ; Mr. Oakly, Pierre, Biron (*Isabella*), Posthumus, Stranger, Wolsey, Leontes, Jaques, Henry V., Iago, King John, King Lear, 1. At COVENT GARDEN : King Lear, 2 ; Hamlet, 1. At the VICTORIA : Virginius, 1. At the OPERA HOUSE : Virginius, 1.

1835–36 : Macbeth, 9 ; *Bertulphe (*Provost of Bruges*), 8 ; Othello, 7 ; Hamlet, Lord Townly, 3 ; Jaques, Hotspur, Leontes, Virginius, King John, Tell, Stranger, Henry IV., Richard III. (first three acts), 1.

COVENT GARDEN : 1836 : *Ion, 8 ; Macbeth, Stranger, 2 ; Virginius, Hamlet, Cassius, 1.

1836–37 : Othello, King John, 14 ; Ion, Brutus, 13 ; *Bragelone (*La Vallière*), 8 ; Macbeth, 7 ; Richard III., Wolsey, *Strafford, 5 ; Virginius, 4 ; Werner, Posthumus, 3 ; Leontes, Pierre, 2 ; Hamlet, Hastings, 1.

CHAPTER V.

1837–1843.

MANAGEMENT.

THE idea of going into management had hovered before Macready's mind for years. It was absolutely necessary, he felt—and the " legitimate " actors all felt with him— that some effort should be made to arrest the rapid decline of the legitimate drama. At the patent theatres, to which these performers were obliged to look for the greater part, at any rate, of their livelihood, matters had long been going from bad to worse. Manager after manager had been driven to the most " illegitimate " expedients in the hope of attracting the public, and had nevertheless drifted into insolvency. The monopoly which confined the "regular drama" to Drury Lane, Covent Garden, and the Haymarket had become a mere dog-in-the-manger absurdity. Its days were clearly numbered; yet Macready and most of his comrades had the foresight to recognize that the remedy for the depression of their particular branch of art was not to be found in free-trade. In his evidence before the Select Committee on Dramatic Literature, of 1832, Macready had expressed himself in favour of the monopoly, with certain modifications. In the mean time, the fact of the decline was obvious, and it was generally felt that some serious attempt ought to be made to stay it. All eyes turned towards Macready. In spite of his unpopularity, he was known to be an able, energetic, honourable man. If anything could be done, he was the man to do it. Private motives conspired with public considerations to induce him to undertake the task. It was certain that, unless he stepped into the breach, the great theatres would be given over to a succession of showman-managers, of Bunns and Osbaldistons, each, probably, more speculative and irresponsible than the last. He could no longer brook such leadership ; and, on the other hand, his power of attraction in the provinces was on the wane. Even if his management should result in a pecuniary loss, the effort, he knew, would not be inglorious. The great productions which he had in his mind's eye would give his reputation a fillip both in the country and in America. A splendid success was possible, a disastrous failure highly improbable. The enterprise might conceivably lead to great results for dramatic art and all concerned in it, while at worst it could do him, personally, no harm in the long-run. Osbaldiston's failure offered an opportunity, and, after much anxious thought, Macready determined to enter into negotiations with the Covent Garden proprietors.

In the mean time, he had accepted a short engagement with Benjamin Webster, who entered upon his historic management at the Haymarket on Monday, June 12, 1837. On that night Macready played Hamlet, with Webster as the Gravedigger, Elton as the Ghost, and Miss Huddart as the Queen. The chief event of this engagement was the first performance in London (June 26) of *The Bridal.* It was an adroit-enough handling of a difficult subject, though much of the tragic intensity of the original was, of course, sacrificed, whilst the style of

Knowles, overlaying that of Beaumont and Fletcher, was like a coat of cheap varnish on a Stradivarius. Its success was declared to be more brilliant and decisive than that of any play since *The Hunchback*. According to the *Times*, the rough frankness of Macready's Melantius was touching, his anger terrific. Miss Huddart's Evadne was probably the great success of her life. Elton made a hit as Amintor, and Miss Taylor played Aspatia. Farren, Buckstone, Mrs. Nisbett, and Mrs. Glover were all at this time members of the Haymarket company, and Macready appeared along with them in *The Provoked Husband*.

By the middle of July the Covent Garden negotiations were practically concluded. I have not been able to discover the precise details of Macready's contract with the proprietors. We find in his diary that he offered to pay £40 per night for a hundred and eighty nights (£7200 in all), and then, after assigning himself a salary of £30 a week, to share any surplus with the proprietors "till the remainder of £8800 should be paid to them." On the other hand, we have his own statement that the rent he actually did pay was only £5500, or about £26 for each of the two hundred and eleven acting nights of the season. During his second and more productive season he paid £7000 on two hundred and twenty-one acting nights, or a little over £31 a night. It appears, then, that the claims of the proprietors must have been in some measure contingent on the receipts ; but the details of the arrangement are, to me at least, obscure. Fifteen years earlier, Elliston had paid the Drury Lane proprietors £11,300 in a single season. Comparing these figures, the reader may estimate for himself the depreciation of theatrical property.

The next care was to select a company, and to induce

the actors so far to moderate their demands as to give
the enterprise a fair start. The fact that he had no real
difficulty on this score is a conclusive proof of the confidence he inspired. He met with only one serious rebuff—from Charles Kean. Having won his way by a
hard struggle into genuine popularity, Kean was but little
tempted by Macready's offer to "give the completest
scope to the full development of his talents." He knew
that the value of such a phrase lay entirely in its inter-
pretation; and being by inheritance and habit essentially
a "star," he saw that it would be folly on his part to
become a stock actor under a tragedian-manager. Macready can scarcely have expected any other reply. His
offer was probably intended as a mere cloak for the expression of a hope that, if Kean could not co-operate,
he would at least not actively oppose—a rather maladroit
appeal to an improbable generosity.

On July 30, 1837, Macready wrote to his friend Wightwick, with reference to an Exeter tragedian, of whom
good reports had reached him—

"I hope he is moderate in his expectations of *remuneration*
for ours is now a *struggle for existence*, not for profit ; and
every salary on our establishment is largely, but willingly,
reduced. I should like much to know what is his aim in
coming to town—whether he has the 'aut Cæsar aut nullus'
view of young Kean, or a resolution in the love of his art to
study and toil for the perfection of it."

This young man was named Samuel Phelps; and, after
a visit to Southampton to see him act, Macready engaged
him. Another provincial actor, James Anderson, who
came of a Scotch theatrical family, and had been on the
stage from his childhood, was secured for the "juvenile
lead." Phelps was at this time thirty-three, Anderson
twenty-eight. Edward William Elton, on the other hand,

was only a year younger than Macready himself. He had
for nearly twenty years been struggling into notice as a
provincial and East-End actor, but had only recently made
his mark in the West End. An amiable and intelligent
man, he had no originality of talent, and his small stature
stood in the way of his advancement. James Warde was
a still older stager. Born in 1790, he had been a leading
actor in Bath and Dublin for a dozen years before his
first appearance at Covent Garden in 1825. He was
a useful and "responsible" performer of the second
rank. Ten years younger than Warde, George Bennett
was an actor of similar merit, though not yet of equal
reputation. He had played the leading tragic characters
in his day, not without applause ; but his place was undoubtedly in the second rank. Pritchard, though an
actor of some ambition, scarcely rose above the third
rank, to which such useful but undistinguished performers
as Waldron and Diddear certainly belonged. On the
level of general utility stood T. J. Serle, playwright and
actor, one of Macready's most assiduous henchmen ; and
a youth of twenty-five, named Henry Howe, was already
showing in small parts that sterling ability which has
earned him the respect of two generations of playgoers.
Among the ladies, Miss Huddart and Miss Helen Faucit
shared the leading place. Miss Huddart, born in 1804,
had been discovered and brought to the front by Macready, and was now the best living actress of what may
be called Siddonian characters. Miss Faucit, whose
mother and elder sister had preceded her on the boards,
was a girl of eighteen, and had made her first appearance
so recently as January, 1836. She was already recognized
as the most promising young actress of her time ; but her
first signal triumph was yet (and very soon) to come.

On the comic side the company was well provided

The genial and rotund Bartley, fifty-five years of age, had made his first appearance in London so early as 1802, had acted all over the English-speaking world of his time, had succeeded Fawcett as stage-manager at Covent Garden during Charles Kemble's reign, and now retained that post under Macready. W. J. Hammond, one of the best low comedians and burlesque actors on the stage, came fresh from a great success at the Strand Theatre in the part of Sam Weller, the popular hero of the hour. Vining, Drinkwater Meadows, and Tilbury were all sterling actors trained in a good school. Harley, " Quicksilver Harley," whom the death of Munden and the retirement of Liston left incontestably the first comedian of the older generation, joined the company in the spring of 1838 ; and Tyrone Power, the extravagantly popular Irish actor ; Strickland, a good comedian of the second order ; and Mrs. Glover, the greatest living actress in 'a wide range of comic characters,—all made brief appearances in the course of the season. Miss Taylor (afterwards Mrs. Walter Lacy) played with distinction in sentimental comedy ; Mrs. Humby was an experienced and popular soubrette ; Mrs. W. Clifford was a good "first old woman ; " and a girl of nineteen, Miss Priscilla Horton, whom many of us remember as Mrs. German Reed, soon proved herself one of the most useful members of the company.

"English opera," said Macready, in his opening manifesto, " has become an essential part of the amusements of a metropolitan audience." He was consequently forced to secure a strong musical company, the leaders of which were Wilson, Manvers, and Leffler, Miss Shirreff, and Miss Vincent. Though these names have little meaning in our ears, they were popular in their day. Indeed, I gather that Miss Shirreff drew the highest salary on the Covent Garden list—£18 a week. Macready offered Miss Faucit (and she seems to have accepted) £15 a week, while Phelps had only £10, and Anderson £6. The musical director was Alexander Lee, once part-manager of Drury Lane, who died some years afterwards in extreme misery. There was also a complete company of pantomimists on the establishment, including W. H. Payne, T. Matthews, and C. J. Smith, who used to play "utility" parts in the Shakespearian productions. The chief scene-painter was Marshall, an artist of some originality.

Macready promised and carried out two reforms which deserve to be noticed. He forswore the extravagant and mendacious play-bill puffs of his predecessors, and he did his best, at considerable trouble and expense, to free the theatre from the "improper intrusion" which had from time immemorial rendered certain parts of it unapproachable for ladies. At Covent Garden he seems to have effected this improvement with comparative ease ; but at Drury Lane, in 1841, his conduct was so misrepresented in the press (especially by the *John Bull* and the *Weekly Dispatch*) as to cause him much annoyance. On the whole, he seems to have effected a distinct improvement in the manners of the average audience. Ten years earlier, Prince Pückler-Muskau wondered how great actors could endure to waste their genius on the inattentive mob whose turbulence would often spoil their best effects.

At the end of this chapter will be found a synopsis, as complete as my limits allow, of Macready's four seasons of management. I have given the dates and casts of all important productions, with the number of their repetitions, so that such details need not burden my text. The bill generally consisted of a five-act play and a farce, a three-act drama, or a musical piece; sometimes both a farce and an operetta would be given. For instance, *Macbeth* would be followed by *Fra Diavolo* or *The Marriage of Figaro*, *Hamlet* by *The Miller and his Men*, *Othello* by Dibdin's *Waterman* and *The Spitfire*, *Werner* by the Christmas pantomime. With us a three-act play will often constitute an "entire evening's entertainment;" fifty years ago the public would have felt defrauded had the manager offered them less than six acts, and did not complain of seven or eight. "Curtain-raisers" were unknown. The solid pudding always headed the bill of fare, with a more or less liberal dessert to follow. The institution of "half-price," however, must have been a boon to all who preferred to take their theatrical enjoyments in moderate doses.

The new management made but a languid start. *The Winter's Tale* was carefully but not brilliantly mounted, and the acting excited no enthusiasm. Anderson alone, who had nearly thrown up his engagement in disgust at being cast for Florizel, made a striking success. The revivals of *Hamlet* and *Othello* passed unnoticed by the *Times*, though, according to the *Examiner*, "the scenes of *Hamlet* were a series of glorious pictures," while the Council-scene in *Othello* (a faithful reproduction of the "Sala del Maggior Consiglio") was one of the finest of all Macready's scenic effects. *Macbeth*, very strongly cast, and with the whole of the musical company in the singing parts, was the first revival that really impressed both critics and public. The *Times* admitted that Macready had made it "almost a new play;" while the *John Bull* said, "The poetry of the drama is now for the first time put in motion, and its supernatural agents begin to assume their real functions." On the other hand, *Henry V.* was "crudely and incompletely"

revived, the battle of Agincourt being fought by gentlemen in silken hose and velvet doublets, while not a
single bowman was visible! Balfe's *Joan of Arc* being
in preparation at Drury Lane, Macready was not above
taking the wind out of Bunn's sails by hurrying on a
spectacular romance of the same title, written by Serle,
with one or two ideas borrowed from Schiller. It was
successful; and, a few days later, Rooke's romantic
opera *Amilie* was received with great favour. Nevertheless, it was stated that the loss, up to Christmas,
amounted to £3000; while scoffers remarked that this
vaunted Shakespearian management had made its only
real successes with a spectacle and an opera. The
pantomime, with Stanfield's diorama, somewhat re-
plenished the treasury, and towards the end of January
King Lear was revived with unprecedented scenic effect.
"The castles," said the *John Bull*, "are heavy, sombre,
and solid; their halls are adorned with trophies of the
chase and instruments of war; druid circles rise in spec-
tral loneliness on the heath; and the 'dreadful pother'
of the elements is kept up with a verisimilitude which
beggars all that we have hitherto seen attempted." The
Fool, restored to the stage for the first time, amid many
misgivings, was charmingly played by Priscilla Horton.
Three weeks later a new play was produced, the authorship of which was attributed by rumour to all manner of
improbable people. It was called *The Lady of Lyons;*
and Macready, rather to his own humiliation, and to the
displeasure of his more fervent admirers, assumed the
part of the youthful hero. He was at least twice the age
of Claude Melnotte, but Anderson assures us that "when
playing to a good house, he did not look more than
twenty-five;" and as Anderson would fain have played
the part himself, his evidence may be taken as unbiased.

I

The play was enthusiastically received, Miss Faucit's Pauline producing a deeper impression than any of her previous performances. The *Times* praised the adroit manipulation of the plot, and allowed that the author "had written several nice speeches," but declared the characters to be "the gaudy, overdrawn personages of melodrame." "Vulgar bravoes," it added, greeted the "republican claptraps which were flung in every here and there;" and these "liberalisms," as another critic contemptuously called them, gave so much offence that at the end of the fourth performance Macready protested, in a short address, that they "belonged to the period of the action," and were to be taken as purely dramatic utterances. For five or six nights the play drew poor houses, and Macready was on the point of withdrawing it; but Bartley, who, in the part of Damas, had good opportunities of watching the demeanour of the audience, assured him that, if he kept it on, it would be "as great a draw as *The Stranger.*" Gradually the audiences increased, and the announcement of the author's name confirmed its success; notwithstanding which, Bulwer declined to receive any payment for it.

Perhaps by way of atonement for so frivolous a triumph, Macready now put all his strength into a great revival of *Coriolanus,* which extorted the admiration even of Bunn. The *Times,* indeed, dismissed it in seventeen lines, admitting that "the organization of the mob was exceedingly clever," but adding that the "decorations were better than the substance." In his mounting of the play Macready reversed the achievement of Augustus—he found the stage Rome marble, and left it brick. The Colosseum, the Arch of Constantine, and Trajan's Column figured in Kemble's revival; in Macready's, the Palatine was covered with thatched hovels. In every outdoor

scene, the Capitol, with its arx and temples, closed the
perspective, "like a chord in music pervading the entire
composition." In the Senate-scene, the white-robed
fathers, between one and two hundred in number, sat in
triple rows round three sides of the stage, an effect of
perspective being obtained by getting half-grown boys
to present the more distant figures. In the middle
of the back row the Consul occupied the curule chair;
before him the fire of the sacred altar, behind him
(sole ornament of the pillared hall) the brazen wolf
suckling the founders of Rome. The starlight view of
the port and mole of Antium, with its pharos, was a lovely
effect. But the great scene of all was the siege of Rome
by the Volscian army, with its battering-rams and moving
towers. The brilliantly equipped soldiers "seemed
thousands, not hundreds;" and when their serried ranks
opened for the "black apparition" of the Roman matrons,
"one long dreary sable line of monotonous misery," the
stage presented a glorious picture. The management of
the Roman mob, all critics agree, was an unparalleled
feat. Each figure lived its own life, and the plebeians
were "now for the first time shown upon the stage as
agents of the tragic catastrophe." In this revival, in
short, Macready seems to have anticipated all the
Meiningen methods. An unfortunate attempt of Forster's
to prove Macready superior to Kemble, on the ground
that it is a mistake to suppose Coriolanus "an abstraction
of Roman-nosed grandeur," drew from James Smith the
following epigram, which had great success in its day :—

> "What scenes of grandeur does this play disclose,
> Where all is Roman—save the Roman's nose!"

Coriolanus was the great effort of the season. Macready
produced *The Two Foscari* for his benefit, with much

applause; but the part of the Doge soon dropped out of his repertory. After this, nothing of importance occurred until well on in the summer, when Sheridan Knowles's comedy of *Woman's Wit* was produced amid wild enthusiasm. To us it is almost inconceivable that people should take pleasure in the romantic extravagances of the plot and the laboured artificiality of the wit; for, Irishman though he was, Knowles assuredly " jocked wi' deeficulty." The success of *Woman's Wit*, however, almost rivalled that of *The Lady of Lyons*, and brought the season to a brilliant close.

On the whole Macready had fought a good fight. Out of two hundred and eleven acting nights, fifty-five had been devoted to Shakespeare,* eleven of his plays being produced. There is reason to believe that, if he would have yielded to the tendency of the time, and repeated *King Lear* and *Coriolanus* without intermission until their attraction was exhausted, he might largely have increased the proportion of Shakespearian performances, to the great advantage of his treasury; but he resisted, with heroic obstinacy, the encroachments of the " long run " system. As it was, he stated officially that " the plays of Shakespeare, genuine and unalloyed, had been the most profitable performances of the season "—and this in spite of the rivalry of Charles Kean, who had played a forty-three nights' engagement at Drury Lane to large houses. The legitimate drama, as a whole, had held by far the most prominent place in the Covent Garden programme; and though Macready had been rather unfortunate in his minor novelties, he had added two new plays of some importance to the dramatic literature of the time.

---

* In these statistics I do not reckon Garrick's afterpiece, *Catherine and Petruchio*, among the Shakespearian plays.

During the recess he played a five-weeks' engagement with Webster at the Haymarket, appearing on July 23 as Kitely in *Every Man in his Humour.* On August 4 Talfourd's *Athenian Captive* was produced with considerable success, Mrs. Warner playing Ismene and Macready Thoas.

The same company, to all intents and purposes, gathered round Macready for his second Covent Garden season. It was strengthened, however, by Vandenhoff and his daughter. Vandenhoff was an older man and older actor than Macready by about three years, though he did not appear in London until 1820. He was popular in the provinces, but had never quite attained the first rank in his profession. Macready writes of him as "a useful mill-horse actor, or rather post-horse"—implying that it was his nature to follow in the track of others. Miss Vandenhoff, now near the commencement of her career, was a mediocre actress, who subsequently came to be regarded as an imitator of Miss Helen Faucit. It was Macready's practice, at the beginning of each season, to distribute complimentary season tickets among men of distinction in literature, art, and science. The ticket sent to Carlyle for the season 1838–39 elicited the following characteristic letter of thanks :—

"5, Cheyne Row, Chelsea, October 12, 1838.
"DEAR SIR,
        "On returning from the country, I find you have again honoured me with a Free Ticket to Covent Garden. I owe you many thanks for such a kindness and distinction ; many thanks for the great pleasure I hope to have this season, as I had last, of occasionally seeing you—were it only in the distance and by lamplight. To an entirely *un*theatrical man, perhaps the most so of all your spectators, there was a touch of wild sincerity in these things which was extremely

striking.   I wondered at the Drama, wondered at your Her-
culean task.   Proceed in it, prosper in it !   I remain always,
" Dear sir,
" Yours, much obliged
" T. CARLYLE."

The first week of the season was given up to Vandenhoff and Phelps, who played Coriolanus and Aufidius,
Iachimo and Posthumus, respectively.   The critics
condemned them roundly, perhaps not altogether to
Macready's disappointment.   At the end of the third
week the first great effort of the season was made—an
elaborate and highly successful revival of *The Tempest.*
It was received with enthusiasm.   " Even papers that were
wont to ' damn with faint praise, assent with civil sneer,'
and to dismiss with a frigid notice of some dozen lines
the most splendid restorations of Shakespeare at this
theatre, whilst devoting columns to nonentities elsewhere,
at length joined in the popular acclaim."   Yet the
general taste of the production was questionable.   The
whole dialogue of the opening scene was suppressed ; and
the shipwreck, exhibited spectacularly, was a more or
less clever piece of mechanism.   In the second scene
Prospero and Miranda entered together down a rocky
incline, so that Miranda's first words—

> " If by your art, my dearest father, you have
> Put the wild waters in this roar, allay them !"

—were treated as part of an ordinary conversation, instead
of the eager cry of her " piteous heart " on first meeting
her father after having witnessed the wreck.   It seems
almost incredible that Ferdinand's sword should have
been struck out of his hand by *actual collision* with
Prospero's wand ; yet so the *John Bull* affirms.   Miss
Priscilla Horton, as Ariel, it adds, was " whisked about

by wires and a cog-wheel like . . . the ladies in *Peter Wilkins*," and throughout the play " poetry was drowned in the vulgar hurly-burly of an Easter piece." Almost the only feature of the production praised by this critic (in my judgment the ablest of his day) was George Bennett's Caliban, which was acknowledged to be at once powerful and poetical. The *John Bull*, however, stood almost alone in its unfavourable opinion. The other critics were loud in their praises, especially of the wire-wafted Ariel. According to the *Examiner*, she

" floated in air across the stage, singing or mocking as she floated—while a chorus of spirits winged after her higher in the air. Now amidst the terrors of the storm she *flamed amazement* ; now with the gentle descent of a protecting god she hung over the slumbers of Gonzago, . . . flitting in another instant across the scene, behold her resting on a leaf, that she may mock with her pretty human mimicry, Caliban and Stephano and Trinculo ; and then, almost before thought has time to follow her, see the pert and deft little spirit performing the part of Ceres. . . . The masque is given as Shakespeare wrote it, with beautiful landscapes, brown and blue, such as Titian would have beheld with pleasure."

We are probably safe in taking the mean between the *John Bull*, which found little to praise, and the *Examiner*, which found nothing to condemn. The majority sided with the *Examiner*. The play was performed fifty-five times to an average of £230 a night, and might have drawn like receipts for another hundred nights, says Anderson, if Macready would have suffered it to run without interruption.

Early in December Macready once more resorted to the not very generous policy of forestalling Bunn in an important enterprise. Rossini's *Guillaume Tell* being in preparation at Drury Lane, Knowles's *William Tell* was hurried on at Covent Garden, with interpolated choruses from Rossini's opera, performed by a company of eighty singers. The pantomime of *Fair Rosamond* was a failure on Boxing Night, but "weathered the storm," and became fairly popular. January and February were, for the most part, given up to *The Tempest*, *King Lear*, and *The Lady of Lyons.* But early in March a new play by Sir Edward Lytton Bulwer, Bart., was produced. *Richelieu; or, The Conspiracy,* had been the subject of long and anxious discussion and correspondence between author and manager. The character of De Mauprat (under another name) was originally intended for Macready, but the impossibility of finding a satisfactory Richelieu led to the abandonment of this design. Every scene, every speech, was anxiously weighed, and, before the production was finally decided upon, the play was submitted to a conclave of advisers, among whom were Robert Browning and W. J. Fox. It was elaborately mounted and very carefully prepared. "We have had twenty rehearsals of this piece," said some one on the morning of the production. "Then I wish you luck at *vingt-et-un*," replied Tom Cooke, the conductor of the orchestra. His wish was amply fulfilled. The extraordinary originality and power of Macready's conception were recognized from the outset, and the great scenes of the concluding acts roused the crowded audience to a wild pitch of excitement. When Richelieu drew "the circle of the Church" round Julie de Mortemar, and threatened to "launch the curse of Rome" at whoever should infringe it, "the vast pit," says Westland Marston, "seemed to rock with enthusiasm as it volleyed its admiration in rounds of thunder;" and the great phrase of the last act, "There, at my feet!" proved no less effective. The press scarcely echoed the public enthusiasm. "The play is clever," said the *Times*— "nothing more nor less; clever is the exact predicate. . . . Sir E. L. Bulwer, according to the new and most absurd fashion, being called for, made his bow from the stage-box." The *John Bull* admitted that the author had shown tact, cleverness, and the power of adapting means to an end; "but the tact is wasted on the little, the cleverness on the pretty; the end is to startle, and the means are squibs." A week later, the same paper remarked, "We said that the herd would go and gape at *Richelieu*, and were oracular, for they do."

The success was complete, and for three months no new effort of any importance was required. For Miss Faucit's benefit, *As You Like It* was revived, Macready playing Jaques, and Phelps the First Lord !—who, however, was not forced, according to stage tradition, to give up his one great speech to Jaques. Miss Faucit, playing Rosalind for the first time, was received with popular applause, but not, as she herself tells us, with critical approbation. A "dramatic romance" named *Agnes Bernauer* was moderately successful; but a new opera named *Henrique*, by the composer of *Amilie*, soon dropped out of the bills. Having determined, early in April, to bring his management to a close at the end of the season, Macready gave his whole mind to an elaborate revival of *Henry V.*, which should enable him to retire in a blaze of triumph. The rehearsals were long and arduous, and the actors were seriously annoyed by the perpetual presence on the stage of a whole cohort of the manager's friends—Bulwer, Dickens, Forster, Maclise, Fox, and others. Forster's overbearing manner made him especially obnoxious, and so utterly upset the nerves of Mrs. Humby, who was to have played Dame Quickly, that the words of her part constantly escaped

her. She was, says James Anderson, so incredibly
ignorant that her comrades advised her to put up with
Forster's interferences on the ground that he was the
author of the play ! Even this consideration, however,
could not reconcile her to his habit of shouting, whenever she made a slip, " Put her through it again, Mac. ;
put her through it again ; " so that the matter ended in
her relinquishing the part. The production did not take
place until early in June, when it was received with
general acclamation. The *Morning Chronicle* declared
it " worthy of being reserved for some great national
fête," adding that " the nation has but rarely the occasions which deserve so splendid a celebration." Once
more the *John Bull* played the devil's advocate, ridicul-
ing especially Stanfield's " Pictorial Illustrations." The
prologue to the first act, with its allusion to " famine,
sword, and fire," crouching for employment at the feet
of " the warlike Harry," was illustrated by " a figure in
armour with three furies clinging to his feet." " Shade
of Æschylus ! " cries the critic, " imagine your Theban
chiefs in a raree-show ! " Macready's performance of
the King was pronounced " conventionally dignified "
and " bustling and didactic, rather than frank and impulsive." Phelps told Mr. Coleman that, after fatiguing
rehearsals, Macready would " devote hours to walking
about the stage ' with his cuisses on his thighs ; ' but
all to no avail, for at night he tossed and tumbled
about literally like a hog in armour." Nevertheless, the
production was very attractive. " It would have filled
the house nightly," said Anderson ; " but the old policy
prevailed : it was acted only four nights a week, up to
the close of the season, which was as good as telling the
public the production was only half a success."

Macready's reasons for relinquishing management are

not very clear. The enterprise was evidently prospering. He calculated that in "actual decrease of capital and absence of profit on his labour," he was £2500 out of pocket by his first season; but the result of his second season must have been very different. The excessively cautious proposition he made to the Covent Garden proprietors for a third season was rejected by them; and as we find him, several months earlier, resolving in his diary that *Henry V.* should be "the last Shakespearian revival of his management," it is natural to infer that he did not desire or intend it to be accepted. One can hardly believe the proprietors so blind to their own interests as to let slip such a tenant if they could retain him by any reasonable concessions; unless, indeed, they were already in treaty with Charles Mathews and Madame Vestris, who eventually took the theatre. We may probably conclude that the cares of management were such a perpetual annoyance to Macready as to make him eager for any fair excuse to cast them off. Both in personal and professional consideration he had reaped the full reward of his enterprise. A public dinner bore witness to the esteem in which he was held, by a clique, perhaps, but certainly a large and influential clique. It took place at the Freemasons' Tavern, July 20, 1839. The Duke of Sussex was in the chair, and Lord Conyngham, Lord Nugent, Dickens, Bulwer, Sheil, Talfourd, Monckton Milnes (Lord Houghton), Forster, Fonblanque, Charles Buller, and Charles Young were among the company. This was just the sort of distinction Macready most appreciated, and though nervousness made him look, as Bulwer said, like "a baffled tyrant," the occasion may be called, in more than a conventional sense, one of the proudest moments of his life.

It was at this time that he applied to the Lord Chamberlain for a "personal licence" to perform the legitimate drama when and where he pleased—an application which was ultimately refused.   Similar ill success attended a scheme for securing him the post of Reader of Plays, in succession to Charles Kemble.   He was eager to obtain the office, and would willingly have engaged to retire from the stage in four years, or even in one, had such a condition been insisted on.   In the end, however, the Anglo-Saxon scholar, John Mitchell Kemble, succeeded his father.

During the two years and a half which intervened between his first and second managements, Macready was engaged, almost without intermission, at the Haymarket.   He seems to have got on better with the Haymarket manager than with any other.   I find him, indeed, in a letter to Webster of October 8, 1840, complaining bitterly of certain unspecified offences, and vowing that, after the expiration of the current engagement, he will never enter upon another.   But this quarrel seems to have blown over quickly, and Macready certainly did not carry out his resolution.

On August 19, 1839, he appeared at the Haymarket as Othello, with Phelps as Iago, Cooper as Cassio, Walter Lacy as Roderigo, Miss Faucit as Desdemona, and Mrs. Warner as Emilia.   Mr. Howe, on this occasion, made his first appearance on the stage with which he was so long and honourably connected, in the small part of Lodovico.   *The Lady of .Lyons* followed, and was frequently repeated.   Other stock plays were performed at intervals, the most popular being *The Merchant of Venice*, with Phelps as Antonio, Helen Faucit as Portia, and Buckstone as Launcelot Gobbo.   On October 31 a new play by Sir E. L. Bulwer was produced with great success. This was *The Sea-Captain ; or, The Birth-right*, now remembered almost solely by reason of Barham's rhyming account of its plot, and Thackeray's scathing satire on its style. Macready played Norman ; Phelps, Onslow ; Mrs. Warner, Lady Arundel ; and Miss Faucit, Violet. In the scene between Norman and Lady Arundel, where the son reveals himself to his mother, and, being scornfully repudiated, invokes the spirits of his ancestors to take his part, " Macready's action, his look, his utterance, was sublimity itself." The play did not hold the stage, however, either in its original shape, or in the revised form in which it was reproduced at the Lyceum in 1868, under the title of *The Rightful Heir.*

Five days after the close of the Haymarket season Macready appeared at Drury Lane, under the manage-ment of the comedian W. J. Hammond. His opening play (January 20) was *Macbeth*, with Phelps as Macduff, and Mrs. Warner as Lady Macbeth. On January 22 a new tragedy by James Haynes was produced under the title of *Mary Stuart.* It had originally and more fitly been called *Rizzio.* Macready's part was Ruthven ; Elton played Rizzio ; Phelps, Darnley ; and Mrs. Warner, the Queen. The play was repeated twenty times, but cannot have been profitable, since at the end of February Hammond failed for £8000. Macready played four nights gratuitously for the benefit of the minor per-formers, and then returned to the Haymarket, where the season commenced on March 16.

The opening play was *Hamlet*, with Warde as Claudius, Mrs. Warner as Gertrude, Priscilla Horton as Ophelia, Strickland as Polonius, Webster as Osric, and Phelps as the Ghost. A revival of *The Sea-Captain* proved un-attractive ; but, on the other hand, *The Lady of Lyons* and *Richelieu* vied with each other in popularity. At the close of the previous year a tragedy named *Glencoe ; or, The Fate of the Macdonalds*, had been placed in Macready's hands by Dickens. He read it with admiration, and thought the anonymous author an imitator of Talfourd, "but without the point that terminated Talfourd's speeches." Great was his surprise on learning that it was by Talfourd himself. It was successfully produced at the Haymarket on May 23, Macready playing Halbert Macdonald ; Phelps, Glenlyon ; Webster, MacIan; Mrs. Warner, Lady Macdonald; and Miss Faucit, Helen Campbell. A gloomy and stilted production, it took no permanent place on the stage. Mrs. Inchbald's comedy, *To Marry or not to Marry*, revived with Macready in Kemble's part of Sir Oswin Mortland, met with some success, but a new play by Serle, named *Master Clarke* (September 26), was practically a failure. In this Macready played Richard Cromwell ; and Miss Faucit, his wife, Lady Dorothy. The play-bill of November 5 announced that a "New and Original Comedy by Sir Edward Lytton Bulwer had been accepted, and would be produced as early as the scenic arrangements, etc., would permit." A week later its title, ₁MONEY! appeared in large letters. The production, after repeated postponements, was fixed for Saturday, November 28 ; but on the previous day the play-bill stated that "In consequence of the *very severe domestic calamity* of MR. MACREADY, the production was necessarily deferred until Mr. Macready could resume his professional duties." The calamity was the death of his daughter Joan, aged three years and four months. Phelps and Wallack occupied the bill for ten days, playing *Othello, Hamlet*, and other stock pieces. On December 7 Macready appeared in *Werner*, and on the following evening *Money* was produced, "with entirely new Scenery, Dresses, Furniture, and Appurtenances." It was out of pure complaisance that Macready accepted the part of Alfred Evelyn. He calls it in his diary "ineffective and inferior," and is said to have denounced the sententious secretary, in private, as a "damned walking-gentleman." His success, however, was indubitable; "the forced gaiety," says Walter Lacy, "being as natural to the man as appropriate to the character." The cast as a whole was very strong : Miss Faucit and Miss Horton played Clara Douglas and Georgina Vesey; Webster and Mrs. Glover established the traditions, now so threadbare, of Graves and Lady Franklin; David Rees, a fine and very popular comedian, created the part of Stout; Dudley Smooth, declined by James Wallack, was admirably performed by Wrench; F. Vining played Lord Glossmore; Strickland, Sir John Vesey; and Walter Lacy, Sir Frederick Blount. Every strap and button of the costumes was anxiously studied, Count d'Orsay supervising the whole; for the Mathews-Vestris management at the Olympic and Covent Garden had made solecisms in modern dress unpardonable. We obtain a curious glimpse of Macready's habiliments in the following letter from Dickens, dated 1845 :—

"MY DEAR MACREADY,
"You once—only once—gave the world assurance of a waistcoat. You wore it, sir, I think, in *Money*. It was a remarkable and precious waistcoat, wherein certain broad stripes of blue or purple disported themselves, as by a combination of extraordinary circumstances too happy to occur again. I have seen it on your manly chest in private life. I saw it, sir, I think, the other day in the cold light of morning, with feelings easier to be imagined than described. Mr. Macready, sir, are you a father? If so, lend me that waistcoat for five minutes. . . . I will send a trusty messenger at half-past nine precisely in the morning. He is sworn to secrecy. He durst not for his life betray us, or

swells in ambuscade would have the waistcoat at the cost of his heart's blood.

> "Thine,
> "THE UNWAISTCOATED ONE."

This marvellous garment no doubt contributed its share to the success of the comedy, which was unprecedented. It ran for eighty consecutive nights, the season being extended for two months, up to March 13, 1841, by special licence from the Lord Chamberlain.

When Macready returned to the Haymarket for the following season (May 3, 1841) *Money* was again placed in the bills—Mrs. Stirling now playing Lady Franklin—and was repeated twenty-nine times. His performances during this season were interrupted for nearly two months, during which Charles Kean and Ellen Tree held the chief place in the bills, their principal production being *Romeo and Juliet*. Macready played no new character until November 1, when, for Miss Faucit's benefit, R. Zouch Troughton's tragedy of *Nina Sforza* was produced. Wallack played the hero, Raphael Doria; and Macready found in Ugone Spinola one of those sardonic villains who had vexed his soul during his early years at Covent Garden. The play, though written with some power, was in truth a mere romance, with little dramatic fibre. On December 7 he brought his Haymarket engagement to a close with *The Lady of Lyons*.

So early as the previous April Macready had arranged to undertake the management of Drury Lane, and to open the theatre at Christmas. I am unable to state the precise terms of his agreement with the proprietors. He notes in his diary that he demanded "liberty to close at a day's notice," and "no compulsion to pay any rent." This somewhat fantastic stipulation probably means that, if he should bring the season to a premature close, no rent was to be due for the nights thus sacrificed. We learn, too, that when he entered upon his new dominion, the female wardrobe was not worth £40, and there was not a serviceable rope in the house ; so that the proprietors had to consent to a " very inadequate deduction " from the rent, in consideration of his putting the theatre in working order. What the rent actually was, however, I have not discovered. The chief members of his Covent Garden company gathered eagerly round him, in some cases rejecting more highly-paid engagements elsewhere —a sufficient proof, surely, that his bark was worse than his bite. Mrs. Warner and Miss Faucit, Phelps, Elton, Anderson, and George Bennett enlisted once more under his banner ; while Henry Marston, who had come to the front under Hammond's management, was the chief new-comer on the tragic side. This sterling actor, afterwards Phelps's trusted lieutenant at Sadler's Wells, might have attained great distinction but for his unfortunately husky voice. The leading comedians were Keeley, Mrs. Keeley, Henry Compton, and James Hudson. Keeley and his wife were already at the height of their popularity ; Compton had been four years on the London stage ; and Hudson, a young actor whom Macready had discovered in Dublin, proved a valuable importation. The musical company included H. Phillips and Allen, Miss Romer, Miss Gould, Miss Poole, and Miss P. Horton. Anderson was stage-manager ; Serle, acting-manager ; and T. Cooke, musical director. The scenic department— doubly important since the decorative achievements of the Vestris management at Covent Garden—was for the most part in the hands of Marshall and Telbin.

The season opened on Boxing Night with *The Merchant of Venice* and the pantomime of *Harlequin and*

K

Duke Humphrey.   Enthusiasm was the order of the evening, and the audience would not suffer the play to proceed until Macready had appeared to receive their welcome.   The *Times*, which, four years ago, had dismissed Macready's opening night at Covent Garden in a mere paragraph, now devoted a column and three-quarters to impressing on the public the importance of the new undertaking.   Macready's Shylock was received with almost unmixed praise, and the mounting of the play was declared superb.   For the first time (so far as I know) in the case of a Shakespearian revival, a synopsis of the scenery was issued—an honour hitherto reserved for pantomime and spectacular drama.   Even now the list of scenes found no place on the play-bill, but was relegated to a small fly-leaf.   On the two following evenings Macready, after a heroic mental struggle, swallowed two very bitter pills—the small parts of Harmony in Mrs. Inchbald's comedy *Every One has his Fault*, and Valentine in *The Two Gentlemen of Verona*.   In Old Harmony (created by Munden !) he seems to have been thoroughly out of place, and he was scarcely repaid for his condescension in undertaking Valentine.   The revival of *The Two Walking-Gentlemen* (as they were rechristened by a green-room wit) was chiefly remarkable for the great success of a Miss Fortescue in the part of Julia.   Its first night, too, was signalized by the first appearance of a new crimson velvet curtain, with a broad gold fringe, ornamented with large gold wreaths of laurel.   A revival of *The Gamester*, in which Macready undertook the part of Beverley with grave misgivings, was well received, but proved unattractive, and the season languished on the whole until, early in February, Gay's *Acis and Galatea* was produced, with Handel's music and Stanfield's scenery.   This was a great triumph, and was received with enthusiasm on every hand. It charmed even the fastidious Edward Fitzgerald. " Never in this country has the illusion which scenic art permits of been so completely and triumphantly displayed," exclaimed the cool and critical *John Bull.* What chiefly excited admiration was a novel device for representing " the hollow ocean ridges roaring into cataracts."

" The Sicilian coast in moonlight," said the *Examiner*, " stretches up the stage, and between the foreground and Etna in the distance—

> ' A promontory, sharpening by degrees,
> Ends in a wedge, and overlooks the seas,'

as they come swelling towards us, the waves breaking as they come ; the last billow actually tumbling over and over with spray and foam upon the shore, and then receding with the noise of water over stones and shells, to show the hard, wet sand, and, in its due time, roll and break again."

Macready himself took great pride and pleasure in the production, and Westland Marston records his delight when a lady said to him, " Now I have *seen* a poem ! " " It ought to have run two hundred nights," says Anderson, who, as stage-manager, had access to the books of the theatre, "and brought thousands of pounds to the treasury, had the manager been so inclined. But no ; in direct opposition to the advice of his officers, . . . he would not permit it to be sung more than *three times* a week. The consequence was its attraction dwindled to nothing. . . . Mr. Macready treated the public much as he did his own children—reared them on vegetable diet, and physicked them with homœopathic doses. He said, ' He knew what probity was. He had promised variety, and he would be conscientious.' He had his own way, but he lost his money."

Douglas Jerrold's *Prisoner of War*, produced two nights later, was a great success ; Mrs. Keeley's reading of Peter Pallmall's letter from Verdun being encored nightly ! On the other hand, Gerald Griffin's powerful play *Gisippus*, splendidly mounted, finely played, and received with acclamation by the critics, brought no money to the treasury. According to Anderson, it should have been reserved till next season ; as it was, *Gisippus* and *Acis and Galatea* each cut the other's throat. *Macbeth* was revived after Easter, in much the same style as at Covent Garden, and three weeks later a terrible disaster took place in the failure of *Plighted Troth*, a would-be Elizabethan tragedy, by a Mr. Darley. It was, in fact, an extravagantly gloomy and forcible-feeble melodrama, against which all possible circumstances conspired. The name of Macready's character, "Gabriel Grimwood," aroused memories of a recent crime, and led to bantering interruptions from the gods ; and while Grimwood, stabbed with a bread-knife, was lying dead under a table, one of the other actors had the misfortune to tread on Macready's hand, causing the corpse to sit up and rate him soundly, in full hearing of the audience. This transformed the hisses and cat-calls, which had previously reigned supreme, into shouts of laughter, and dealt the finishing blow to *Plighted Troth*. The criticisms were one chorus of condemnation ; yet Macready had been "confident in hope about it." He was never guilty of a greater error of judgment. A revival of *Hamlet*, and the production of *Marino Faliero*, for Macready's benefit, were the chief events of the remainder of the season, which was brought to an early close on May 23.

Provincial engagements occupied a portion of the summer, the intervals being devoted to preparations for a "longer, stronger pull" during the coming season at

Drury Lane, which was to commence on October 1.
The company was strengthened by the addition of Mrs.
Nisbett, the most popular comic actress of the day;
Charles Mathews and Madame Vestris, engaged at a
salary of £60 a week; and John Ryder, then a raw-
boned stripling, fresh from the provinces. *As You Like
It*, elaborately mounted, and very strongly cast, was the
opening play, Macready acting Jaques; but once more
the audience insisted on seeing him before the comedy
began, and the stage was littered with bouquets and
wreaths, which were collected and carried off by a foot-
man! The weak point of the cast was Mrs. Nisbett's
Rosalind, which Robson, "the Old Playgoer," does not
hesitate to describe as "infamous." Her merriment,
said the *Times*, was thoughtless and unrestrained, with
no hint of underlying seriousness. Anderson's Orlando,
Mrs. Stirling's Celia, Hudson's Le Beau, and Compton's
William, were all much praised, but Keeley's Touchstone
can scarcely have been the true sententious philosopher,
and the sprightly Mrs. Keeley could by no means assume
the stolidity of Audrey. The second Shakespearian
revival, *King John*, with scenery by Telbin, took p'
towards the end of the month. The stage-mana
was very careful and effective. Especially str
the rupture of the short peace between Phil
"The Englishmen and Frenchmen, w
together," said the *John Bull*, "parte
of lightning. . . . A quiet mass
ments had suddenly burst in
animation and energy." M
to be one of his best Sh
"an actor with more Pr
stage," was greatly
The Mathews

They drew poor houses, and their dignity was outraged by the small parts for which they were cast.   Mathews actually appeared as Fag in *The Rivals* and Roderigo in *Othello*, and, playing carelessly no doubt, was roundly condemned by the critics.   His wife complained that she was asked to play Maria in *The School for Scandal*, and Venus in *King Arthur*—a part which was ultimately assigned to Miss Fairbrother, a columbine.   The engagement, in short, was found to have been a mistake on both sides, and was rescinded by mutual consent in little more than a month.

By way of following up the vein so successfully opened in *Acis and Galatea*, Dryden and Purcell's *King Arthur* was revived about the middle of November.   Unfortunately, it had not the advantage of Stanfield's scenery, and was a "retrograde movement" in point of "artistic display."   The costumes were very tawdry.   A generation which has passed through the awakening crisis of æstheticism cannot read without a shudder of Mrs. Nisbett's "bright yellow, almost orange, gown, surcoat of decided blue, and tippet and scarf of extreme scarlet." nevertheless, it was well received and fairly successful. and *Times* described it as "a succession of magnificent shouts of A young singer, who had hitherto passed *Troth*. The the crowd, was entrusted on an emergency yet Macready the Warrior, and made a decided hit in He was never gu if you dare," though he narrowly revival of *Hamlet*, and declining to sing it with his back for Macready's benefit; is since been known as Sims mainder of the season, w close on May 23.   it was generally agreed

Provincial engagements occurs. Nisbett especially), summer, the intervals being devot ready took no part a "longer, stronger pull" during the tle appetite for

Congreve's wit. Very different was the fare provided in the first new play of the season, *The Patrician's Daughter*, by J. Westland Marston, produced early in December. The work of a young and as yet unknown writer, it had been published some months before, and had "made a sensation which, for an unacted drama, might be considered remarkable." Critics had long been advocating an attempt to utilize, for the purposes of poetic drama, the spiritual conflicts of modern life, and some were sanguine enough to hope that this simple yet powerful play might mark a new departure in dramatic literature. Charles Dickens took deep interest in the experiment, and wrote a prologue for it. The play was to all appearance a success, though its central incident—a repetition, in some sort, of the painful cathedral-scene in *Much Ado* —was misunderstood and generally condemned. When Macready, in his own person, spoke the prologue, he was, said the *John Bull*, "easy and gentlemanly;" but "such a person as he represented Mordaunt to be had emptied any modern drawing-room in five minutes." On the whole, however, the performance was praised, and as the audience had shown no inclination to ill-timed laughter, it was declared that "the principle .er characters talking poetically in plain dress" was se.c the But the victory, as we know, has proved a barre.count of

Of the pantomime of *Harlequin and Williq* with him, *Times* remarked, "The scenery is clever.uc said he was may be said of it as of the scenery of *K*.n a snowstorm." it is better conceived than executed.ered the chivalrous want of finish prevails throughout.certainly have regarded *The Lady of Lyons*, and *C*.xed feelings. elaborate as some of its pre.rand opera was made shortly by taste and art of th*Sappho* being splendidly produced, events of January, .ello, fresh from her early continental prosperously, and Macready was in no happy mood; hence the regrettable circumstances connected with the production of Mr. Browning's tragedy, *A Blot in the 'Scutcheon,* which took place on February 11. Macready had engaged to produce it, and was too proud frankly to confess the embarrassments which now rendered his promise irksome to him.

" It would seem, by all the evidence I had afterwards," Mr. Browning writes to me, " that I was supposed to myself understand the expediency of begging to withdraw, at least for a time, my own work—saving Macready the imaginary failure to keep a promise to which I never attached particular importance. As so many hints to my dull perception of this, Macready declined to play his part, caused the play to be read in my absence to the actors by a ludicrously incapable person—the result being, as he informed me, 'that the play was laughed at from the beginning to the end'—naturally enough, a girl's part being made comical by a red-nosed, one-legged, elderly gentleman [Willmott, the prompter]— then, after proposing to take away from his substitute the opportunity of distinction he had given him (to which I refused my consent), leaving the play to a fate which it somehow managed to escape. Macready was *fuori di se* from the moment when, in pure ignorance of what he was a..ving at, I acquiesced in his proposal that a serious play of shou retension should appear under his management with *Troth.* protagonist than himself. When the more learned yet Macrew enlightened me a little, I was angry and dis- He was never advice—but it is happily over so long ago ! revival of *Hamlet*ghtforward word to the effect that what for Macready's be..advantage would, under circumstances mainder of the seasor ger ignorant, prove the reverse—how what regret it would have spared close on May 23.

Provincial engagements

summer, the intervals being de..sham, and, in spite of a "longer, stronger pull" during ne time made up his mind to understudy the part, he played it very finely. The *Morning Post* missed in him "a little of that refinement which carries Macready so triumphantly through his blotchy mannerisms," but added that "he gave a singular passion and power to the proud brother, which could have been shown by no other actor than himself." Miss Faucit's Mildred was also much praised, and the performance, as a whole, was received with applause. *The Thumping Legacy*, with Keeley in his afterwards celebrated part of Jerry Ominous, was performed for the first time on the same evening; and this combination was thrice repeated. On the third evening (February 17) the play-bill announced that the tragedy and farce would be acted three times a week until further notice; yet from that night forward the tragedy was shelved.

For his benefit, to every one's surprise, Macready attempted the part of Benedick in *Much Ado.* As to the merits of the performance opinions were greatly divided. The *John Bull* declared that "he clutched at drollery, as Macbeth at the dagger, with convulsive energy;" while the *Examiner* argued, not very convincingly, that because his Benedick made Don Pedro and Claudio laugh, it must have been comic. Forster adds, however, what is much more to the point, that the audience laughed as well. James Anderson's account of the matter is that "his friends were pleased with him, and he with himself; but the general public said he was as melancholy as a mourning-coach in a snowstorm." Playgoers who still vividly remembered the chivalrous grace of Charles Kemble must certainly have regarded Macready's Benedick with mixed feelings.

A spirited attempt at grand opera was made shortly before Easter, Pacini's *Sappho* being splendidly produced, with Miss Clara Novello, fresh from her early continental triumphs, as Sappho, and Mrs. Alfred Shaw, one of the most popular singers of the day, as Climene. The experiment, however, was unremunerative. The Easter piece was Planché's graceful extravaganza, *Fortunio*, with Priscilla Horton in the leading part. " The rehearsals," says the author, " were most energetically and judiciously superintended by Macready himself. . . . He knew every one's part, and acted each in turn, to my great delight, and the infinite amusement of Miss Helen Faucit, who sat almost daily on the stage, and encouraged us all by her unaffected enjoyment of the dialogue." A small part was allotted to Mrs. Alfred Wigan, who, with her husband, had now joined the company, both appearing in very subordinate characters. *Fortunio* was a success, but *The Secretary*, by Sheridan Knowles, produced a few days later, was a complete failure. It was Knowles's last play, and one of his wordiest and emptiest. One other new play closes the list of novelties under Macready's management. This was William Smith's *Athelwold*, produced on the occasion of Miss Faucit's benefit, and repeated only once. It dealt with a striking subject, but was undramatic in treatment and heavy in diction.

At a conference with the Drury Lane Committee, on May 6, Macready found that there was no hope of coming to terms with them for another season. The details of their disagreement are unknown to me. Macready stated, in his farewell speech, that " he could not subject himself to the liabilities required of him ; " and his friend W. J. Fox attributed his retirement to " proprietary arrangements, or disarrangements, which yielded no security for an expenditure that could only have repaid itself in a series of years, and the immediate profits of which were liable to be pressed upon by undefined and encroaching claims." We can scarcely believe that the proprietors were unwilling to grant Macready a lease at a fixed rental if he would have accepted it. The truth probably is that he declined to undertake what they considered his fair share of the risk. He was determined not to burn his ships, and the Committee were dissatisfied with a lessee who insisted upon such unlimited facilities for retreat. In the light of after-events, we may think them unwise. It would have been to their interest, we may argue, to give such a man as Macready every possible encouragement in his enterprise. They should have preferred small profits and steady returns to rack-rents tempered by bankruptcy. Yet Macready's bargains bore on the surface a heads-I-win-tails-you-lose appearance, from which we cannot wonder that they recoiled, In his heart of hearts Macready cared too little about the enterprise to give it any chance of permanency. He went into it with the feeling and pose of a martyr. At every touch of discouragement he said to himself that he was endangering his own and his children's future in order to fight a losing battle on behalf of an art he regarded with mingled feelings, and a body of artists with whom he had little personal sympathy. In such moments the alternative course of making a modest fortune as a star, retiring, and devoting himself to the education of his family, presented itself in the light of a positive duty. This was not the temper in which to set about the regeneration of the drama. He " feared his fate too much."

Without venturing too far into the vasty labyrinths of the might-have-been, we may ask whether any possible compliance on the part of the Drury Lane or Covent Garden proprietors would have ensured success. I doubt it. The era of long runs, of conversational playwriting and

acting, of division of labour, or rather specialization of
function, in the theatrical sphere, was already and in-
evitably upon us.   Macready struggled gallantly to carry
on the traditions and methods handed down, under all
external modifications, from Davenant to Elliston.   His
huge establishment, his varied bill of fare, were fitted for
the time when there were but two winter theatres to
cater to the taste of a smaller but more homogeneous and,
theatrically speaking, more intelligent town.   In short,
he tried to continue the system of monopoly management under the conditions of free-trade ; for the already
decrepit monopoly was on the verge of extinction by
Bulwer's Act of 1843.   He declared, in his concluding
speech, that the result of his experiment, though it did
not as yet "amount to a remunerating return," might be
" confidently taken as an earnest of future and permanent
success."   In order to secure this success he would
almost certainly have had to modify and modernize his
principles of management.   He fought a good fight, but
the tendencies of the time were against him.

His conduct as a manager was much, and bitterly,
criticized.   The following passage from the *John Bull*
states in short compass the current objections of his
detractors.   It occurs in an article on his Covent Garden
management, but so far as it applies at all it applies
equally well to his tenure of Drury Lane.   I have read
carefully the whole series of this writer's criticisms, and
can find in them no trace of personal animus.   He is
often generous in praise, sometimes convincing in cen-
sure.   We may accept his judgment as that of an impartial outsider, neither a member of the Macready
clique nor an adherent of the opposition :—

" His real services we were the first to bear testimony to,

and will be the last to deny. Following in the track laid
down by Kemble, he has rendered it impossible for any suc-
ceeding manager to bring out a play of Shakespeare's otherwise than in an adequate manner. For this his profession is
largely indebted to him. He has made the theatre a *decent*
place of amusement, which it hardly was before. . . . As an
actor, though a very unequal, he is now an unrivalled one ;
and so far from joining in the ungenerous judgments we
have heard passed on him in this respect, we believe that,
could the greatest in his art repeople the scene again, he
would still be a foremost and a distinguished man. But here
we stop. He has given encouragement to no dawning
genius ; has brought forward no new author ; has done all
to serve himself, little to advantage his brethren. . . . We
gave him credit for the enlarged views of the scholar, for the
liberal sentiments of the gentleman. We have found him the
mere actor ; the slave of the little feelings and paltry as-
sumptions engendered of the green-room. He has professed much ; we have weighed him by his professions, and
found him wanting. He began his career with well-assumed
modesty ; he has ended it with ill-concealed and insensate
vanity."

The reproach as to his neglect of " dawning genius "
may at once be dismissed. There is no proof that any
such genius existed to suffer from his neglect. Far more
relevant is the remark upon his conduct to his brother-
actors. He treated them justly, in some cases gene-
rously, but never graciously. He crushed their professional vanity with an iron hand, but he took no trouble
to soften the blow by mortifying his own. In one or two
cases he made a show of taking minor parts, such as Friar
Laurence and Jaques, but these condescensions were
rare, and in great measure illusory. He was the star of
Covent Garden and Drury Lane, just as Mr. Irving is the
star of the Lyceum. It is true that this position was in
some degree forced upon him. To have cast himself

for minor parts would have cost him a far greater sacrifice than one of mere vanity.   Those which he could
have played to any advantage were few, and the
public would probably not have cared to see him in
them.   Before really critical audiences, a great actor
may bestow his whole care upon second-rate or third-rate
characters without any sense of waste ; but the average
English audience has no eye for aught but the large
effects to be obtained in leading characters.   Moreover,
the critics and the public would not accept Vandenhoff
or Phelps, Elton or Anderson, in characters which Macready had made his own.   He is scarcely to be blamed,
then, for not having brought his subordinates more to
the front.   Juster reproach attaches to his habit of
taking to himself the whole credit of his achievements,
and ignoring the co-operation of his comrades.   His
churlishness in this respect contrasts unfavourably with
Mr. Irving's generosity of acknowledgment towards his
company on all public occasions.   Many of Macready's
actors risked a third of their ordinary salary in order to
serve under his banner ; and though he fulfilled his promise of making good the deficiency so far as the results
of each season permitted, he did so in such an ungraceful way as to minimize their gratitude.   The attitude of
his fellow-actors towards him is amusingly illustrated in
an anecdote related by James Anderson.   One day
Macready failed to appear at rehearsal, on account of
illness.   Some one inquired what was the matter with
him, and Willmott, the prompter, replied that he believed
it was heart-disease.   "What!" cried Mrs. Keeley,
who was standing by, "Macready suffering from heart-
disease !   You might as well try to make me believe that
Walter Lacy could suffer from brain fever !"   The faith-
fulness with which the leading members of his company

clung to him throughout proves that they had little serious ground of complaint; but there was undoubtedly a lack of amenity in his behaviour towards them which gave some colour to the strictures of his harsher critics.

Among his personal friends and the theatre-going public his popularity was undiminished. On his retirement from Drury Lane his friends presented him with a marvellous piece of symbolic sculpture in silver, testifying that his management had "Formed an Epoch in Theatrical Annals." The public, who always crowded to his opening and closing nights, however they might neglect the intermediate performances, filled every corner of Drury Lane, when, on June 14, 1843, Macready made his last appearance as a manager. Their enthusiasm, he says, "was grand and awful. . . . It was unlike anything that ever occurred before." He was nerved by the splendid reception to play his part—Macbeth—in his best style; then, having "spoken his speech," he "retired with the same mad acclaim."

COVENT GARDEN THEATRE.

1837–1838.

SEPT. 30 (opening night): Address [by Talfourd] spoken by Macready. *The Winter's Tale:* Leontes = Macready; Polixenes = Diddear; Camillo = Pritchard; Antigonus = G. Bennett; Florizel = Anderson (first appearance in London); Shepherd = Tilbury; Clown = Meadows; Autolycus = Bartley; Hermione = Miss H. Faucit; Perdita = Miss Taylor; Paulina = Miss Huddart; Mopsa = Miss P. Horton; Dorcas = Miss Vincent. 4 times. Feb. 10: Dorcas = Mrs. Humby.

OCT. 2: *Hamlet:* Claudius = Diddear; Hamlet = Macready; Polonius = Meadows; Laertes = Anderson; Horatio = G. Bennett; Osrick = Vining; Gravedigger = Bartley;

Ghost = Elton ; Ophelia = Miss Taylor ; Gertrude = Miss Huddart.   3 times.   Oct. 8 : Ghost = Warde.

Oct. 7 : *The Bridal:* Arcancs = G. Bennett ; Melantius = Macready ; Amintor = Anderson ; Evadne = Miss Huddart ; Aspatia = Miss Taylor.   7 times.

Oct. 11 : New Play, *The Novice* [translation by W. Dimond?]: Warde, Bartley, Anderson, Miss H. Faucit. 3 times.

Oct. 14 : *Catherine and Petruchio* (afterpiece) : Miss Faucit and Vining.   Twice.

Oct. 16 : *Othello:* Duke = Bartley ; Brabantio = G. Bennett ; Othello = Macready ; Cassio = Anderson ; Iago = Warde ; Roderigo = Vining ; Desdemona = Miss Faucit ; Emilia = Miss Huddart.   3 times.   Oct. 30 : Othello = Phelps ; Iago = Macready.

Oct. 19 : *The Provoked Husband:* Lord Townly = Macready ; Lady Townly = Miss Faucit ; Lady Grace = Miss Huddart.   3 times.   New Play, *Afrancesado* [by T. J. Serle]: Anderson, Bartley, Warde, Miss Taylor, Miss Vincent.   Twice.

Oct. 21 : *Werner:* Werner = Macready ; Ulric = Anderson ; Gabor = G. Bennett ; Josephine = Miss Huddart ; Ida = Miss Vincent.   9 times.

Oct. 26 : *The Hunchback:* Warde, Anderson, Vining, Miss Faucit, Miss Taylor.   Twice.

Oct. 27 : *Venice Preserved:* Jaffier = Phelps (first appearance at this Theatre) ; Pierre = Macready ; Belvidera = Miss Faucit.   Twice.   Nov. 9 : Pierre = Warde.

Oct. 31 : *The Stranger:* The Stranger = Macready ; Steinfort = Warde ; Mrs. Haller = Miss Faucit.   Once.

Nov. 2 : *Virginius:* Appius Claudius = G. Bennett ; Dentatus = Warde ; Virginius = Macready ; Icilius = Anderson ; Virginia = Miss Faucit ; Servia = Miss Huddart.   Twice.

Nov. 4 : New Play (afterpiece), *Parole of Honour* [by T. J. Serle]: Bartley, Anderson, G. Bennett, Meadows, Miss Faucit, Miss Taylor.   10 times.

Nov. 6: *Macbeth:* Duncan = Waldron ; Malcolm and Donaldbain = Anderson and Miss Fairbrother ; Macbeth

= Macready; Macduff = Phelps; Banquo = Warde; Lenox = Howe; Witches = G. Bennett, Meadows, and Payne; Hecate = H. Phillips; Singing Witches = Wilson, Leffler, Stretton, Manvers, Ransford, Mesdames Shirreff, P. Horton, Taylor, Vincent, Land, and East; Lady Macbeth = Miss Huddart. Acted every Monday for 14 weeks running, and 18 times in all. Monday, Jan. 1, 1838: "Lady Macbeth = Mrs. Warner (late Miss Huddart)."

Nov. 11: New Comic Opera, *The Barbers of Bassora* [by J. Hullah]: H. Phillips, Wilson, Bartley, Leffler, Miss Shirreff. 7 times.

Nov. 13: New Interlude, *The Original*: Bartley, Meadows, Anderson, Miss P. Horton. 20 times.

Nov. 14: *King Henry V.*: Henry V. = Macready; Exeter = Warde; Archbishop of Canterbury = G. Bennett; Fluellen = Meadows; Williams = Bartley; Bardolph, Pistol, and Nym = Macarthy, Hammond, and Ayliffe; Mrs. Quickly = Mrs. Garrick; Katherine = Miss P. Horton. Twice.

Nov. 28: *Riches (The City Madam)*: Luke = Macready; Lady Traffic = Miss Taylor. Once. *Joan of Arc*, "Grand Historical and Legendary Spectacle" [by T. J. Serle]: Pritchard, Anderson, Waldron, Miss Huddart. 31 times.

Dec. 2: New Romantic Opera, *Amilie; or, The Love-Test* [music by T. B. Rooke]: Phillips, Hammond, Wilson, Miss Shirreff, Miss P. Horton. 53 times.

Dec. 26: *Jane Shore*: Hastings = Macready; Glo'ster = G. Bennett; Dumont = Phelps; Alicia = Miss Huddart; Jane Shore = Miss Faucit. Once. Pantomime, *Harlequin and Peeping Tom of Coventry*: Herbert Bellenclapper = Paul Bedford. 43 times. "The Manager acknowledges expressly and particularly, *under the particular circumstances*, his obligations to MR. STANFIELD. That *distinguished Artist*, at a sacrifice, and in a manner the most liberal and kind, has for a short period laid aside his easel to present the Manager with his LAST WORK *in a department of art so conspicuously advanced by him*, as a mark of the interest he feels in the success of the cause which this Theatre labours to support." Stanfield's Diorama consisted of "Scenes at Home and Abroad."

L

1838. JAN. 25 : *King Lear:* Lear = Macready ; Kent = Bartley ; Glo'ster = G. Bennett ; Edgar= Elton ; Edmund = Anderson ; Fool = Miss P. Horton ; Goneril and Regan = Mrs. W. Clifford and Mrs. Warner ; Cordelia = Miss Faucit. 10 times.

JAN. 27 : *The Wonder:* Don Pedro = Strickland (first appearance at this Theatre) ; Don Felix = Macready ; Violante = Miss Faucit ; Flora = Mrs. Glover (first appearance this season) ; Inis = Mrs. Humby (first appearance here these four years). 4 times. But after first performance, Don Felix = Anderson.

FEB. 13 : *The Irish Ambassador:* Sir Patrick O'Plenipo = Tyrone Power (first appearance here these two years). His engagement ended March 3.

FEB. 15 : New Play, *The Lady of Lyons; or, Love and Pride:* Beauséant = Elton ; Glavis = Meadows ; Damas = Bartley ; Deschappelles = Strickland ; 1st Officer = Howe ; Landlord = Yarnold ; Gaspar = Diddear ; *Claude Melnotte = Macready ; Madame Deschappelles = Mrs. W. Clifford ; Pauline = Miss Faucit ; Widow Melnotte = Mrs. Griffith. 33 times. "Edward Lytton Bulwer, Esq.," announced as author at the foot of play-bill of Feb. 24.

FEB. 16 : New Opera, *The Black Domino* [by Scribe and Auber]: Strickland, Wilson, Hammond, Miss Shirreff, Miss P. Horton. 3 times.

FEB. 20 : *Julius Cæsar:* Cæsar = G. Bennett ; Octavius = Anderson ; Antony = Elton ; Brutus = Macready ; Cassius = Phelps ; Casca = Bartley ; Cinna = Howe ; Calphurnia = Mrs. W. Clifford ; Portia = Mrs. Warner. Twice.

FEB. 21 : New Farce, *Mackintosh and Co.:* Power, Bartley. 3 times.

MARCH 12 : *Coriolanus :* Menenius = Bartley ; Caius Marcius = Macready ; Aufidius = Anderson ; Volumnia = Mrs. Warner ; Virgilia = Miss E. Clifford ; Valeria = Mrs. W. Clifford. 8 times.

APRIL 7 (Macready's benefit) : *The Two Foscari:* Francis Foscari = Macready ; Jacopo Foscari = Anderson ; Loredano and Barbarigo = Warde and Elton ; Marina = Miss Faucit. 3 times. New Operetta, *Windsor Castle ; or, The*

Prisoner King: Wilson, Leffler, Bartley, Miss Shirreff, Miss P. Horton. Once.

APRIL 16: Easter piece, *Sindbad the Sailor:* Bartley, Anderson, Paul Bedford, Miss P. Horton. 5 times.

APRIL 21: *The Hypocrite:* Cantwell = Bartley; Mawworm = Harley (first appearance this season), Waldron, Vining, Mrs. W. Clifford, Miss E. Clifford, Miss Taylor. 5 times.

APRIL 28: Talfourd's *Athenian Captive* announced for this evening, but not produced on account of the sudden illness of Mrs. Warner.

APRIL 30: *Romeo and Juliet:* Romeo = Anderson; Paris = Howe; Tybalt = G. Bennett; Mercutio = Vining; Friar Laurence = Macready; Apothecary = Meadows; Nurse = Mrs. W. Clifford; Juliet = Miss Faucit. Twice.

MAY 3: *The Jealous Wife:* Major Oakly = Warde; Charles Oakly = Anderson; Mr. Oakly = Macready; Sir Harry Beagle = Harley; Russet = Bartley; Mrs. Oakly = Miss Faucit. Once.

MAY 4: *Ion:* Adrastus = Phelps; Ion = Macready; Clemanthe = Miss Faucit. Once.

MAY 5: *As You Like It:* Banished Duke = G. Bennett; Amiens = Wilson; Jaques = Macready; Orlando = Anderson; Adam = Warde; Touchstone = Harley; Silvius = Howe; Rosalind = Miss Taylor; Celia = Miss E. Clifford; Phœbe = Miss E. Phillips; Audrey = Mrs. Humby. Once.

MAY 10: New Farce, *The Veiled Portrait; or, The Château of Beauvais:* Harley, Warde, Vining, Miss Taylor. 6 times.

MAY 14: *King Henry VIII.:* Henry VIII. = Bartley; Wolsey = Macready; Buckingham = Elton; Sands = Harley; Gardner = Meadows; Cromwell = Anderson; Queen Katharine = Miss Faucit; Anne Bullen = Miss Taylor; Patience = Miss Shirreff (with song, " Angels ever bright and fair "). Twice.

MAY 17: New Operatic Entertainment, *The Outpost* [by J. Hullah]: Wilson, Leffler, Meadows, Bartley, Miss Shirreff. 7 times.

MAY 23: New Play by James Sheridan Knowles, Esq.,

Woman's Wit ; or, Love's Disguises : Lord Athunree =
Warde ; Sutton = Bartley ; De Grey = Anderson ; *Wal-
singham = Macready ; Eustace = Miss Taylor ; Clever =
Harley ; Hero = Miss Faucit.   31 times.   Elton played
Walsingham 6 times.

JUNE 23 (Sheridan Knowles's benefit) : *Woman's Wit* and
The Wife : Leonardo and Ferrardo Gonzago = Elton and
Warde ; Julian = S. Knowles ; Mariana = H. Faucit.
Once.

JUNE 28 (Theatre open gratuitously, in honour of the
Queen's Coronation) : *The Hypocrite* and *The Quaker.*

JULY 6 (last night of season) : *Woman's Wit.*

MINOR PIECES : *A Roland for an Oliver*, 3 ; *Miller and
his Men*, 3 ; *Love in a Village*, 2 ; *Irish Tutor*, 3 ; *Brother
and Sister*, 3 ; *Fra Diavolo*, 22 ; *The Spitfire*, 11 ; *The
Beggar's Opera*, 3 ; *The Lord of the Manor*, 3 ; *The Quaker*,
7 ; *The Poor Soldier*, 5 ; *The Waterman*, 6 ; *No Song no
Supper*, 3 ; *Aladdin*, 2 ; *Guy Mannering*, 2 ; *The Marriage
of Figaro*, 7 ; *Rob Roy*, 2 ; *The Irish Ambassador*, 3 ; *Born
to Good Luck*, 2 ; *The Omnibus*, 3 ; *Teddy the Tiler*, 1 ; *The
Nervous Man*, 1 ; *High Life Below Stairs*, 7 ; *Animal
Magnetism*, 3 ; *John of Paris*, 3 ; *The Midnight Hour*,
2 ; *Matrimony*, 1 ; *The Padlock*, 1 ; *The Will*, 5.

MACREADY'S CHARACTERS : *Claude Melnotte, 33 ;
*Walsingham, 25 ; Macbeth, 18 ; Lear, 10 ; Werner, 9 ;
Coriolanus, 8 ; Melantius, 7 ; Leontes, 4 ; Hamlet, Lord
Townly, *Francis Foscari, 3 ; Othello, Virginius, Henry V.,
Brutus, Friar Laurence, Wolsey, 2 ; Iago, Pierre, Stranger,
Luke, Hastings, Don Felix, Mr. Oakly, Ion, Jaques, 1.
Total, 144 performances.

1838–1839.

SEPT. 24 (opening night) : *Coriolanus :* Caius Marcius
= Vandenhoff (first appearance here these two years) ;
Virgilia = Miss Vandenhoff ; Aufidius = Phelps.   Rest as
March 12, 1838.   Twice with this cast.   (See May 6, 1839.)

SEPT. 26 : *Cymbeline :* Cymbeline = Waldron ; Guiderius
= Elton ; Arviragus = Anderson ; Cloten = Vining ; Be-

larius = Warde ; Posthumus = Phelps ; Pisanio = G.
Bennett ; Imogen = Miss Faucit ; Minstrels = Mrs. Serle,
Miss P. Horton ; Iachimo = Vandenhoff; Philario = Howe.
Twice.

SEPT. 27 : New Farce, *Brown, Jones, and Robinson* [by J.
Oxenford] : Bartley, Harley, Vining, Mrs. Humby, Mrs. W.
Clifford. Thrice.

SEPT. 29 : *Town and Country* : Vandenhoff, Elton, Harley,
Mrs. Warner, Miss Vandenhoff. Once.

. OCT. 1 : *Hamlet* : Polonius = Bartley ; Horatio = Serle ;
Gravedigger = Harley ; Ghost = Warde ; Ophelia = Miss
Rainforth. Rest as Oct. 2, 1837. 5 times.

OCT. 3 : *The Lady of Lyons* : Deschappelles = Waldron.
Rest as Feb. 15, 1838. 29 times.

OCT. 4 : *Othello* : Othello = Macready ; Iago = Vandenhoff. Rest as Oct. 16, 1837. 8 times. Oct. 25 : Othello =
Vandenhoff; Iago = Macready.

OCT. 6 : *The Winter's Tale* : Leontes = Vandenhoff
Polixenes = Warde ; Camillo = Diddear ; Autolycus =
Harley; Perdita = Miss Vandenhoff; Dorcas = Mrs. Humby.
Rest as Sept. 30, 1837. Thrice.

OCT. 13 : *The Tempest*, from the text of Shakespeare.
The music selected from the works of Purcell, Linley, and
Dr. Arne, and arranged by Mr. T. Cooke. The *entr'actes*
from Corelli. Previous to the play, Weber's Overture to
The Ruler of Spirits. Alonzo = Warde ; Sebastian = Did-
dear ; Prospero = Macready ; Antonio = Phelps ; Ferdi-
nand = Anderson ; Gonzalo = Waldron ; Caliban = G.
Bennett ; Trinculo = Harley ; Stephano = Bartley ; Mi-
randa = Miss Faucit ; Ariel = Miss P. Horton ; Spirits in
the Vision : Iris = Mrs. Serle ; Ceres = Miss P. Horton ;
Juno = Miss Rainforth. 55 times. On Nov. 29 and
Dec. 1 and 4 : Miranda = Miss Vandenhoff.

OCT. 19 : New Drama [from the German], interspersed
with music, *The Foresters; or, Twenty-five Years Since* :
Vandenhoff, Frazer, Anderson, Warde, Harley, Bartley,
Mrs. Warner, Miss Rainforth, Miss P. Horton. 4 times.

OCT. 20 : New Petite Comedy, *Jealousy* : Vandenhoff,
Anderson, Meadows, Mrs. Warner. Thrice.

OCT. 26 : *The Hunchback:* Helen = Miss Vandenhoff. Rest as Oct. 26, 1837. Once.

OCT. 29 : *Macbeth:* Lenox = Serle ; Hecate = Leffler. Rest practically as Nov. 6, 1837. 5 times.

NOV. 2 : *Cato :* Cato = Vandenhoff ; Porcius = Elton ; Marcus = Phelps ; Juba = Anderson ; Sempronius = G. Bennett ; Syphax = Warde ; Marcia = Miss Vandenhoff ; Lucia = Mrs. Warner. Once.

NOV. 3. New Opera, *Barbara ; or, The Bride of a Day* [music by Boieldieu *fils*] : Harley, Frazer, Miss Rainforth, Miss P. Horton. 7 times.

NOV. 10 : *Catherine and Petruchio.* 8 times. Petruchio = Vining ; Catherine = sometimes Miss Faucit, sometimes Mrs. Warner.

NOV. 19 : New Farce, *Chaos is Come Again ; or, The Race Ball :* Bartley, Vining, Meadows, Miss Charles. 30 times.

NOV. 23 : *Ion :* Adrastus = Vandenhoff ; Ion = Anderson ; Clemanthe = Miss Faucit. 3 times. May 20 : Ion = Macready.

NOV. 30 : *Werner :* Gabor = Vandenhoff ; Ida = Miss Vandenhoff. Rest as Oct. 21, 1837. 4 times.

DEC. 3 : *William Tell,* with alterations by the author : Gesler = Warde ; Tell = Macready ; Michael = Anderson ; Albert = Miss R. Isaacs ; Emma = Mrs. Warner. 14 times.

DEC. 7 : *Venice Preserved :* Jaffier = Elton ; Pierre = Vandenhoff ; Belvidera = Miss Faucit. Once.

DEC. 26 : *Jane Shore :* Glo'ster = Vandenhoff. Rest as Dec 26, 1837. (Repeated March 4, 1839 : Hastings = Elton.) Pantomime, *Harlequin and Fair Rosamond ; or, Old Dame Nature and the Fairy Art.* 41 times.

1839. JAN. 4 : *Rob Roy :* Vandenhoff, Harley, Frazer, Mrs. Warner, Miss Rainforth. 5 times.

FEB. 1 (Royal command) : *The Lady of Lyons* (49th time) and last two acts of *Rob Roy.*

FEB. 4 : *King Lear.* Cast as Jan. 25, 1838. 6 times.

FEB. 8 : New Drama, *The King and the Duke ; or, The Siege of Alençon :* Bartley, Anderson, Vining, Harley, Miss Rainforth, Miss Taylor. 6 times.

MARCH 7 : New Play, *Richelieu ; or, The Conspiracy,* by Sir Edward Lytton Bulwer, Bart. : Louis XIII. = Elton ; Gaston = Diddear ; *Richelieu = Macready ; Baradas = Warde ; Mauprat = Anderson ; De Berighen = Vining ; Father Joseph = Phelps ; Huguet = G. Bennett ; François = Howe ; Julie de Mortemar = Miss Faucit ; Marion de Lorme = Miss Charles. 37 times.

APRIL 8 : " The Public is respectfully informed that the present management will terminate with this season."

APRIL 18 (Miss Faucit's benefit) : *As You Like It :* 1st Lord = Phelps ; Amiens = Frazer ; Rosalind = Miss Faucit ; Celia = Miss Rainforth ; Phœbe = Miss P. Horton. Rest as May 5, 1838. 4 times. New Farce, *Sayings and Doings :* Meadows, Vining, Harley, T. Lee, Mrs. W. Clifford, Miss Charles. 15 times.

APRIL 20 : New Dramatic Romance, *Agnes Bernauer ; or, The Secret Tribunal ;* Overture and incidental music by Mr. G. A. Macfarren : Phelps, Anderson, Serle, Elton, G. Bennett, Mrs. Warner. 17 times.

APRIL 27 (Vandenhoff's benefit) : *Julius Cæsar :* Antony = Vandenhoff. Rest as Feb. 20, 1838. Once.

MAY 2 : New Grand Opera, *Henrique ; or, The Love-Pilgrim ;* Music by Mr. W. M. Rooke : H. Phillips, W. Harrison (first appearance in London), Leffler, Manvers, Harley, Miss Rainforth, Miss P. Horton. 5 times.

MAY 6 (Macready's benefit) : *Coriolanus :* Menenius = Strickland ; Virgilia = Miss Vandenhoff. Rest as March 12, 1838. Once with this cast. (See Sept. 24, 1838.)

MAY 13 : *Virginius.* Cast as Nov. 2, 1837. Once.

MAY 25 : *The Provoked Husband :* Squire Richard = Harley ; Moody = Meadows ; Miss Jenny = Mrs. Humby. Rest as Oct. 19, 1837. Once.

MAY 27 : *The Two Foscari.* Cast as April 7, 1838. Once.

JUNE 10 : *King Henry V.* " To impress more strongly on the auditor, and render more palpable these portions of the story which have not the advantage of action, and still are requisite to the Drama's completeness, the narrative and descriptive poetry spoken by the chorus is accompanied with PICTORIAL ILLUSTRATIONS from the pencil of MR.

STANFIELD." The music selected from Purcell, Handel, and Weber. Chorus in the character of Time = Vanden-hoff; Henry V. = Macready; Exeter = Elton; Erpingham = Bartley; Gower = Anderson; Fluellen = Meadows; Macmorris = T. Lee; Bates and Williams = C. J. Smith and Warde; Bardolph, Nym, and Pistol = Bedford, Ayliffe, Harley; Boy = Miss P. Horton; Mrs. Quickly = Mrs. C. Jones; Charles VI. = G. Bennett; Dauphin = Vining; Orleans = Howe; D'Albret = Phelps; Isabel = Mrs. W. Clifford; Katharine = Miss Vandenhoff. 21 times.

JUNE 25: *The Stranger:* Vandenhoff, Warde, Miss Faucit. JULY 16 (last night): *King Henry V.*

MINOR PIECES: *High Life Below Stairs,* 11; *Fra Dia-volo,* 20; *A Roland for an Oliver,* 6; *The Original,* 11; *Animal Magnetism,* 1; *The Waterman,* 7; *The Marriage of Figaro,* 12; *The Cabinet,* 5; *Laugh when you can,* 5; *The Quaker,* 12; *The Omnibus,* 12; *The Miller and his Men,* 1; *The Royal Oak,* 3; *An Agreeable Surprise,* 4; *Charles II.,* 3; *The Portrait of Cervantes,* 7; *Raising the Wind,* 3; *The Invincibles,* 10; *Lodoiska,* 6; *Inkle and Yarico,* 5; *The Slave,* 2; *The Mountaineers,* 1; *No Song no Supper,* 3; *Amilie,* 10.

MACREADY'S CHARACTERS: Prospero, 55; *Richelieu, 37; Melnotte, 29; Henry V., 21; Tell, 14; Othello, 7; Lear, 6; Hamlet and Macbeth, 5; Werner, 4; Jaques, 3; Iago, Hastings, Brutus, Coriolanus, Virginius, Ion, Lord Townly, F. Foscari, 1. 194 performances.

DRURY LANE THEATRE.
1841–1842.

DEC. 27 (opening night): *The Merchant of Venice,* from the text of Shakespeare: Duke = G. Bennett; Antonio = Phelps; Bassanio = Anderson; Salarino = Marston; Shy-lock = Macready; Launcelot Gobbo = Compton; Old Gobbo = W. Bennett; Portia = Mrs. Warner; Nerissa = Mrs. Keeley. 15 times. Pantomime, *Harlequin and Duke Humphrey's Dinner; or, Jack Cade, the Lord of London.* 42 times.

DEC. 28 : *Every One has his Fault:* Macready, Phelps, Compton, Keeley, Anderson, Mrs. Warner, Mrs. Keeley. 8 times.

DEC. 29 : *Two Gentlemen of Verona:* Duke = Phelps ; Valentine = Macready ; Proteus = Anderson ; Thurio = Compton ; Speed = H. Hall ; Launce = Keeley ; Julia = Miss Fortescue ; Silvia = Miss Ellis. 13 times.

1842. JAN. 12 : *The Gamester:* Beverley = Macready ; Lewson = Anderson ; Jarvis = Elton ; Stukeley = Phelps ; Mrs. Beverley = Mrs. Warner ; Charlotte = Miss Ellis. 5 times. May 6 : Beverley = Anderson.

JAN. 25 : *Point of Honour:* Phelps, Hudson, Anderson, Compton, Mrs. Warner. Twice. New Farce, *The Windmill* [by E. Morton]: Sampson Low = Keeley ; Marian = Mrs. Keeley. 33 times.

FEB. 5 : *Acis and Galatea.* "In aid of the endeavour to establish upon the ENGLISH STAGE the WORKS of the GREATEST COMPOSERS of the ENGLISH SCHOOL OF MUSIC, MR. STANFIELD, R.A., has been engaged to furnish the SCENIC ILLUSTRATIONS for the representation of the first of a series of Operas proposed to be revived at this Theatre." Cupid = Miss Gould ; Acis = Miss P. Horton ; Damon = Allen ; Polyphemus = H. Phillips ; Galatea = Miss Romer. 43 times.

FEB. 8 : New Play, *The Prisoner of War* [by Douglas Jerrold]: Captain Channel = Phelps ; Firebrace = Anderson ; Peter and Polly Pall-Mall = Mr. and Mrs. Keeley. 31 times.

FEB. 14 : *Venice Preserved:* Jaffier = Anderson ; Pierre = Phelps ; Belvidera = Miss Faucit (first appearance at this Theatre). 3 times.

FEB. 21 : *Catherine and Petruchio* (afterpiece) : Petruchio = Anderson ; Grumio = Compton ; Catherine = Miss Faucit. 4 times.

FEB. 23 : *Gisippus,* by the late Gerald Griffin : Fulvius = Anderson ; *Gisippus = Macready ; Pheax and Chremes = Elton and Hudson : Sophronia = Miss Faucit. 20 times.

MARCH 28 (Easter Monday) : *Macbeth:* Duncan = Waldron : Malcolm = Graham ; Macbeth = Macready ; Banquo = Anderson ; Macduff = Phelps ; Rosse = Elton ; Lenox

= Marston ; Fleance = Miss Phillips ; Lady Macbeth = Mrs. Warner ; 1st and 2nd Witches = G. and W. Bennett ; 3rd Witch = M'Ian ; Singing Witches = Giubilei, Allen, Reeves, Jones, etc., Mesdames Romer, P. Horton, Keeley, Poole, etc. 8 times ; every Monday to May 16. New Operetta, *The Students of Bonn* [by G. H. Rodwell]: Hudson, Allen, Mr. and Mrs. Selby, Mrs. C. Jones, Mrs. Keeley, Miss Romer. 22 times.

APRIL 20 : New Play, *Plighted Troth* [by Darley]: Macready, Anderson, Hudson, Phelps, Elton, Miss Faucit, Mrs. Stirling. Once.

APRIL 29 : *Hamlet:* Claudius = G. Bennett ; Hamlet = Macready ; Polonius = Compton ; Laertes = Elton ; Horatio = Graham ; Osrick = Hudson ; Gravedigger = Keeley ; Ghost = Phelps ; Gertrude = Mrs. Warner ; Ophelia = Miss P. Horton. 4 times.

MAY 17 (Miss Faucit's benefit) : *The Stranger:* Stranger = Macready ; Steinfort = Phelps ; Solomon = Compton ; Peter = Keeley ; Mrs. Haller = Miss Faucit ; Countess Wintersen = Mrs. Stirling ; Charlotte = Mrs. Keeley.   Once.

MAY 19 (Mr. and Mrs. Keeley's benefit) : *The Provoked Husband:* Lord Townly = Macready ; Manly = Phelps ; Sir F. Wronghead = Compton ; Squire Richard = Keeley ; Lady Townly = Miss Faucit ; Lady Wronghead = Mrs. C. Jones ; Lady Grace = Mrs. Stirling ; Miss Jenny = Mrs. Keeley. Once. New Farce, *The Attic Story:* Mr. and Mrs. Poddy = Mr. and Mrs. Keeley. Twice.

MAY 20 (Macready's benefit) : *Marino Faliero :* *Marino = Macready ; Bertuccio Faliero = Hudson ; Lioni = Anderson ; Benintende = G. Bennett ; Israel Bertuccio = Phelps ; Bertram = Elton ; Angiolina = Miss Faucit.   Twice.

MAY 23 (Anderson's benefit, and last night) : *Othello :* Othello = Anderson ; Iago = Macready ; Cassio = Hudson ; Roderigo = Compton ; Brabantio = Elton ; Desdemona = Miss Faucit ; Emilia = Mrs. Warner.   Once.

MINOR PIECES : *La Sonnambula,* 4 ; *The Poor Soldier,* 4 ; *No Song no Supper,* 6 ; *The Quaker,* 3 ; *The Duenna,* 2.

MACREADY'S CHARACTERS : *Gisippus, 20 ; Shylock, 15 ; Valentine, 13 ; Macbeth and Harmony, 8 ; Hamlet and

Beverley, 4; *Marino Faliero, 2; *Grimwood, Iago, Stranger, and Lord Townly, 1. 78 performances.

1842–1843.

OCT. 1 (opening night): *As You Like It*; Overture, first movement of Beethoven's Pastoral Symphony, *entr'actes* selected from the same work : Duke = Ryder ; 1st Lord = Elton ; 2nd Lord = H. Phillips ; Amiens = Allen ; Jaques = Macready ; Duke Frederick = G. Bennett ; Le Beau = Hudson ; Oliver = Graham ; Jaques de Bois = Lynne ; Orlando = Anderson ; Adam = Phelps ; Touchstone = Keeley ; William = Compton ; Pages to Banished Duke = Miss P. Horton and Miss Gould ; Foresters = Stretton, J. Reeves, etc. ; Rosalind = Mrs. Nisbett ; Celia = Mrs. Stirling ; Phœbe = Miss Fortescue ; Audrey = Mrs. Keeley. 22 times.

OCT. 3 : *Hamlet.* Cast as April 29. 7 times. April 3 and 19, 1843 : Hamlet = Anderson. *Acis and Galatea :* Polyphemus = Stretton. Rest as last season ; but see May 5, 1843. 15 times.

OCT. 5 : *Marino Faliero.* Cast as May 20. *Follies of a Night* [by J. R. Planché] : Druggendraft = Compton ; Palliot = C. Mathews ; Duchesse de Chartres = Madame Vestris. 16 times.

OCT. 7 : *The Rivals :* Sir Anthony = Lambert (first appearance); Captain Absolute = Anderson ; Faulkland = Phelps ; Acres = Keeley ; Sir Lucius = Hudson ; Fag = C. Mathews ; David = Compton ; Mrs. Malaprop = Mrs. C. Jones ; Lydia Languish = Mrs. Nisbett ; Julia = Miss Faucit ; Lucy = Mrs. Keeley. Thrice.

OCT. 11 : *The Stranger.* Cast as May 17. Once.

OCT. 18 : *The Road to Ruin :* Dornton = Phelps ; Harry Dornton = Anderson ; Sulky = Lambert ; Silky = Compton ; Goldfinch = C. Mathews ; Widow Warren = Mrs. C. Jones ; Sophia = Mrs. Stirling. Twice.

OCT. 20 : *Othello :* Othello = Macready ; Cassio = Anderson ; Iago = Phelps ; Roderigo = C. Mathews. Rest as May 22. 10 times [Macready played Iago twice ; and once Othello = Anderson ; Iago = Phelps].

OCT. 24 : *King John;* Overture, Martial Movement from Beethoven's C Minor Symphony : King John = Macready ; Arthur = Miss Newcombe ; Salisbury = Elton ; Hubert = Phelps ; Faulconbridge = Anderson ; Philip Augustus = Graham ; Dauphin = Hudson ; Pandulph = Ryder ; Elinor = Miss Ellis ; Constance = Miss Faucit ; Blanch = Miss Fairbrother ; Lady Faulconbridge = Mrs. Selby. 26 times.

OCT. 27 : *Patter v. Clatter :* C. Mathews. Twice.

OCT. 29 : *The Provoked Husband :* Lord Townly = Anderson ; Manly = Phelps ; Lady Townly = Mrs. Nisbett. Rest as May 19. Once. New Farce, *The Eton Boy :* Popham = C. Mathews [afterwards Hudson] ; Dabster = Keeley ; Fanny = Mrs. Stirling. 18 times.

NOV. 16 : Dryden's *King Arthur ;* Overture and music by Purcell, except three songs by Dr. Arne: Arthur = Anderson ; Conon = G. Bennett ; Merlin = Ryder ; Warrior = J. Reeves ; Emmeline = Mrs. Nisbett [afterwards Mrs. Stirling] ; Osmond = H. Phillips ; Priest = Allen ; Philadel = Miss P. Horton ; Grimbald = Stretton ; Cupid = Miss Romer ; Venus = Mrs. Fairbrother. 31 times.

NOV. 19 : *Love for Love :* Legend = Lambert ; Valentine = Anderson ; Ben = Keeley ; Scandal = Phelps ; Tattle = Hudson ; Foresight = Compton ; Angelica = Miss Faucit ; Mrs. Foresight = Mrs. Stirling ; Mrs. Frail = Mrs. Nisbett ; Miss Prue = Mrs. Keeley ; Nurse = Mrs. C. Jones. 8 times.

DEC. 10 : New Play, *The Patrician's Daughter,* by J. Westland Marston, Esq. : Earl Lynterne = Phelps ; Pierpoint = Hudson ; *Mordaunt = Macready ; Heartwell = Elton ; Lister = G. Bennett ; Physician = Ryder ; Lady Mabel = Miss Faucit ; Lady Lydia = Mrs. Warner. 11 times.

DEC. 26: *Jane Shore :* Glo'ster = Phelps ; Hastings = Macready ; Dumont = Anderson ; Belmour = Ryder ; Jane Shore = Miss Faucit ; Alicia = Mrs. Warner. Once. Pantomime, *Harlequin and William Tell ; or, The Genius of the Ribstone Pippin.* 35 times.

1843. JAN. 9 : *Macbeth :* 3rd Witch = Ryder. Rest practically as March 28, 1842. 10 times. (See April 17.)

JAN. 13: *Werner:* Gabor = Phelps ; Idenstein = Compton ; Ida = Miss Fortescue. Rest as Covent Garden, Oct. 21, 1837. Twice.

JAN. 17 : *The Lady of Lyons:* Beauséant = Elton ; Glavis = Keeley ; Damas = Phelps ; Gaspar = G. Bennett ; Melnotte = Macready ; Madame Deschappelles = Mrs. C. Jones ; Pauline = Miss Faucit ; Widow Melnotte = Miss Ellis. 12 times.

JAN. 21 : *Cymbeline:* Cymbeline = Ryder ; Cloten = Compton ; Posthumus = Anderson ; Iachimo = Macready ; Bellarius = Phelps ; Guiderius and Arviragus = Hudson and Allen ; Pisanio = Elton ; Queen = Miss Ellis ; Imogen = Miss Faucit. 4 times.

FEB. 11 : New Play, *A Blot in the 'Scutcheon* [by Robert Browning]: Thorold = Phelps ; Mertoun = Anderson ; Austin = Hudson ; Gerard = G. Bennett ; Mildred = Miss Faucit ; Gwendolen = Mrs. Stirling. Thrice. New Farce, *The Thumping Legacy:* Jerry Ominous = Keeley ; Rosetta = Miss P. Horton. 17 times.

FEB. 18 : *She Stoops to Conquer :* Hardcastle = Compton ; Young Marlow = Hudson ; Tony Lumpkin = Keeley ; Mrs. Hardcastle = Mrs. C. Jones ; Miss Hardcastle = Mrs. Nisbett ; Miss Neville = Miss Fortescue. Once.

FEB. 24 (Macready's benefit) : *Much Ado about Nothing :* Don Pedro = Hudson ; Don John = Lynne ; Claudio = Anderson ; Benedict = Macready ; Leonato = Phelps ; Balthazar = Allen ; Dogberry and Verges = Compton and Keeley ; Sexton = Morris Barnett ; Friar = Ryder ; Hero = Miss Fortescue ; Beatrice = Mrs. Nisbett. 11 times. *Comus :* Attendant Spirit = Miss P. Horton ; Comus = Macready [he played the part this night and on May 5 ; on all other occasions, Comus = Phelps] ; Elder Brother = Anderson ; Lady = Miss Faucit ; Sabrina = Miss Romer ; Bacchanals = H. Phillips, Allen, J. Reeves, etc. 14 times.

FEB. 25 : *The Gamester:* Mrs. Beverley = Miss Faucit ; Charlotte = Mrs. Stirling. Rest as Jan. 12, 1841. Once. New Operetta, *The Queen of the Thames :* Phillips, Allen, Keeley, Miss Romer. 6 times.

MARCH 6 : *Virginius:* Appius = Ryder ; Virginius =

Macready; Dentatus = Phelps; Numitorius = Elton; Icilius = Anderson; Virginia = Miss Faucit; Servia = Mrs. Warner. Twice.

APRIL 1: Pacini's *Sappho:* Phillips, Allen, Stretton, J. Reeves, Clara Novello (first appearance on the English stage), Mrs. Alfred Shaw (first appearance at this Theatre). 13 times.

APRIL 17 (Easter Monday): *Macbeth:* Lady Macbeth = Miss Faucit; Gentlewoman = Mrs. Alfred Wigan. New Piece, *Fortunio* [by J. R. Planché]: Hudson, T. Matthews, Miss P. Horton, etc. 40 times.

APRIL 24: New Play, *The Secretary,* by Sheridan Knowles: Earl of Byerdale = Phelps; Colonel Green = Macready; Wilton Brown = Anderson; Lady Laura Gaveston = Miss Faucit. Thrice.

MAY 1 (Anderson's benefit): *Julius Cæsar:* Cæsar = Ryder; Antony = Anderson; Brutus = Macready; Cassius = Phelps; Lucius = Mrs. A. Wigan; Calphurnia = Miss Ellis; Portia = Miss Faucit. Thrice. May 16: Casca = Sheridan Knowles.

MAY 5: *Acis and Galatea* (see Oct. 3, 1842): Acis = Allen; Polyphemus = Staudigl (first appearance at this Theatre); Galatea = Clara Novello.

MAY 6 (Mrs. Nisbett's benefit): *The School for Scandal:* Sir Peter = Compton; Sir Oliver = Lambert; Backbite = Keeley; Crabtree = W. Bennett; Joseph = Macready (this night only); Charles = Hudson; Moses = Morris Barnett; Trip = A. Wigan; Sir Harry (with song) = Allen; Lady Teazle = Mrs. Nisbett; Lady Sneerwell = Miss Ellis; Mrs. Candour = Mrs. Stirling; Maria = Miss P. Horton. Once.

MAY 10 (Mr. and Mrs. Keeley's benefit): *The Jealous Wife:* Mr. Oakly = Macready; Major Oakly = Phelps; Charles Oakly = Anderson; Sir Harry Beagle = Keeley; Captain O'Cutter = A. Wigan; Mrs. Oakly = Miss Faucit; Lady Freelove = Mrs. Stirling; Toilet = Mrs. A. Wigan. Once.

MAY 18 (Miss Faucit's benefit): New Play, *Athelwold,* by W. Smith, Esq.: *Athelwold = Macready; Elfrid = Miss

Faucit ; Anderson, Phelps, Ryder, Keeley, Mrs. Keeley, Mrs. Stirling. Twice.

MAY 29 (Performance in aid of the Siddons Memorial) : *2nd Henry IV.*, act iv. : King = Macready ; Prince = Anderson ; Gascoigne = Phelps ; Pages = Selby and A. Wigan. Two chief acts of *Der Freischütz. Is he Jealous ?* Hudson, Mrs. Warner, Mrs. Nisbett, Mrs. Keeley. *Fortunio.* Tributary address, spoken by Miss Faucit.

MAY 30 (Phelps's benefit) : *The Winter's Tale* : Leontes = Macready ; Polixenes = Ryder ; Florizel = Anderson ; Camillo = Elton ; Antigonus = Phelps ; Autolycus = Compton ; Shepherd = W. Bennett ; Clown = Keeley ; Hermione = Miss Faucit ; Perdita = Mrs. Nisbett ; Paulina = Mrs. Warner ; Mopsa and Dorcas = Mrs. Keeley and Miss P. Horton. Twice.

JUNE 3 (Saturday) announced as last night but one of the season ; but on

JUNE 5 (Monday) "The public is respectfully informed that, in pursuance of arrangements with the Proprietary of this Theatre, MR. MACREADY will relinquish its direction upon the close of the present season, which, in consequence, is extended to Monday, June 12, on which night he will make HIS LAST APPEARANCE in a LONDON THEATRE for a very considerable period."

JUNE 12 (Royal command) : *As You Like It* and *A Thumping Legacy.*

JUNE 14 (last night) : *Macbeth* and *Fortunio.*

MINOR PIECES : *The Attic Story*, 10 ; *La Sonnambula*, 8 ; *The Duenna*, 1 ; *The Windmill*, 2 ; *Catherine and Petruchio*, 1 ; *La Gazza Ladra*, 5 ; *Der Freischütz* (whole or part), 16 ; *The Prisoner of War*, 3 ; *The Midnight Hour*, 1 ; *The Loan of a Lover*, 2.

MACREADY'S CHARACTERS : King John, 26 ; Jaques, 22 ; Melnotte, 12 ; *Mordaunt and Benedick, 11 ; Macbeth, 10 ; Othello, 7 ; Hamlet, 5 ; Iachimo, 4 ; Brutus and *Colonel Green, 3 ; Iago, Leontes, Werner, Comus, Virginius, and *Athelwold, 2 ; Henry IV., Stranger, Hastings, Beverley, Joseph Surface, and Mr. Oakly, 1. 133 performances.

MACREADY'S CHARACTERS.

1837–1843.

(Not under his own management.)

HAYMARKET : 1837 : *Melantius, 23 ; Hamlet, Othello, 2 ; Richard III., Ion, Lord Townly, Mr. Oakly, 1.

1838 : *Thoas, 17 ; Lord Townly, 4 ; Kitely, Mr. Oakly, Duke Aranza, 2 ; Melantius, 1.

1839–40 : *Norman, 38 ; Melnotte, 26 ; Shylock, 16 ; Othello, Stranger, Mr. Oakly, 3 ; Lord Townly, 2 ; Iago, 1.

DRURY LANE : 1840 : *Ruthven, 20 ; Macbeth, 7.

HAYMARKET : 1840–41 : *Alfred Evelyn, 80 ; Melnotte, 29 ; *Halbert Macdonald, 22 ; Richelieu, 15 ; Sir Oswin Mortland, 14 ; Werner, 12 ; Hamlet, 10 ; *Master Clarke, 9 ; Jaques, 8 ; Mr. Oakly, Stranger, 4 ; Shylock, 3 ; Norman 2 ; Lord Townly, 1.

1841 : Alfred Evelyn, 30 ; *Spinola, 18 ; Melnotte, 15 ; Werner, Virginius, 11 ; Luke (*Riches*), 7 ; Hamlet, Tell, 4 ; Sir O. Mortland, Stranger, 3.

\ _____

NOTE.—After the most diligent inquiry, I have failed to ascertain whether the Mr. Darley who wrote *Plighted Troth* (p. 132) was George Darley, the mathematician and poet. I am inclined to think that it was not he. The play was announced for repetition on April 21, but was withdrawn, on the pretext of "the indisposition of a principal performer."

CHAPTER VI.

1843–1851 ; 1851–1873.

" OH, my cottage, my cottage !" Macready mused in his diary some time after his retirement from Covent Garden : "shall I die without seeing thee?" Drury Lane had been abandoned in its turn, and the coveted retreat seemed as far off as ever. He was now just fifty, and there was evidently no time to be lost. A large sum was still needed to secure what he considered a fair provision for his old age and for his family. He must gird up his loins, and make the most of his hard-earned position while his vigour was yet unimpaired ; for both his self-respect and his disrespect for his calling made him shrink from the bare idea of lagging superfluous on the stage.

The first thing to be done was to exploit in America the new renown acquired in his managerial experiments. He sailed from Liverpool early in September, 1843, Dickens relinquishing his intention of seeing him off, lest this public show of friendship should do him injury amid the justly incensed countrymen of Elijah Pogram and Jefferson Brick. Ryder accompanied him (Phelps having declined), to play "seconds," and look after the details of the tour. They opened in New York on Sep-

M

tember 25, travelled as far south as New Orleans, as far
west as St. Louis, as far north as Montreal, and ended
the tour at Boston on October 14, 1844. Macready's
repertory consisted of Hamlet, Macbeth, Othello, Iago,
Lear, Shylock, Brutus, Cassius, Benedick, King John,
King Henry IV., Wolsey, Virginius, Tell, Werner, Marino
Faliero, Melantius, Claude Melnotte, Richelieu, The
Stranger, Lord Townly in a three-act version of *The
Provoked Husband*, and Joseph Surface in a similar cur-
tailment of *The School for Scandal*. His heavy Shakespearian parts seem to have been the most attractive.
" Hamlet," he notes, " has brought me more money than
any play in America ; " and I find that at Mobile, in
March, 1844, his Hamlet drew $833 ; Macbeth, $666 ;
Othello, $475 ; while William Tell brought in but $269,
and Richelieu only $138. The tour was very successful
on the whole, and ended in a clear profit of over £5500.
I emphasize the fact of his success, because the origin of
the Forrest feud has sometimes been traced to Macready's
rage at the " failure " of this visit to America. It was
during this tour that he encountered Charlotte Cushman,
then a struggling actress of twenty-seven. " She has to
learn her art," he noted in his diary, after playing Macbeth to her Lady Macbeth ; " but she showed mind and
sympathy with me." She, on her part, attributed to
Macready's influence and encouragement the true beginning of her artistic life. Everywhere throughout the
Republic he was received with great social distinction.
Charles Sumner and Judge Story were his intimate friends,
and he met Emerson, Longfellow, Bryant, Prescott,
Webster, Clay, and many other " prominent citizens."

Soon after his return from America he paid his second
professional visit to Paris. The company, under Mitchell's
management, included Miss Helen Faucit, whose " grace

anglaise un peu maniérée des keepsakes et des livres de beauté " enraptured Théophile Gautier and the other critics, in spite of the fact that the plays in which she most excelled (all except *Romeo and Juliet*) were cut out of the repertory by Macready. She played Desdemona to his Othello on the opening night (Théâtre Italien, December 16, 1844), and afterwards Ophelia to his Hamlet, Virginia to his Virginius, and Lady Macbeth to his Macbeth. She seems, however, to have escaped the shadowy Josephine of *Werner.* The visit was (at least) a success of esteem.

"On the night on which we were present," says a writer in the *Edinburgh Review* for January, 1846, "the house was crowded. At least half the audience held books in their hands, between which and the stage they managed to divide their attention. Some were incessantly occupied in interpreting what was going on to their less learned neighbours. Many appeared resolutely absorbed, and one might discern considerable anxiety to look as if they understood all that passed, and to be moved by pity or by terror in the right place. Some, on the contrary, looked honestly vacant, and not a few deeply and sincerely interested. In front of the pit sat the critics, triumphantly conscious of English, and boldly enthusiastic for Macready, or *passionés* for Miss Faucit. The boxes were lined with rows of the *blanches épaules*, long locks, and impassive countenances which marked the countrywomen of the mighty poet."

The critics' "consciousness of English" seems to have been somewhat vague, since we find even Gautier admiring in *Werner* "la fermeté mâle du style." Janin preferred Macready's Hamlet to his Othello, and Gautier, though he does not say so explicitly, seems to have been of the same opinion. "If the French public," George Sand wrote, "has seemed to Mr. Macready attentive and deeply affected rather than excited and noisy, he must

not conclude that he has not been understood by us . . .
I should like him to carry away a good opinion of us;
and from myself, individually, my sincere homage.
Eugène Delacroix, Louis Blanc, Chassoir, and all who
saw him with me were enraptured with him. I cannot
console myself for not having seen his Othello." Alexandre Dumas, Eugène Sue, and other leaders of the
literary world were also warm in their praises; and there
is a legend that, at the gala performance in the Tuileries,
Victor Hugo, who was in the parterre, could not restrain
his enthusiasm within the bounds of court etiquette. This
performance took place on January 16, 1845, in presence
of the royal family, the diplomatic body, M. Guizot,
Marshal Soult, and five or six hundred military and civil
notables. The programme consisted of *Hamlet* (with
the Gravediggers omitted), and *The Day after the Wed-
ding*, in which Mdlle. Plessy, of the Comédie Française,
played Lady Elizabeth Freelove in English. She excited
Gautier's admiration by remaining beautiful, "même en
s'extirpant de l'anglais de la bouche, opération qui . . .
ne parait même pas fort aisée pour ces insulaires, s'il faut
en juger d'après les grimaces et les contractions muscu-
laires qui accompagnent leur débit." We can scarcely be
wrong in reading this as a side-fling at Macready's facial
mannerisms. Mdlle. Plessy repeated this feat on the
following evening, when the English company gave a
farewell performance, Macready playing the death-scene
of Henry IV., and Miss Faucit, Juliet. The series of
performances would have been prolonged had not the
director of the Grand Opéra contended that his privilege
was infringed by the opening of the Théâtre Italien on
the three "off-nights" of the week. On January 18
Macready played the death-scene of Henry IV. at the
Opéra Comique, for the benefit of the Society for the

Relief of Distressed Authors. In recognition of this courtesy, the Dramatic Authors' Society presented him with a gold medal struck in his honour, and a letter of thanks, signed by Scribe, Mélesville, Victor Hugo, Halévy, and others. The visit, in short, was an artistic, if not a financial, triumph. It was not so memorable, in a literary sense, as the English performances of 1827–28, for the romantic movement now needed no reinforcement. In 1844–45 Shakespeare was placed in opposition, not to classicism, but to the prevalent triviality of the Scribe school of mere adroitness. " *Othello, Hamlet, Macbeth,*" cries Gautier, " cela nous lave de bien des vaudevilles et de bien des mélodrames."

From the beginning of 1845 till the middle of 1848, when he started on his farewell visit to America, Macready made only desultory appearances in London, devoting himself for the most part to provincial wanderings. The Princess's Theatre, Oxford Street, erected in 1840, had been opened for dramatic performances in 1842 under the management of J. M. Maddox, a Jewish speculator. With him Macready made a series of short engagements, generally for a stated number of weeks at three nights a week. In 1845 he appeared at the Princess's between October 13 and November 21, playing Hamlet, Lear, and Othello, to the Laertes of Leigh Murray, the Edgar and Iago of Wallack, and the Cordelia and Desdemona of Mrs. Stirling. Cooper, Granby, Compton, Ryder, and Mrs Ternan were also in the company. Next year, from January 26 to February 27, he repeated the same parts, and added Richelieu to the list. During a third engagement (April 13 to June 19, 1846) he performed the above-mentioned parts, along with Macbeth and Virginius, and created the character of James V. of Scotland, in *The King of the Commons,*

by the Rev. James White, of Bonchurch.   There was a
good deal of life and vigour in the dialogue of this
romantic drama ; but its construction was rambling, and
the underplot unduly hindered the action.   " The part
of James," says the *Athenæum*, " fiery, moody, passionate,
cheerful, generous, and mistrustful—all things by turns—
was exactly suited to Mr. Macready's style of acting.   It
was, indeed, composed of Macreadyisms—painfully so."
Mrs. Stirling played the heroine, and Ryder, Cooper,
Leigh Murray, and Compton were in the cast.   In the
autumn of 1846 (September 7 to November 7) Macready gave a very successful series of performances
at the Surrey Theatre, under the management of Mrs.
Davidge.

In 1847 he played two engagements with Maddox.
During the first (May 24 to June 18) his parts were
Hamlet, Lear, Macbeth, Werner, and Melantius, and
his supporters Creswick, Ryder, Mrs. Warner, and Mrs.
Stirling.   The second engagement (October 11 to
December 3) was of more importance.   He played
Macbeth, Wolsey, and Othello to the Lady Macbeth,
Queen Katharine, and Emilia of Charlotte Cushman ;
and on November 22 he produced a stage-arrangement,
by himself, of the first part of [Sir] Henry Taylor's
Philip van Artevelde.   Perhaps we should rather say a
stage-disarrangement—

"The nine written scenes of the first act," says the
Athenæum, "have been reduced to four—and this not by
the mere omission of five scenes, but by a recomposition of
the material.   The curtain opens on what is in the book the
third scene of the act ; but this is again recast and pieced
out with passages taken from other scenes. . . . Speeches
are torn from the dialogue and treated as soliloquies. . . . As
we advance further into the performance we find even the
text changed—enlarged as well as abridged. . . . In fact,

Mr. Taylor has been treated (perhaps with his own consent) as a dead dramatist. . . . He has, while yet living, had the honour of having his work mutilated for the stage."

It was with his own consent that Mr. Taylor had been so treated, and he was not dissatisfied with the result. The piece was finely mounted (though extreme parsimony was the rule at the Princess's in those days), but was very inadequately acted by Cooper as Occo, James Vining as the Earl of Flanders, Miss Emmeline Montagu as Adriana, and Miss Susan Cushman as Clara. Ryder as Van den Bosch seems to have been good.

"I thought Macready acted his part admirably," wrote Sir Henry Taylor, in his Autobiography, "and I did not find so much fault as he and many did with others of the performers ; and whatever might be his own feeling, so long as the audience was of the cultivated class, the play seemed to persons of that class to be successful ; but of course the literary audiences could only be few ; and the Press, which either leads or follows the many, took the part of blaming the attempt to bring on the stage a work which was designed only for the library."

The fact is that those of the audience who did not know the play beforehand had difficulty in following the action, which never properly seized their interest. It attained only five performances, to Macready's bitter disappointment. Philip van Artevelde was his last new part, and it is pleasant to think that the roll of his creations ends with so noble an effort, even if unsuccessful. "I never saw you more gallant and free than in the gallant and free scenes last night," Dickens wrote to him on the morning after the production. "It was perfectly captivating to behold you."

On December 7, 1847, Macready played the death-scene of King Henry IV. at Covent Garden, on what was called a "Shakespeare Night," designed to raise money for the purchase of Shakespeare's birthplace. Macready's scene came first (Leigh Murray appearing as the Prince of Wales), and was followed by selections from no fewer than nine plays of Shakespeare, played by Harley, Buckstone, Farren, Webster, Keeley, Granby, Charles Mathews, Phelps, George Bennett, and Henry Marston; Mrs. Butler (Miss Fanny Kemble), Miss Faucit, Mrs. Glover, Mrs. Nisbett, Madame Vestris, Mrs. Stirling, Miss Priscilla Horton, Miss Laura Addison, and Mrs. Warner. The performance was a remarkable one, and added £800 to the fund.

In 1848, before his departure for America, Macready played two engagements in London. The first—at the Princess's—lasted from February 21 to April 14. During the first four weeks he played Macbeth, Wolsey, Othello, Hamlet, and Lear, to the Lady Macbeth, Queen Katharine, Desdemona, Ophelia, and Cordelia of Mrs. Butler, the daughter of his old adversary, Charles Kemble. On the expiry of Mrs. Butler's engagement he added Virginius, Richelieu, and Werner to the list, and on April 5 resumed a part which he had long dropped—that of Brutus in *Julius Cæsar*—to Ryder's Cassius and Cooper's Antony. From April 24 to May 8 he appeared at the Marylebone Theatre, where Mrs. Warner, having seceded from Sadler's Wells, was carrying on an enterprise similar to that which she had assisted Phelps to launch in Islington. On July 10, before starting for America, he took a farewell benefit at Drury Lane, "commanded" by the Queen. His parts were Wolsey in the first three acts of *Henry VIII.*, to the Queen Katharine of Charlotte Cushman; and Mr. Oakly in *The Jealous Wife*, to the Mrs. Oakly of Mrs. Warner. Phelps assisted in both pieces, and the great

Braham came forth from his retirement to take part in the National Anthem. The house was so crowded that, after some disturbance, many of the audience departed, receiving their money back. Nevertheless, over £1100 were realized.

Macready's farewell tour in America in 1848–49 is chiefly noteworthy for its lurid ending. In order fully to understand the causes and circumstances of the Astor Place catastrophe, it is necessary to follow up the Forrest feud from its insignificant beginnings. This I shall now do; premising that the greater part of the evidence may be read at length in two pamphlets published in New York in 1849—the first entitled, *The Replies from England, etc., to Certain Statements circulated in this Country respecting Mr. Macready;* the second entitled, *A Rejoinder to " The Replies from England, . . ."* together *with an Impartial History and Review of the Lamentable Occurrences at the Astor Place Opera-House on the* 10th *of May,* 1849, *by an American Citizen.*

Edwin Forrest was thirteen years younger than Macready. His parentage was obscure, his boyhood unsettled. He had tried his hand at printing and other trades; had been (we are assured) a circus athlete; and had found a place on the stage before he was fifteen, in virtue of his handsome face and commanding presence. When Macready was in New York in 1826, Forrest, then barely twenty, had just made his first marked success at the Bowery Theatre. Writing long after the events which made the name of Forrest one of tragic import to him, Macready professes to have recognized his promise at this early date, and to have foreseen danger in the preponderance of his physical over his mental powers. Ten years passed, in which Forrest acquired great popularity in his own country. He was the first distinguished *American* actor, his predecessors and rivals, Cooper and Booth, being English by birth. Accordingly, when he came to England in 1836, his countrymen felt the honour of America concerned in his success. On the night of his appearance at Drury Lane, under Price's management (October 17), Macready heard from Dow that the play, *The Gladiator*, had failed, but that Forrest had succeeded. Recording this in his diary, Macready notes, "When I saw him nine years ago, he had everything within himself to make a very great actor." Forrest dined with Macready at Elstree; Macready made a cordial speech at a dinner given to Forrest at the Garrick Club; and all was friendship and amenity. "Mr. Macready," Forrest wrote, "has behaved in the handsomest manner to me." Their paths did not cross again until Macready visited America in 1843-44. Soon after his arrival in New York he dined with Forrest, and notes, "Our day was very cheerful; I like all I see of Forrest very much. He appears a clear-headed, honest, kind man : what can be better?" Five months later he met Forrest again in New Orleans, still in friendly fashion, though the local critics seem to have done their best to make mischief between them. We have seen that the theory which finds the germ of the subsequent strife in Macready's rage over the "failure" of this tour is totally untenable. The feud really dates from Macready's visit to Paris in 1844-45. Forrest also was in Paris at the time, and naturally wished to show the Parisians that America had her tragedian as well as England. To that end he tried to open negotiations with the manager, Mitchell, who (oddly enough) refused to see him. This refusal Forrest attributed to the hostility of Macready; but he never adduced one tittle of evidence, and Mitchell afterwards solemnly asserted in writing that Macready neither directly nor indirectly influenced his action in the matter.

Still smarting under this rebuff, Forrest came to London to fulfil an engagement with Maddox at the Princess's, where Charlotte Cushman had made her first appearance in England only a few days earlier. Among his American supporters, and perhaps in his own mind, the belief subsequently grew up that Macready and Forster had suborned the press in his disfavour, and had packed the house on his opening night (February 17, 1845) with a body of roughs hired to drive him from the stage. After careful examination of the evidence, I am convinced, not only that Macready had no hand in any such attempt, but that no such attempt was ever made. The writer of the *Rejoinder to the Replies* (reproduced almost word for word by Forrest's biographer, James Rees), asserts that "it was evident from the number of hisses, and the pertinacity with which they persisted in expressing their disapprobation of Mr. Forrest himself —not his acting, for they scarcely heard him—that the movement was preconcerted." If this were so, how comes it that not one of the critics who were present seems to have heard any hisses at all? The *Times* (one of the papers supposed to have been bought by Macready) stated that Forrest's Othello was greatly applauded; the *John Bull* says that it "merited the immense applause it received;" and I have sought in vain for the record of a single hiss. On the other hand, when he played Macbeth four days later, Oxenford remarks that "the tragedy was not announced for repetition, probably on account of the general disapprobation that Mr. Forrest's peculiarities elicited, in spite of the unanimous applause awarded to Miss Cushman." It seems, then, that Forrest's imagination, and that of his partisans, converted the

"general disapprobation" of his third performance into
an attempt to drive him from the stage on his opening
night ! That the *Times* critic was an impartial witness
is sufficiently proved by his warm praise of Forrest's
subsequent performances of King Lear and Metamora.
The engagement came to an end—prematurely, I suspect
—after eighteen performances, and Forrest retreated with
rage in his heart, which the praise bestowed on Miss
Cushman by no means tended to allay. He probably
felt himself a better actor than he had been at the time
of his first success, nine years before, and was irritated to
find himself treated with comparative indifference. In
this morbid frame of mind he found solace in imagining
himself the victim of jealous machinations on the part of
a rival tragedian ; and these imaginings soon grew into
a sort of monomania.

It must be admitted that the conduct of Forster, as
critic of the *Examiner*, gave a faint tinge of colour to
Forrest's suspicions. In 1836 Forster had stood almost
alone among the critics of the day in condemning the
blusterous style of the American tragedian. He found a
good deal to praise in his non-Shakespearian parts, but
utterly condemned his Othello and his Lear. I know of
few criticisms which convey so clear an idea of the
performances criticized as these two articles of Forster's.
They are full of masterly analysis and vivid description.
Damaging they certainly were ; but it was the writer's
obvious sincerity and thoughtfulness that made them so.
Macready, according to Albany Fonblanque, the editor
of the *Examiner*, "repeatedly entreated Mr. Forster to
be lenient or silent, but Mr. Forster very properly
maintained his independent judgment." He must have
known that his intimacy with Macready might subject
both of them to injurious imputations in the matter ;

but no one who reads his articles will blame him for taking the risk. Very different was his conduct on Forrest's second visit. Instead of criticizing him frankly, as before, or ignoring him altogether, he wrote, or allowed to be written, two or three contemptuous paragraphs, after this fashion—

"Our old friend, Mr. Forrest, afforded great amusement to the public by his performance of Macbeth on Friday evening at the Princess's. Indeed, our best comic actors do not often excite so great a quantity of mirth. The change from an inaudible murmur to a thunder of sound was enormous ; but the grand feature was the combat, in which he stood scraping his sword against that of Macduff. We were at a loss to know what this gesture meant, till an enlightened critic in the gallery shouted out, 'That's right ! sharpen it !'"

Jibes like this, proceeding from the friend and satellite of another tragedian, were in flagrant ill taste. The most perfect sincerity does not justify a man in wantonly exposing himself and others to misrepresentation. Forster certainly helped to start the snowball of misunderstanding which was soon to become an avalanche.

It was now Forrest's turn to put himself openly in the wrong. On March 2, 1846—a year after Forrest's retreat from London—Macready was playing Hamlet in Edinburgh. At the phrase, "I must be idle," immediately before the entrance of the court for the play-scene, it was his custom to wave his handkerchief fantastically, and assume an air of exaggerated jauntiness. Great was his astonishment on this evening when the waving of the handkerchief called forth a loud and determined hiss from some one in the upper boxes. He "bowed derisively and contemptuously to the individual," who was soon put to silence by the applause of the audience. The incident was, of course, discussed in the green-room, and the rumour began to get abroad that Forrest was the hisser. Macready at first refused to believe it, averring that Forrest was "too much of a gentleman." Conviction grew upon him, however, until the question was set at rest by a letter from Forrest to the *Times*, confessing that he hissed his rival's "fancy dance," stating that he was not alone in so doing, arguing that, having paid for his admission, he had a right to express his opinion, and alleging that he more than once started applause at points which he held to deserve it. It was afterwards maintained that, some nights later, the Edinburgh audience again hissed what Forrest called the *pas de mouchoir*. As to this there is some conflict of evidence; but I am strongly inclined to believe that, as Ryder put it in an affidavit, "there was not one single hiss from any other person [than Forrest] through that evening, nor during any night of Mr. Macready's engagement." The point is quite immaterial. What is certain is that Forrest did, deliberately and obtrusively, hiss his brother-actor, and that in so doing he was guilty of an unpardonable error. Not even Forrest's warmest partisans have found a word to say for him in this instance. They have tried to prove that the *pas de mouchoir* deserved to be hissed, but they have freely admitted that Forrest should have left the duty to some one whose motives were less open to suspicion.

The report of these events naturally crossed the Atlantic in all sorts of garbled forms. Forrest himself had now far passed the stage of exasperation at which it is still possible to distinguish fact from fancy. No one who has ever had to sift the testimony of untrained intellects, even on the simplest matters of fact, can have failed to observe how soon the mythopœic faculty, spurred by interest or by passion, takes the bit between its teeth and dashes off into the region of pure romance. Forrest's intellect was essentially untrained. His perceptions were at the mercy of his passions. Without any mendacious intent (as we can easily believe) he put in circulation the most flagrant falsehoods. He "had met with persecution in every corner—in Paris, in London, in Edinburgh;" though in Edinburgh, at any rate, he was, by his own admission, the aggressor. "The whole house had hissed" the *pas de mouchoir;* whereas the immense preponderance of testimony goes to show that his was the solitary hiss. He had been "most outrageously assailed by the venal London press in 1845;" whereas the files are there to show that the leading papers treated him with respect, and in some cases praised him very highly. His American adherents, however, were in no frame of mind to examine his assertions critically. The lampoons of Mrs. Trollope and of Dickens had touched the national susceptibilities on the raw. There was a large class or party to whom Forrest was endeared no less by his patriotism than by his talent. He was in their eyes the genius of democracy, while Macready was the toady and tool of the bloated aristocracy of an effete civilization, and his American admirers were little short of traitors to their country and its institutions. I am not conjecturing these sentiments; they are set forth at length and with emphasis in the documents of the case. The feud between the two tragedians may be said to have passed from the artistic into the political sphere, and we are now approaching the sanguinary close of the sordid "international episode."

Scarcely had Macready landed in America, in the autumn of 1848, when the Forrest party on the press began to decry him. Their taunts were of the sort best met by perfect silence, and Macready certainly

blundered when, on the night of his first appearance
(New York, October 4), he made a short speech, thanking the audience for having, by their applause, con-
futed his detractors.   This mistake, of openly braving
hostility, he repeated at the close of his New York engagement, three weeks later.   The foe retaliated by
publishing in the *Boston Mail*, on the very day of his
first appearance in Boston (October 30) a violent and
detailed account of the "persecutions" endured by
Forrest.   The Bostonians, however, were not stirred up
to any demonstration; it was in Philadelphia, on
November 20, that the first disturbance took place.
The play was *Macbeth*, and a noisy opposition was kept
up throughout it, though the great majority of the audience were in Macready's favour.   A copper cent and
a rotten egg were thrown on the stage, but no serious
violence was attempted.   At the close, Macready managed
to deliver a speech, thanking the well-disposed among
the audience for their support, and asserting strongly
that he had never in act or word shown the slightest
hostility towards Forrest.   Two days later there appeared in the Philadelphia papers a so-called "Card"
from Forrest, categorically reaffirming his accusations
against Macready and his "toady" Forster, while deny-
ing the existence of any "organized opposition" to
the English invader.   "Many of my friends," Forrest
continued, "called upon me when Mr. Macready was
announced to perform, and proposed to drive him from
the stage. . . . My advice was—Do nothing; let the
superannuated driveller alone; to oppose him would be
but to make him of some importance."   The document,
as a whole, was conceived in the worst possible temper
and taste.   It elicited from Macready a denial that any
notice of Forrest had appeared in the *Examiner* in 1845,

and a statement that he intended to seek "legal re-
dress" for Forrest's other allegations. Macready was
wrong as to the *Examiner.* Knowing that Forster had
been ill at the time of Forrest's performances in London,
he felt sure that no "notice" of his acting had appeared; he had not seen, or did not remember, the
contemptuous paragraphs of which I have given a specimen. With a view to his contemplated libel suit, he
wrote to England for evidence on the points in dispute,
and the *Replies from England,* published in New York
on May 8, 1849, two days before the grand catastrophe,
were the result of these inquiries. His American lawyer,
however, advised him to abandon his action, not because
it did not lie, but because the proceedings would certainly
outlast his stay in America, and involve indefinite trouble
and expense. In the mean time, the matter seemed to
have blown over. Macready enjoyed a prosperous and
pleasant tour in the south and west. At New Orleans,
in March, he was entertained at a great banquet, amid
much enthusiasm. At Cincinnati, during the performance of *Hamlet,* a sportive gentleman threw half the
carcase of a sheep upon the stage; but this seems to
have been a mere ebullition of amiable vivacity, not an
expression of opinion. The beginning of May found
him once more in New York, ready for the farewell
engagement which was to be so tragically cut short.

He was curiously free from apprehension, though
Forrest was in the city, and the enthusiasm of his ad-
mirers was running high. Macready's opening night at
the Astor Place Opera-House was Monday, May 7.
Macbeth was the play announced, and on the same night
Forrest appeared in the same character at the Broadway
Theatre. It was probably on this occasion that the
whole audience rose and cheered the lines—

N

"What rhubarb, senna, or what purgative drug
    Would scour these English hence?"

A pretty drastic purgative was, in fact, being exhibited
at the Opera-House. The theatre was crowded with a
very demonstrative audience, but until he was actually on
the stage Macready did not anticipate hostility. He was
received with thunders of applause, which at first gratified him. He bowed and bowed; the applause went on
and on; and gradually he realized that his friends were
doing their best to drown the groans and howls which
nevertheless made themselves audible from the parquette.
He tried to address the audience, but his words were lost
in the clamour. Placards were displayed, with the
words, "You have been proved a liar," and "No apo-
logies: it is too late." "Down with the English hog!"
yelled the malcontents, and again "Three groans for the
codfish aristocracy!" A rotten egg fell on the stage at his
feet. He waited calmly for a quarter of an hour, in the
hope that the tumult would subside, then went on with
the play in dumb-show. "Copper cents were thrown," he
says; "some struck me; four or five eggs, a great many
apples, nearly—if not quite—a peck of potatoes, pieces of
wood, a bottle of assafœtida, which splashed my own dress,
smelling, of course, most horribly." So the first and
second acts passed. At last, during the third act, a
man in the gallery tore up a chair, and sent it crashing
upon the stage. "Mr. Macready," said the *New York
Herald*, on the whole a hostile organ, "stood quite
unmoved—not the slightest tremor visible, nor the least
bravado either, in his manner." Presently a second
chair descended from aloft; and then Macready thought
"he had fulfilled his obligation to Messrs. Niblo and
Hackett;" the curtain dropped, and the rioters were
triumphant.

The better class of newspapers, and all men of the more intelligent sort, were indignant at this outrage. It was Macready's intention to relinquish his engagement altogether, but a requisition, signed by forty-eight leading citizens (among them Washington Irving and Richard Grant White), induced him to alter his mind. It was represented that the riot had been totally unforeseen ; that such a surprise could not occur again ; and that it would be unjust to deny Americans who had the credit of their country at heart an opportunity of making him reparation, and at the same time signally rebuking his assailants. Thus invited, Macready could scarcely decline ; and the following Thursday, May 10, was fixed for his reappearance as Macbeth. In the interval the *Replies from England* were published in a twenty-one page pamphlet.

The seats for Thursday evening were bought up with ominous rapidity, many of the purchasers being suspiciously like the " b'hoys " of Monday. Determined to nip rowdyism in the bud, the city authorities stationed posses of police at various points of vantage in the auditorium, especially so as to command the parquette, or pit. The house was filled to the very dome soon after the doors were opened, but it is said that only seven ladies were present. An increasing crowd assembled outside ; but until the curtain rose there was no disturbance. Macready's appearance was greeted with tremendous applause, but it soon became evident that there was a determined opposition present, though its numerical strength was not so great as before. This time no pause was made in the performance. Macready went right on with his part, the rioters howling and shaking their fists at him savagely, and the well-disposed, admonished by a placard, remaining silent, so as to

make the offenders more conspicuous. At the end of
the first act, as Macbeth was leading Lady Macbeth off,
the chief of the police gave the signal by raising his hat,
and his men bore down upon the rowdies in the parquette, clearing them out at one swoop. Four ringleaders were arrested, and, being temporarily confined in
a room under the pit, tried to set fire to the house. The
attempt, fortunately, was discovered in time, and frus-
trated. The others, being forcibly ejected into the
street, seem to have excited the fury of the mob outside,
for a bombardment almost instantly began. It happened, by a fatal chance, that a sewer was being repaired
in the street, so that a plentiful supply of loose paving-
stones was ready to hand. To shiver the windows was
the work of an instant, but the barred shutters inside
resisted for some time. Presently they too gave way,
and missiles began to crash into several parts of the
auditorium. Meanwhile the play went steadily on, in
spite of the pandemonium outside and the howlings of
the rioters who still held their places in the gallery.
The name of the Lady Macbeth who remained gallantly
at her husband's side throughout this dismal scene deserves to be recorded. It was Mrs. Coleman Pope—"a
very beautiful and queenly-looking woman "—who thus
showed an "undaunted metal" not unworthy of the
character she represented. At the end of the third act
Macready found his dressing-room drenched with water,
some pipes having been shattered in the bombardment.
Throughout the fourth act the hubbub increased. A
stone struck the chandelier. The audience shrank together into sheltered spots, and many left the theatre.
During the fifth act the inside noises ceased, and Macready acted his best, in spite of the roar from without.
His death was loudly cheered, and he was called before

the curtain, where he mutely thanked his supporters, and
then made his last bow on the American stage. He
retired to his room to change his dress, the riot meanwhile raging more furiously than ever outside. He had
barely finished his hasty toilet, amid a crowd of pale and
anxious onlookers, when a rattling detonation suddenly
crashed through the hubbub. "Hark! what's that?"
he asked. It was a volley of musketry. Soon there
came another, and yet another; then the noise of the
riot rolled gradually back, and stillness fell upon the
scene.

The civic authorities had arranged early in the day
that the military should be at hand if required. It is
almost certain that, if the police had acted with prompti-
tude and determination when the bombardment began,
they could have dispersed the rioters, who at that time
were comparatively few. They were mostly youths
between fifteen and twenty, animated by sheer love of
mischief rather than by any great enthusiasm for Forrest
or hatred of Macready. They seem to have entertained
no serious design of storming the theatre. The great
majority of the crowd (which was not at this time
unmanageably dense) were mere indifferent onlookers.
The police, however, made no decided sortie; the mob
increased; and many policemen, disabled by stones, had
to be carried into the theatre. At last, shortly before
nine o'clock, the Sheriff sent for the military, who were
soon on the ground. First came a troop of cavalry,
forty strong, followed by infantry to the number of a
hundred and seventy, in two detachments. As soon as
the cavalry entered Astor Place, they were assailed with
a shower of stones and brickbats. Almost every one of
them was hurt, their horses became unmanageable, and
they rode ignominiously from the field. Thus the foot-

soldiers were left unsupported in the midst of a dense
crowd of from ten to twenty thousand people, howled
at, cursed, and stoned by the aggressive section of the
mob, whom their very presence infuriated.   To make
confusion worse confounded, the night was as dark as
pitch, the street-lamps around having been extinguished.
For some time the troops tried, by marching and counter-
marching, to clear the space round the theatre.   It was
useless.   Little by little they were more and more closely
hemmed in, until, when orders were given for a bayonet-
charge, they found themselves at too close quarters with
the mob even to attempt it.   Many of them, both soldiers
and officers, were severely injured by stones; a pistol,
loaded with small shot, was fired by one of the rioters,
and wounded two or three men ; some of the mob were
even wrenching the muskets from the soldiers' hands.
When things had come to this pass, Generals Sandford
and Hall, who were in command, told the Sheriff and the
Recorder that unless their men were ordered to fire they
could not hold their ground.   Still the civic authorities
hesitated for several minutes, warning the mob that they
would be fired upon, and exhorting them to desist.
There was not even a pause in the shower of missiles ;
the Sheriff saw that the troops could not stand there to
be annihilated ; and finally he gave the requisite per-
mission.   The number of soldiers at this point was
about seventy, the others being engaged at the back
of the theatre, where the disturbance was less acute.
General Hall gave orders to fire above the heads of the
crowd, against the wall of a house opposite ; but the
hubbub was so terrible that the order was imperfectly
heard.   Most of the troops obeyed it ; but some fired
into the crowd, one or two of whom fell.   The majority
of the mob, however, imagining that no harm was done,

concluded that the soldiers had only blank cartridges, and, raising a howl of scorn and execration, rushed again to the attack. This time the order was given to aim low; a second volley was fired; several people dropped; and the mob, now alive to the seriousness of the situation, recoiled considerably. Still the hailstorm of missiles continued, and it was evident that the rioters were not really quelled. They rallied, indeed, and began to advance once more, in two bodies. The troops were ordered to fire obliquely, one half to the right, the other to the left; and this volley, which was so desultory that some witnesses describe it as two separate discharges, did great execution, and finally broke the spirit of the mob. An advance was made in two directions, the rioters falling gradually back, though still keeping up a running fire of stones. Presently the military were left in undisputed possession of the space around the theatre. Two brass pieces, loaded with grape-shot, were brought upon the scene, and placed so as to command, one the Broadway, the other the Bowery. The battle over, the crowd vanished very quickly, bearing its dead and wounded away with it; and the soldiers, largely reinforced, bivouacked for the night on the scene of their melancholy victory. The number of the dead is variously stated, but seems to have been about seventeen; many of them, of course, mere chance onlookers, who cared no straw for the rival tragedians.

Within the theatre, Macready and his friends were in a state of not unnatural trepidation. Shots had been fired; men had been killed; even if the military were for the moment victorious, could Macready hope to get out of New York without falling into the hands of rioters eager to avenge their comrades? "There was nothing for it," he writes, "but to meet the worst with dignity." He was persuaded to exchange overcoats with one of the actors, and to wear a cap in place of his hat. Otherwise undisguised, he joined the last stragglers of the audience leaving the theatre, and passed with them into the street. Accompanied by one friend, he made his way unrecognized to that friend's house, where a council of war was held. It was decided that he must leave New York at once. He sat up all night, smoking and talking, until, at the peep of day, a carriage and pair, ordered "to take a doctor to some gentleman's house near New Rochelle," sped him out of the city. At New Rochelle he took train for Boston. Some fellow-passengers recognized him on the way, but he was quite unmolested, and soon found himself safe in the house of his friend George Curtis. Even in Boston he did not at first feel quite secure, though the Mayor called to assure him that the authorities had both the will and the power to protect him from outrage. He remained in Boston for ten days, and then started for home in the steamer *Hibernia.* " I never felt such relief," he writes, " as in planting my foot upon that vessel's deck."

Supersensitive as his conscience was, Macready could not feel that any drop of the blood shed on the 10th of May was on his head. In the last analysis, the riot is to be regarded simply as an acute outbreak of a long-standing international irritation. But for that pre-existent condition, not even Forrest's alleged "persecution" could have worked people up to such a pitch of frenzy. Local rancours, too, came into play. It is evident that the support given to Macready by the upper classes and the upper-class press did much to exasperate the mob. If we must distribute the responsibility among individuals, there can be no doubt that Forrest's wounded vanity lay at the root of the misunderstanding. The jibes of the *Examiner* gave him some shadow of excuse for suspecting Macready of hostility to him ; and this suspicion grew into a monomania which rendered him subject to delusions on the plainest matters of fact. Forrest, however, seems to have given no direct encouragement to violence. Apart from his angry letters to the newspapers, he pursued a policy of masterly inactivity. Macready, on the other hand, cannot be acquitted of injudiciously braving an opposition which he ought to have ignored. His speeches on the opening and closing nights of his first New York engagement should have remained unspoken. Otherwise, I cannot find that any tittle of blame attached to him, and, at the crisis, even his opponents admitted the dignified intrepidity of his conduct. Surveying the whole matter with every desire to be impartial, I should say that Forrest was thrice as much to blame as Macready, while fatality —the unhappy convergence of a hundred deplorable circumstances—was thrice as much to blame as Forrest.

Macready returned from America in June, 1849, and retired from the stage in February, 1851. The intervening twenty months were occupied with farewell visits to the provinces and two engagements at the Haymarket. The first of these extended from October 8 to December 8, 1849. He played only four parts—Macbeth, Hamlet, Lear, and Othello, supported by James Wallack, Howe, Rogers, Keeley, Mrs. Warner, Miss Reynolds, and Miss Priscilla Horton. On February 1, 1850, he took part in the Windsor Castle theatricals, arranged by Charles Kean, playing Brutus in *Julius Cæsar* to Kean's Antony, Wallack's Cassius, and Mrs. Warner's Portia. This was the only time he ever appeared on the same stage with Kean, whom he did not love. It is reported

that on this occasion, after the play was over, Kean sent
some message of courtesy to him in his dressing-room,
which was met by the gruff rejoinder, " If Mr. Kean has
anything to say to me, let him say it through my solicitor!"
Kean's share in the Windsor theatricals was rewarded by
the gift of a diamond ring, which he afterwards lost;
whereupon a wit reported that it had been found "stick-
ing in Macready's gizzard." The second Haymarket engagement began with Macbeth on October 28, 1850, and
ended with Lear on February 3, 1851. In the course
of the engagement he played Hamlet, Othello, Shylock,
Richelieu, Werner, Virginius, Brutus, and afterwards
Cassius, in *Julius Cæsar* (Mr. Howe making a great
success as Mark Antony), Wolsey, King John, the
Stranger, Benedick, Henry IV. (in the death-scene), Mr.
Oakly, and (for the first time in London) Richard II.
The revival of *Richard II.* (which was acted with "singular fidelity to the text") excited little interest, and was
repeated only once. The American actor, E. L. Davenport, played seconds during this engagement, in place of
Wallack; the support, for the rest, being much as before.
Macready, I fear, cannot be acquitted of conniving at
what he calls "play-bill trickery" in the announcement
of "last appearances," which, as a matter of fact, were
only penultimate, or even antepenultimate. But the
phrase, "last time for ever," meant what it said; and
during the last weeks of January it was appended to each
of his great characters in turn, except Macbeth. That
favourite part was reserved for his last farewell.

So early as two o'clock on February 26, 1851, crowds
had gathered round the pit and gallery doors of Drury
Lane Theatre, then under the management of James
Anderson. An old playgoer, who witnessed the throng
later in the day, said that " Jenny Lind was nothing to

it "—there was no slight crowd to *see* the crowd. Phelps closed his own theatre in order to play Macduff to his old leader's Macbeth ; Howe was the Banquo ; Mrs. Warner, the Lady Macbeth. When the curtain rose every corner of the house was densely packed.

"And what a sight that was !" writes George Henry Lewes. " How glorious, triumphant, affecting, to see every one starting up, waving hats and handkerchiefs, stamping, shouting, yelling, their friendship at the great actor, who now made his appearance on that stage where he was never more to reappear ! There was a *crescendo* of excitement enough to have overpowered the nerves of the most self-possessed ; and when, after an energetic fight—which showed that the actor's powers bore him gallantly up to the last—he fell pierced by Macduff's sword, this death, typical of the actor's death, this last look, this last act of the actor, struck every bosom with a sharp and sudden blow, loosening a tempest of tumultuous feeling such as made applause an ovation.

"Some little time was suffered to elapse wherein we recovered from the excitement, and were ready again to burst forth as Macready the Man, dressed in his plain black, came forward to bid 'Farewell, a long farewell, to all his greatness.' As he stood there, calm but sad, waiting till the thunderous reverberations of applause should be hushed, there was one little thing which brought the tears into my eyes, viz. the crape hatband and black studs, that seemed to me more mournful and more touching than all this vast display of sympathy [his eldest daughter, 'Nina,' died February 24, 1850, aged twenty]. . . . Perhaps a less delibe-rate speech would have better suited the occasion ; . . . but under such trying circumstances a man may naturally be afraid to trust himself to the inspiration of the moment. Altogether I must praise Macready for the dignity with which he retired, and am glad that he did not *act*. There was no ostentation of cambric sorrow ; there was no well got-up broken voice to simulate emotion. The manner was calm, grave, sad, and dignified."

His children were among the audience. They had also been allowed to witness his farewell performances at the Haymarket.*

The inevitable public dinner followed on the 1st of March, in the Hall of Commerce. Sir E. L. Bulwer was in the chair; Dickens, Thackeray, and Bunsen spoke. Forster read Tennyson's sonnet of farewell to "Macready, moral, grave, sublime;" and the whole company stood up and cheered when Charles Kemble, at the age of seventy-six, rose to stammer a few words of reply to the toast of "The Stage." On the following day Macready betook himself to his "cottage"—a substantial house at Sherborne, Dorsetshire—and entered upon the twenty-two years of his retirement.

The evening of his life was full of sorrows. Death was busy around him. The first victim was his wife, who survived his retirement only some eighteen months, dying on September 18, 1852. A son, Walter Francis Sheil, died on February 3, 1853, aged thirteen; another son, Henry Frederick Bulwer, died after a lingering illness on August 12, 1857, aged nineteen; a daughter, Lydia Jane, died of scarlatina, June 20, 1858, aged sixteen; and his "sister and friend," Letitia, died four months later (November 8, 1858), aged sixty-four. Death now stayed its hand for eleven years—a period of tranquillity and happiness. In 1860 (April 3) Macready married again. His wife, Miss Cecile Louise Frederica Spencer, was many years his junior; yet the union was a happy one. About the same time he removed from Sherborne to Wellington Square, Cheltenham, where he spent the rest of his life. A son was born of the second marriage

* One of his sons, Edward, went on the stage in Australia, apparently without success.

(May 7, 1862), and life rolled on unruffled until the sixties drew to a close. Then his eldest surviving daughter, "Katie," a young lady of strong character and some poetic talent, fell ill, and was sent to Madeira in search of health. She died on the homeward voyage, March 24, 1869, at the age of thirty-four. From this blow Macready never fully recovered; and it was followed two years later (November 26, 1871) by the death, in Ceylon, of his eldest son, William Charles, aged thirty-nine.

At Sherborne Macready had busied himself greatly, not only with the bringing up of his own children, but with the spread of education among the people. He founded, or revived, a literary institution, at which he induced Dickens, Thackeray, Forster, Bellew, and others to give readings and lectures. He himself frequently read and lectured, not only at Sherborne, but in other towns of the south and west. After the removal to Cheltenham these public appearances were almost, if not entirely, discontinued; but he still gave frequent private readings, to which the boys of Cheltenham College were sometimes admitted. During the last two or three years of his life he could not hold a book or read for himself; but he still enjoyed being read to, and, failing a reader, would go over the stores of literature in his memory. "I have been reading *Hamlet*," he said on one occasion; and added, touching his forehead, "Here." Asked if he could remember the whole play, he said, "Yes, every word, every pause; and the very pauses have eloquence." Time had softened the asperities of his countenance. "We now think with pleasure," says a not too friendly writer, "of his venerable and noble head as we saw it last in 1872, and of the sweet smile of his beautiful mouth, which spoke of the calm wisdom of a gentle and

thoughtful old age." Death came upon him in the
shape of gradual decay, but a slight bronchial attack was
the immediate cause of the end. After three days' con-
finement to bed, he passed away peacefully on Sunday,
April 27, 1873. His second wife, one son and one
daughter by his first marriage, and one son by his
second marriage, survived him.

MACREADY'S CHARACTERS.

1843–1851.

PRINCESS'S : 1845 : Hamlet, 8 ; Lear, 7 ; Othello, 3.

1846 (January and February) : Richelieu, 5 ; Hamlet, 4 ;
Lear, Othello, 3. (April—June) : *James V. (*King of the
Commons*), 13 ; Macbeth, 5 ; Virginius, 4 ; Lear, Othello, 3 ;
Richelieu, 2 ; Hamlet, 1.

SURREY : 1846 : Macbeth, Lear, 8 ; Hamlet, 7 ; Othello,
Richelieu, 3 ; Werner, Virginius, 2 ; Shylock, 1.

PRINCESS'S : 1847 (May and June) : Lear, Macbeth, 3 ;
Hamlet, Werner, Melantius, 2. (October—December)
Wolsey, 12 ; *Philip van Artevelde, 5 ; Macbeth, 3 ;
Hamlet, 2 ; Othello, Richelieu, 1.

COVENT GARDEN (December 7) : Henry IV. (death-scene).

PRINCESS'S : 1848 (February—April) : Othello, Hamlet,
5 ; Lear, 4 ; Macbeth, Wolsey, Brutus, 2 ; Virginius,
Richelieu, Werner, 1.

MARYLEBONE : 1848 : Macbeth, Lear, 2 ; Hamlet, Othello,
Wolsey, Henry IV., Mr. Oakly, 1.

DRURY LANE : 1848 (July 10) : Wolsey, Mr. Oakly, 1.

HAYMARKET : 1849 (October—December) : Macbeth, 10 ;
Lear, 8 ; Hamlet, 6 ; Othello, 3.

1850–51 : Lear, Richelieu, 7 ; Macbeth, Henry IV., Mr.
Oakly, 6 ; Othello, 5 ; Wolsey, King John, Virginius, 4 ;
Hamlet, Werner, 3 ; Shylock, Brutus, Cassius, Richard II.,
2 ; Benedick, Stranger, 1.

DRURY LANE : 1851 (February 26) : Last appearance,
Macbeth.

CHAPTER VII.

ART AND CHARACTER.

Was Macready an actor of the first, or only of the second, order ?   Could he have held his own beside the giants of the stage—beside Betterton, Garrick, Kemble, Kean ?   Or did he seem great only in comparison with the lesser men of a degenerate age—Wallack, Phelps, Vandenhoff, and Charles Kean ?   Let us assemble and sift the evidence.

The very fact that this question presents itself shows that his position is not assured.   We may discuss and analyze the genius of Garrick or Mrs. Siddons, Talma or Rachel, but its general supremacy we take for granted. Macready holds no such unassailable eminence.   His place is assigned him by a preponderance of suffrages, not by acclamation.

The first thing to be observed is that he did actually hold his own beside Kean, and was treated as an actor of the highest order by critics who had seen John Kemble and his greater sister in their prime.   There is a curious passage in *Oxberry's Dramatic Biography*, 1826, as to the esteem in which Macready was then held—

"About five-eighths of London declare Kean to be the first English actor, two of the remaining three perhaps vote

for Young, and one-eighth for Macready ; but, singular to
say, all the Keanites say Macready is next to their favourite,
and all the Youngites rank Macready above Kean : so that,
in fact, Mr. Macready is more *generally* considered a great
actor than either Kean or Young."

No one of any authority, however, places Macready quite
on a level with Kean. Hazlitt, writing of the beginnings
of his London career, ranks him next to Kean among
the younger actors of the day, but evidently at a long
interval.

"Mr. Kean," writes "T" in the *New Monthly* (1820),
"represents simple man in his fiercest passions, his most
terrific agonies, or his deepest sympathies. Mr. Kemble
delineated him chiefly as surrounded with the pomp and
external circumstance which gave a stateliness to all his
actions and distresses. Mr. Macready depicts him as elate
with high enthusiasm, attired on great occasions in sudden
brightness, or wearing the pensive livery of fanciful sorrow.
. . . If Mr. Kean is the most intensely human, and Mr.
Kemble the most classical, Mr. Macready is the most
romantic of actors."

Leigh Hunt, writing ten years later (the *Tatler*, 1830),
thus formulates the difference between Kean and
Macready—

"The former has an instinctive natural reason for all that
he does, and never acts at random ; is never loud when he
might as well be low, or *vice versâ*; . . . in a word, has a
finer conception of the character throughout, and adapts
himself to it as naturally, as gracefully, and with as much
self-possession as the limbs do to the motions required of them.
Now, we do not hold this to be the case with Macready. He
is striking throughout : often fine, sometimes extremely
affecting and masterly : but the level of his style is of a more
gratuitous order than Kean's. We do not always ee the
reason for his *fortes* and *pianos*: his grace looks more the
effect of study than of habit . . . Mr. Macready has sensi-

bility, tenderness, passion : he suffers : his passion masters him : he knows how to undergo it with delicacy . . . Kean, on the other hand, though undergoing passion more terribly, still surmounts it with the grace of moral grandeur. He feels the poetry of it more ; that is to say, all the elegance and idealism of which it is capable, compatible with nature. . . . His tragedy [is] as superior to Mr. Macready's in general, as poetry is to mixed poetry, and prose, or as the mixed poetry and prose of Macready is the declamatory verse of the purely artificial tragedian."

It must not be forgotten that while Kean was at the zenith of his powers, Macready gained a signal victory in a part which his rival seemed to have made peculiarly his own—Richard III. to wit. Impartial and intelligent critics compared the two performances to Macready's advantage. Macready, too, was far ahead of Kean as a creator, an originator, of characters ; and when Kean tried to annex one of his parts—Virginius—he was anything but successful. Still, it may be taken for granted that Kean had inborn powers and graces denied to Macready, playing more by instinct and less by intellect. Macready always declined to play Kean's great parts of Sir Edward Mortimer and Sir Giles Overreach. He said that Kean's delivery of three words in the part of Mortimer, "I answer—No !" was sufficient to make him despair of rivalling him. We may perhaps say that Kean was a greater actor, but not so great an artist. And we may add with tolerable confidence that the gap between Kean and Macready was not nearly so wide as the gap between Macready and the other tragic actors of his time.

Let us now try to summarize the leading characteristics of Macready's style. He was consciously and of set purpose an eclectic actor, trying to combine the dignity of the Kemble school with the vivacity of Kean. He is reported to have said that "his aim was to present an amalgam of Kean and Talma." Natural grace, unfortunately, he did not possess. Though, as years went on, he could scarcely be called ugly, he was always harsh-featured. Mr. George Scharf, whose lifelong study of physiognomy gives his words authority, informs me that he greatly resembled the portraits of Lorenzo de' Medici. His eyebrows had a curious upward slope from the nose ; that feature itself was very irregular ; his mouth was much depressed at the corners ; and his jaw was excessively large and square. In his make-up he seems never to have aimed at comeliness. Character-portraits, drawn by friendly artists with no bent towards caricature, are apt to make him out ill-favoured, if not positively hideous. Théophile Gautier complained that in Othello Macready "s'était composé un masque de singe anthropophage." His motions were abrupt, his attitudes frequently ungraceful, or, as Oxenford put it, "unsculptural." He seems to have been particularly fond of standing in profile, or semi-profile, to the audience, with his shoulders thrown very far back, the weight of his body resting on one leg, and the other bent forward at a sharp angle. It is evident, too, that the stage-costume of his day did nothing to soften these eccentricities. In parts belonging to a definite historical period (such as Strafford) he would sometimes dress admirably ; but where any licence was admissible he seems to have been apt to go astray. Gautier ridicules as grotesque his dress in Othello ; and Mr. John Coleman, who was present when Forrest hissed Macready in Edinburgh, gives the following sketch of his Hamlet costume on that occasion :—

"He wore a dress the waist of which nearly reached his arms ; a hat with a sable plume big enough to cover a hearse ; a pair of black silk gloves much too large for him ;

a ballet shirt of straw-coloured satin, which looked simply dirty ; and, what with his gaunt, awkward, angular figure, his grizzled hair, his dark beard close shaven to his square jaws, yet unsoftened by a trace of pigment, his irregular features, his queer, extraordinary nose, . . . and his long skinny neck, he appeared positively hideous. But, after all, ' mind is the brightness of the body,' and, O ye gods ! when he spoke, how he brightened, illumined, irradiated the atmosphere ! "

His voice was by nature very fine and rich. Miss Mitford, in 1820, spoke of it as " so delicious that there is a pleasure in listening to it, quite unconnected with the words he utters." Again, four years later, she writes, " I have a physical pleasure in the sound of Mr. Macready's voice, whether talking, reading, or acting (except when he rants). It seems to me very exquisite music, with something instrumental and vibrating in the sound, like certain notes of the violoncello." In 1828 a hostile critic in the *Athenæum* admitted that his voice had been " magnificent," but added that he had " injured it intrinsically by the constant use of that pumping roar with which he interlards all passages of passion." So early as 1826 we find him accused, in *Oxberry's Dramatic Biography*, of a habitual catching of the breath, resembling a burr, which became painful to the hearer. The same writer also states that he imitated from Kean the system of sudden transitions—" Kean's worst peculiarity "—his voice " suddenly rising and dropping, like the waterspout in the Temple." So late as 1846, that fine critic William Robson (The Old Playgoer) inveighs against his practice of " falling in the midst of a burst of passion from the loudest tones to audible whispers—one of the vilest of stage tricks." But Robson was too bigoted a Kembleite to admit any merit at all in Macready. He even goes the length of remonstrating with Young for

" degrading himself" by speaking at the Macready dinner in 1839. Other critics complain of Macready's "peculiar and unnatural intonations," and even of his vocal dissonances. Yet there can be no doubt that, in spite of faults in his method of using it, his voice was one of his chief natural advantages. His enunciation was somewhat too laboriously precise. In his anxiety to avoid any slur or liaison between a final consonant and the initial letter of the next word, he fell into the irritating mannerism of inserting an explosive *a* (or, as some writers represent it, an *er*) at the end of certain words, and even of prolonging the intercalated sound into a sort of rumble, something after this fashion—

> " Be innocenttta of knowledge, dearesttta chuck,
> Till thou applauddda the deed."

James Murdoch gives an amusing account of Macready's struggle with an American utility actor, who, in announcing the approach of Birnam Wood, insisted on saying—

> " Within these three miles you may see it *a*-coming."

"Good Heavens, sir !" cried Macready, " have you no ears ? You are not speaking common language : it is *blank verse*, sir, and a single misplaced syllable destroys the metre. . . . You know how to spell *coming*, which begins with a *c*—no preceding sound of *a ;* therefore you should say—

> ' Within these three miles you may see it-a-a-coming.' "

The actor tried it over and over again, but could not eliminate the *a*. Goaded to despair at last, he turned upon the tragedian, and said, " Mr. Macready, I don't see the difference between my way of doing it and yours, unless it is that I put only one *a* before ' coming,' and you put half a dozen little ones."

As he belonged, in the main, to what is called the "natural" school of actors, Macready was more apt to slur than to emphasize the rhythm of blank verse—a habit which probably grew upon him. So early as 1827 the friendly critic of the *New Monthly* complained of his "too fitful, hurried, and familiar" delivery of the verse in Macbeth. The *Athenæum*, in 1830, made similar complaint, suggesting, in allusion to the newly opened railway, that his "speed had probably been acquired between the Manchester and Liverpool theatres." Leigh Hunt, in the *Tatler* (1831), blames him for being "afraid of the poetry of some of his greatest parts, as if it would hurt the effect of his naturalness and his more familiar passages." This remark (taken in its context) involves a criticism of his treatment of metre, though its whol bearing is much wider. It is difficult, however, to believe that Fanny Kemble is not exaggerating when she says that "his want of musical ear made his delivery of Shakespeare's blank verse defective, and painful to persons better endowed in that respect. It may have been his consciousness of his imperfect declamation of blank verse that induced him to adopt what his admirers called the natural style of speaking it; which was simply chopping it up into prose." He was certainly not conscious of any defect of ear, and I doubt whether it existed. He records with gratitude the value of his mother's training in cultivating his sense of rhythm, and it is incredible that any one who lacked that sense should have read Milton finely, as Macready unquestionably did. The truth probably is that in speaking dramatic verse he paid more attention to logical than to rhythmic structure ; whereas the Kemble tendency was to take care of the measure, and let the sense take care of itself. The practice of survivors of the Macready school, as well as the testimony of old playgoers, amply proves that, how-ever "natural" his delivery, Macready was incapable of murdering the metre after the fashion of so many actors of to-day.

What seems to be a very fair estimate of his general characteristics was published in the *Daily News* at the time of his retirement—

"In speaking," says the writer, "he paid less attention to the modulation of his tones, and to the rhythmical flow of verse, than any other great actor whom we remember. In the whirl and tempest of passion he cared not what became of his voice ; he often forced it, as one would do in real life, to a harsh and dissonant scream. He gave some pain to the ear, but then he gained his object by placing before the audience the very being he represented, and carrying them with him in a flood of sympathy. Nor did Macready's utterance deprive really fine poetry of any part of its beauty. Take the lines we heard last night—

'To-morrow, and to-morrow, and to-morrow,' etc.

(*Macbeth*, act v. sc. 5)—when did these words ever fall upon the ear with a deeper or more mournful cadence?"

In collecting evidence as to Macready's art, we must bear in mind that he was always progressing, or at any rate trying to progress ; so that a criticism might be just at one period, and very unjust at another. No one ever laboured more assiduously at his art. Murdoch tells an anecdote of an American senator, on a visit to London, being disturbed in the small hours of the night by hearing some one, as he thought, shout "Murder!" repeatedly in all sorts of tones. He rushed into the passage, and shouted, "Hallo, there! hallo!" when his landlady put her night-capped head out at a door, and begged him not to be alarmed, as it was only Mr. Macready the tragedian. The next morning an apologetic note brought an explanation. Macready had that night been playing Macbeth, and, being dissatisfied with his treatment of the murder-scene, had been "submitting the words 'murder' and 'murdered' to a kind of aspirated and husky utterance in different degrees." This took place during his early years at Drury Lane; but to the very end he never "put a part to bed." We find him writing to his friend Wightwick, in 1840—

" I think it cannot be wrong to endeavour to preserve in my acting an equal, or to supply a greater, quantity of passion, with less of exaggerated attitude and overstrained expression—*i.e.* distortion of countenance—a more sustained deportment with less quantity of voice—and to avoid the melodramatic practices you speak of, which in Kean (*the* Kean) himself were blots upon the bright genius of a super-latively great actor, and which were never—*never*—to be detected in Mrs. Siddons, in Talma, in Kemble, or in Miss O'Neill."

He liked to think that his latest performance of any character was the best he had ever given, and he laboured untiringly to that end.

Macready's detractors were fond of asserting that he was not a Shakespearian, but a melodramatic actor.

" In any sense that I can affix to this phrase," says George Henry Lewes, " it is absurd. He was by nature unsuited for some great tragic parts; but by his intelligence he was fitted to conceive, and by his organization fitted to express *characters*, and was not, like a melodramatic actor, limited to *situations*. Surely Lear, King John, Richard II., Cassius, and Iago are tragic parts ! In these he was great; nor could he be surpassed in certain aspects of Macbeth and Coriolanus, although he wanted the heroic thew and sinew to represent these characters as wholes."

F. G. Tomlins, on the other hand, writing in 1851, declares that Macready could not be called a Shakespearian actor because he had no " plasticity "—he could not personate.

" Instead of being subdued to the character, he subdues the character to himself. Like Le Brun, he can give you certain abstract passions, but of these only a limited number : grief on its petulant side, rage on its demoniac, pathos and affections ; but all modifications of himself, not representations of a person. . . . Now, this generalizing personification is the mode of the old French tragedies. . . . In all Shakespeare's characters we have the particular. . . . It may be said, in answer to this charge of want of personification, that Mr. Macready has a great deal of reality, that he is logically correct. True ; but we want imaginative truths, not harsh facts. It is true Macbeth might find his state of man shaken when he goes to murder Duncan, but he is very different from a cowardly burglar. Lear is a choleric, barbaric chief, but he would not bully every one he comes near. Iago is a designing ruffian, but he is not an exaggeration of deceit."

His vehemence and earnestness, the critic continues, would always move audiences by mere emotional contagion, and he had always " the utmost comprehension of his author that a highly cultivated understanding could give." But he was prosaic, unimaginative, and consequently lacked the power of personification, which, in Mr. Tomlins's judgment, was the first essential of the Shakespearian actor. Those who know how cheap and futile is the accusation that such-and-such an actor is " always himself," will be at no loss to estimate the value of this criticism. I quote it as a fair specimen of the arguments of Macready's detractors.

It was quite natural that people should find more to cavil at in his Shakespearian parts than in his Virginius, Werner, and Richelieu. We have each our private ideal of Macbeth, Hamlet, Othello, Lear ; we have all of us read of, if we have not seen, great performances of these parts; so that every actor who undertakes them has to pass through a triple ordeal, encountering, first, our imagination, kindled by Shakespeare; second, our idealized memory of performances which used to please our, perhaps unripe, judgment; third, our conceptions of the great actors of the past, gathered from the often extravagant panegyrics of contemporaries. On the other hand, it was left to Macready to create Virginius, Werner, and Richelieu, so to speak, in his own image. He had no preconceptions, no reminiscences, to contend against. In these parts he could, and probably did, expand, illuminate, and subtilize the author's conception; in the heroes of Shakespeare he could at best hope not to fall notoriously short of the ideal. Thus it was only natural that his Shakespearian characters should be much criticized, while others, the chief of which he himself created, met with almost unqualified admiration. The legitimate conclusion is that he was good in the latter parts, not that he was bad in the former; for what actor was ever admitted to solve unimpeachably the vast and complex problems presented by Shakespeare?

His best Shakespearian parts, beyond a doubt, were Macbeth and Lear, though authorities differ as to which of these two deserves the preference. He himself would have voted for Macbeth; but the lack of kingliness in the murder-scene, noted by almost all critics from Leigh Hunt onwards, was commonly held a grave defect. "He stole into the sleeping-chamber of Duncan," says G. H. Lewes, "like a man going to purloin a purse, not like a warrior going to snatch a crown." Westland Marston, on the other hand, found "the moral of the play made visible" in the contrast between "the erect martial figure that entered in the first act," and "the crouching form and stealthy, felon-like step of the self-abased murderer." Lady Pollock, a keen and delicate critic, notes how, in the first act, Macready produced a great effect by "his singular power of looking at nothing," so that "when he spoke 'Into the air' we could almost see the hags pass away" like a wreath of vapour. In the scene with Banquo's Ghost he surpassed even his greatest predecessors, and there are no two opinions as to the magnificence of his playing in the last act. "He turned upon Fate, and stood at bay." In Lear he found ample scope for that subtlety of psychological suggestion which was one of his great qualities. He marked the gradual encroachments of insanity by the most delicate touches ; and the irresistible tenderness of the last act contrasted beautifully with the overwhelming vehemence of the first and second. Westland Marston suggests (not with special reference to Lear) that his psychological analysis was sometimes overdone, that "various mental states seemed too sharply defined and separated ;" but this is so obviously the mere exaggeration of a rare quality that it can scarcely be reckoned a defect. Hamlet was, perhaps, Macready's own favourite among his characters, but neither public nor critics could entirely get over his physical disqualifications. Lewes found him "lachrymose and fretful ; too fond of a cambric pocket-handkerchief to be really affecting." James Spedding, on the other hand, says, "An advantage attaches to him which I have observed in no other Hamlet : it is easy to credit him with the thoughts he utters." Othello, though he played it frequently, was one of his "worser parts." He made the initial mistake of giving him the complexion of a negro rather than a Moor. "His passion," says Lewes, "was irritability, and his agony had no grandeur." His Iago was almost universally admired ; so was his King John ; so, too, his Cassius ; and his death-scene in Henry IV. was one of his greatest achievements. It must be admitted, as bearing out in a certain measure the strictures of Mr. Tomlins, that he always succeeded best in expressing some phase of his own character. He had a strong sense of the supernatural, the " metaphysical," and he was fine in the witch-scenes of *Macbeth*, the ghost-scenes of *Hamlet.* Irritability was his chief foible, and he was great in Lear and Cassius. He possessed a keen analytic intellect, and he shone in Iago. He was deficient in what may be called majesty of character and passion, and he failed in Othello.*

* I append a statement of the number of times that Macready played each of his principal parts in London, the statistics for the country and America not being attainable. These figures afford a fair test of the comparative popularity of his different parts with metropolitan audiences. A chance circumstance may in one or two cases place a part unduly high or low in the scale ; for instance, the spectacular success of *The Tempest* at Covent Garden gives Prospero an apparent advantage over Lear and other far more important characters ; but the reader, with the help of the foregoing narrative, will easily allow for these aberrations. The first of the two figures attached to each character represents the number of performances *before* Macready went into management in 1837—a point which may be taken as marking a new departure in his career—the second represents the number of performances *after* that date. I do not vouch for the absolute accuracy of my reckoning in all cases ; but I have done my best to avoid errors, and any that may have crept in are certainly trifling. Macbeth, for instance, may in fact have been played 147 or 149 times ; it remains none the less clearly at the head of the roll.

Macbeth, 60 : 88 = 148 ; Hamlet, 16 : 69 = 85 ; Othello, 29 : 48 = 77 ; Prospero, 16 : 55 = 71 ; Lear, 3 : 61 = 64 ; King John, 25 : 30 = 55 ; Jaques, 16 : 33 = 49 ; Henry IV. (including the times when he played the fourth act alone), 35 : 9 = 44 ; Shylock, 1 : 37 = 38 ; Wolsey, 15 : 22 = 37 ; Henry V., 5 : 23 = 28 ; Leontes, 21 : 6 = 27 ; Brutus, 13 : 10 = 23 ; Richard III., 21 : 0 ;

The same principle of self-expression may be clearly traced in his non-Shakespearian performances. Domestic tenderness, and especially paternal affection, formed a most potent factor in his character; it is not surprising, then, that for more than thirty years Virginius should have held a prominent place in his repertory, ranking among his noblest performances. Along with family affection, sensitive pride and moroseness entered largely into his disposition; and all these characteristics found utterance in Werner, whom he transmuted from shadow

Iago, 13 : 6 = 19; Coriolanus, 9 : 9 = 18; Valentine, 0 : 13; Benedick, 0 : 12; Posthumus, 9 : 0; Iachimo, 2 : 4 = 6; Antony (*Antony and Cleopatra*), 3 : 0; Romeo, 3 : 0; Edmund, 3 : 0; Friar Laurence, 0 : 2; Richard II., 0 : 2; Duke (*Measure for Measure*), 2 : 0; Hubert, Petruchio, Ghost (*Hamlet*), and Antonio (*Merchant of Venice*), once each, all before 1837. This is, I believe, a complete list of the Shakespearian parts he played in London. They number 32, and he appeared in them 889 times. The following list includes all his more important non-Shakespearian parts :—

Melnotte, 0 : 144; Rob Roy, 114 : 0; Alfred Evelyn, 0 : 110; Virginius, 70 : 27 = 97; Werner, 30 : 46 = 76; Richelieu, 0 : 71; Tell, 46 : 18 = 64; Gambia, 54 : 0; Henri Quatre, 47 : 0; Joseph Surface, 39 : 1 = 40; Norman (*Sea-Captain*), 0 : 40; Melantius, 23 : 10 = 33; Ludovico (*Evadne*), 30 : 0; Mr. Oakly, 8 : 19 = 27; Walsingham (*Woman's Wit*), 0 : 25; Sardanapalus, 23 : 0; Ion, 22 : 1 = 23; Halbert (*Glencoe*), 0 : 22; Stranger, 7 : 14 = 21; Ruthven (*Mary Stuart*), 0 : 20; Gisippus, 0 : 20; Pescara (*Apostate*), 19 : 0; Spinola (*Nina Sforza*), 0 : 18; Alfred the Great, 17 : 0; Thoas (*Athenian Captive*), 0 : 17; Lord Townly, 4 : 12 = 16; Pierre, 13 : 1 = 14; James V. (*King of the Commons*), 0 : 13; Mordaunt (*Patrician's Daughter*), 0 : 11; Bragelone (*La Vallière*), 8 : 0; Caius Gracchus, 7 : 0; Strafford, 5 : 0; Van Artevelde, 0 : 5; F. Foscari, 0 : 4; Polignac (*Huguenot*), 3 : 0; Marino Faliero, 0 : 2.

Macready appeared in Bulwer's plays 373 times; in Knowles's (including *The Bridal*), 241 times; in Byron's, 105 times; in Talfourd's, 62 times; and in Sheil's (including *Evadne*, but not *Damon* and *Pythias*), 52 times.

into substance. "In Werner," says Lewes, "he represented the anguish of a weak mind prostrate, with a
pathos almost as remarkable as the heroic anguish of
Kean's Othello. The forlorn look and wailing accent
when his son retorts upon him his own plea, 'Who pro-
claimed to me, That there were crimes made venial by
the occasion?' are not to be forgotten." Other critics
join with one voice in declaring Werner to have been
one of his greatest achievements. Richelieu, on the
other hand, was one of the characters in which he exhibited his art of composition. Here, too, we can trace
a certain measure of self-expression; but for the most
part it was a piece of what we now call character-acting,
interspersed with magnificent passages of rhetoric. Richelieu was probably the most modern of his performances.
In most of his other parts, were he to appear to-day, we
should doubtless find much to annoy and bewilder us,
much that we should have to accustom ourselves to, not
without difficulty. But in Richelieu, I imagine, we should
find nothing antiquated—except his declamatory vigour.
His Claude Melnotte, and still more his Ion, were feats
of will and skill, performed in spite of nature and in the
teeth of time. "In Melnotte," says Lewes, "you lost all
sense of his sixty years [he never played it in London
after fifty, but that was late enough] in the fervour and
resilient buoyancy of his manner;" but the part was
never one in which he could develop his full powers.
Among many fine parts which did not take a permanent
place in his repertory, Melantius in *The Bridal* was
probably the most remarkable. It deserved to rank, we
are assured, beside Virginius and Werner.

Some critics altogether denied Macready's claim to
praise, or even toleration, as a comedian; others went
into ecstasies over his Benedick and his Mr. Oakly. It

is almost always the case that when a tragedian essays comedy, one section of the public resents his claim to versatility, while another finds a peculiar piquancy in seeing him descend from the tragic pedestal. That Macready had a strong, though limited, sense of humour cannot be doubted. Without humour he could not have succeeded in Rob Roy, in Iago, in Richelieu. His Joseph Surface, too, was popular and much admired at a time when there was as yet no clique of worshippers sworn to find merit in whatever he chose to attempt. Thus we have no difficulty in accepting, as pretty near the truth, Oxenford's statement that "when he did really play comedy, when he allowed his native humour a free course, it was a high treat for the audience. The state of fidget in which the temper of his wife maintains Mr. Oakly, and the mental perplexity of Benedick, are instances . . . of his admirable skill in representing comic dilemma, worthy to be classed with the deeper anguish of his Lear or his Werner." "Macready," says Lady Pollock, "could be humorous, but could not be light, and where an airy manner was wanted he was sure to fail." This delightful critic admits that in the Prince of Como scenes in *The Lady of Lyons* he was stiff, serious, and over-emphatic ; but she thought his Benedick "perfectly conceived, and on the whole very well executed," while his Mr. Oakly she declares to have been "a perfect performance throughout." Westland Marston, too, praises the "spontaneous humour" of his Benedick, which "roused the house to such shouts of mirth, one might have thought Keeley, not Macready, was on the stage." The same critic praises his Alfred Evelyn, which must have been a highly effective performance. But Macready was certainly not at his ease in modern dress upon the stage. The Duke of Wellington, no slight authority on the subject of manners, is reported to have said that George the Fourth was no gentleman, though an excellent actor of one for ten minutes—" like Mr. Macready, he could not support it longer." Had it reached Macready's ears, this unkind comparison would probably have brought him to a premature grave.

Even if the publication of his diaries had not given him a prominent place among those fascinating persons, the self-revealers of literature, Macready would stand forth in our theatrical chronicles as a remarkable *character*. No one who came in contact with him could help being deeply impressed, though it might be far from favourably, by the sheer force of his personality. What rendered him peculiarly interesting was his inability to conceal the perpetual struggle between the Jekyll and Hyde in his composition. That struggle, which we trace in every page of his diary, was no less obvious in daily life. Hence the fact that Macready was loved by many people, hated by still more, but respected by all. To some people (and especially, one admits with regret, to his fellow-actors) he was apt almost constantly to wear the face of Mr. Hyde ; but even they felt that this was not the real man : that there was a higher nature behind, resisting and suffering from the excesses of the lower : and that this higher nature was the substantial and abiding force, which might be trusted in the long-run to gain the mastery. To those who habitually brought the better side of his nature into play, his personality was singularly attractive. They were accustomed to see him in the moment of victory, for their presence and influence helped to put the evil spirit to rout. Few men have had more faithful and devoted friends. Dickens writes to and of him in terms of almost fulsome affection, and

Dickens may be said to have given the key-note, in this respect, to a whole chorus of adherents. But it is note-worthy that the band of the faithful did not include a single actor. He had serviceable henchmen among the subordinate members of his companies, but not one friend who stood on anything like equal terms with him. This puts us on the track of what I believe to have been the true tragedy of Macready's spirit. It lay in his false relation to his life-work. It seems to me almost certain that in another career he would have been able habitually to conquer the tendency to irritability which he doubtless inherited from his father. In youth he seems to have been high-spirited, but neither morose nor exacting. It was as the sense of personal degradation in his calling grew upon him that Mr. Hyde began to get the upper hand. Whenever his foot touched the boards, his self-respect, like Acres's courage, began to ooze out at his finger-tips, and the great check upon his lower nature was removed. The knowledge, in the background of his mind, that conscience lay in wait for him with a rod in pickle, would often tend to intensify his paroxysms while they lasted. "As well be hanged for a sheep as for a lamb," he would think, or rather feel; "since I am doomed to a fit of remorse, why not unpack my whole heart while I am about it?" As soon as he was freed from the galling yoke of his profession, his better self resumed undivided mastery. He was the affectionate if somewhat over-scrupulous and exacting husband and father, the urbane and even formally courteous gentle-man, the man of sane and liberal instincts, just to him-self, generous towards others. His fragment of autobio-graphy, written during the early years of his stay at Sherborne, is a work of excellent temper. The man who was accused of never having a good word for a fellow-actor here writes with warm and evidently unaffected admiration of men who were his rivals, and to some extent his successful rivals, in years gone by. One is inclined to think him a trifle unjust to Booth, and he makes one or two allusions to Bunn which might have been spared. Otherwise these pages show no sign of the lower part of Macready's nature, except in the scattered remarks depreciating the profession of acting. That was the fundamental error of his life. The great Snob family falls into two classes—the worshippers of nobility (or tuft-hunters) and the worshippers of gentility. Macready belonged, not at all to the former class, but very distinctly to the latter. He never fully realized that the contempt of the world (which his morbid sensitiveness exaggerated) was in itself a thing to be contemned. By brooding over it he in some measure justified it. In his soreness of spirit over the fact that his profession did not ennoble him, he forgot, or failed, to ennoble his profession.

It must be remembered, in extenuation of Macready's foibles of temper, that the best hours of his life were given up to a task which is notoriously trying to the most angelic disposition—that of drilling careless, inefficient, and over-worked actors in country theatres. The life of a "star" must in those days have been one unceasing round of annoyances and humiliations, only to be mitigated by abundant humour or extreme artistic callousness. Macready could now and then see the humorous side of his embarrassments, but only now and then. "Surely you wouldn't shake hands with Hamlet!" he said to an American Guildenstern who insisted on coming close up to the Prince of Denmark. "Well, I don't know;" replied the citizen of the Great Republic. "I shake hands with our President." At such a sally

P

even the austere tragedian would surely unbend. But if humour now and then came to his aid, callousness never did. Much of his unpopularity with " the pro- fession " arose from a perfectly justified artistic puncti- liousness, which, to a lax and haphazard generation, seemed like pedantic tyranny. Even as a young man in London, he incurred some ridicule and odium by always acting at rehearsal. His success in America, according to his detractors, was largely due to his close attention to the minutiæ of stage-business and stage- management, which before his time were habitually neglected. He did what Mr. Irving has since done on a much larger scale—he showed the Americans the im- portance of scrupulous care and thought in every detail of a performance. There are many anecdotes of the resentment he incurred on the part of actors who felt their personal liberty infringed by what they called his trigonometrical calculations as to their position on the stage at any given moment. They would chalk crosses or drive in nails at the points indicated, and decline to budge from them on any account. This artistic scrupu- lousness, however, was accompanied by a large amount of the inartistic unscrupulousness of the typical " star." His own part was everything ; the opportunities of his fellow-actors, and even the poet's text, must all give place to the complete development of his effects. " When he played Othello," says George Vandenhoff, " Iago was to be *nowhere !* . . . Iago was a mere *stoker*, whose business it was to supply Othello's passion with fuel, and keep up his high-pressure. The next night, perhaps, he took Iago ; and lo ! presto ! everything was changed. Othello was to become a mere puppet for Iago to play with ; a pipe for Iago's master-skill to ' sound from its lowest note to the top of its compass.' " He would probably have glozed the egoism of this policy by arguing that the opportunities should be to him who can make use of them, and that, with country companies, it was useless to strive for an "all-round" effect. But the tendency, alas! was dominant whatever his surroundings. Even Fanny Kemble, as Lady Macbeth, had to sacrifice her legitimate opportunities to his self-aggrandizement.

The incessant worry and strain of London management was even more trying to his temper than the annoyances of "starring." His stiff-necked struggle against the long run system involved an infinite amount of labour from which a modern manager of any fairly successful theatre is free. A theatrical paper of the time gives an amusing and (by all accounts) a scarcely exaggerated sketch of "Macready at Rehearsal." The scene is the Covent Garden stage; the manager speaks—

"Where is the tailor-man, that Head, fool, brute, beast, ass? How dare you annoy me, sir, in this manner? Have you got a soul or sense? . . . Look, who wrote these calls? Gentlemen, look about you, read for yourselves: here is 'Macbeth' spelt 'Mackbeth' and Mr. Serle's 'Afrancesado' spelt 'Haffrancishardo.' . . . Who is that talking at the wings? Henry! Henry! go down and tell the stage door-keeper I expect him to go away—to leave the theatre immediately. . . . Mr. Forster—oh, show Mr. Forster to my room; no, stop! My dear Dickens, how d'ye do? Talfourd! your hand; another and another! Browning! Bulwer!—a—a—walk into the green-room. Mr. Bender, get on; why do you wait? Where is Mr. Willmott? I—I —this is exceedingly bad! Will you make a beginning? Where are the—the officers? Where is that—a—Paulo man? Mr. Beckett? Mr. Smith? What cat is that? Do —do—do—a—a—a—a—damn it! are you all asleep? . . . Why do we wait, gentlemen? The band? I—I really will enforce fines without any respect of persons. . . . Where's the supernumerary-master? Sir, I desired you not to employ that person without stockings. Do—do find me decent, intelligent men. Gentlemen of the band, be kind enough to discuss your—a—a—*on dits*—outside the theatre. It is—it is—a—a—preposterous. . . . What is that horrible hubbub in the green-room? I—I really I—Where is the gas-man? Are we rehearsing the—the—a—Black Hole of Calcutta? Do—do—do pray lighten our darkness. Man, I have spoken several times about these pewter pots. I— I will not have the theatre turned into a—a cookshop. . . . You—you—you cannot possibly dine at ten o'clock in the morning. . . . Send in your beds, gentlemen ; let us have a —a—a caravansery at once."

There is no doubt that, in his fits of temper, Macready used very violent language. " Beast !" muttered be-tween his teeth, was his favourite term of opprobrium ; and by way of a superlative, he would now and then add, " Beast of hell !" Mr. Howe avers that he only on one occasion heard him use this expression. He was standing at the wing one warm night, holding a pair of lighted candles, on which the effect of his entrance depended. Half stifling in the sultry atmosphere, he murmured to his dresser, " Puff, puff !" meaning that he should put some powder on his face. The man, mistaking his intent, instantly " puffed " out the candles ; and at that moment the cue was given. Macready withered the culprit with a look, and went on, growling, " Beast—beast—beast of hell !" A curious anecdote is told of his struggle with an actor named Roberts, who, having to deliver a simple message, insisted on striking a spread-eagle attitude before opening his mouth. Again, again, and yet again he was sent back, pro-mising amendment ; but, in spite of himself, he always fell into the old pose. At last, says Anderson, Macready " raised his eyes and hands to the flies, and made us all scream with laughing, as he exclaimed in agony, ' O

God !—a—will you not out of your—a—goodness and mercy, release me—a—from the infliction—a—of this blank split-crow—a !'" For a somewhat similar story we have the authority of Mr. Edmund Yates. A brother of Mr. George Augustus Sala, calling himself Wynn, was a member of the Princess's company; and to him Macready had an intense objection. At rehearsal he would close his eyes tightly while Wynn was on the stage, and before reopening them would ask the prompter, "Has it gone?" When *Henry VIII.* was in preparation, Macready implored Maddox to see that Cardinal Campeius was furnished with a costume which should not seem entirely ridiculous beside the splendid robes he himself wore as Wolsey ; but Maddox, of course, disregarded the injunction.

"At the dress rehearsal," says Mr. Yates, " Macready, enthroned in a chair of state, had the various characters to pass before him : he bore all calmly until, clad in scarlet robes bordered by silver tissue-paper and wearing an enormous red hat, Wynn approached. Then, clutching both arms of his chair, and closing his eyes, the great tragedian gasped out, 'Mother Shipton, by God !'"

In such episodes as these there is a sad discrepancy between the real man and the " Macready, moral, grave, sublime " of the poet's fancy and of his own ideal. Westland Marston's suggestion, that he was inclined deliberately to exaggerate his bursts of temper, "that they might contrast with his after-smoothness," can scarcely be accepted as a plea in mitigation.

One could devote whole chapters to balancing the faults against the virtues of this fascinatingly complex character. But it is time, to sum up. I shall not do so in my own words, but in those of two keen observers of character, both of whom knew him intimately.

"Macready's sensitiveness," said Harriet Martineau, "shrouded itself within an artificial manner ; but a more delightful companion could not be—not only on account of his learning and accomplishment, but of his uncompromising liberality of opinion and his noble strain of meditative thought. . . . But there was, besides the moralizing tendency, a chivalrous spirit of rare vigilance, and an unsleeping domestic tenderness and social beneficence, which accounted for and justified the idolatry with which he was regarded, through all trials occasioned by the irritable temper with which he manfully struggled."

The second estimate is that of Robert Browning, kindly communicated to me by the poet himself—

"I found Macready as I left him—and happily, after a long interval, resumed him, so to speak—one of the most admirable and, indeed, fascinating characters I have ever known ; somewhat too sensitive for his own happiness, and much too impulsive for invariable consistency with his nobler moods."

Macready in a nutshell !

INDEX.

THE END.

PRINTED BY WILLIAM CLOWES AND SONS, LIMITED, LONDON AND BECCLES.

www.ingramcontent.com/pod-product-compliance
Lightning Source LLC
Chambersburg PA
CBHW030106030726
47498CB00007B/2272